OUTLAW XMAS

AN INSURGENTS MC ROMANCE

CHIAH WILDER

Insurgent MC Series:

Hawk's Property

Jax's Dilemma

Chas's Fervor

Axe's Fall

Banger's Ride

Jerry's Passion

Throttle's Seduction

Rock's Redemption

An Insurgent's Wedding

Insurgents MC Romance Series: Insurgents Motorcycle Club Box Set (Books 1 – 4)

Night Rebels MC Series:

STEEL

MUERTO

DIABLO

GOLDIE

Steamy Contemporary Romance:

My Sexy Boss

PROLOGUE

A BLANKET OF fresh snow covered the neighborhood as the subtle crunch of footsteps blended with the whispering wind. Branches groaned with the weight of the snow, and the solitary figure in black wrapped his scarf tighter around his neck. The cold was bitter that night. Had he not spotted the house earlier in the week when he was taking in all the Christmas decorations, he'd be home with his feet up on an ottoman, a crackling fire in the hearth, and a glass of buttered rum in his hand. Instead, he was out in the wet, cold snow, slipping behind a trio of pine trees that stood stark against the winter night. Moonlight struggled through the dense gray clouds above.

Puffs of moisture blew through his parted lips as he breathed heavily, and then the frosted air forced its way into his lungs, stinging his eyes. He shivered and stamped his feet, wiping his watering eyes as he strained to peer through the cluster of pine branches at the house across the street.

It was two stories and had lights on every possible inch of its façade. It looked out of place in the neighborhood where just a string of lights or a Christmas tree glowing in a front window seemed to be the norm.

He shook his head as he watched the house. The porch had two rocking chairs with two bright floodlights trained on them. Figures of Santa Claus and Mrs. Claus sat in them with a wooden table between them decked out in plastic cookies and glasses of milk. In every window facing the street, figures of snowmen, elves, and angels loomed, bright floodlights illuminating them even more. Two oversized Nutcracker sentries stood guard at the foot of the steps leading to the porch, and there were all sizes and shapes of various Santas scattered across the lawn.

Added into the holiday mix were life-sized Tinkerbell and Peter Pan figures. It was one of the tackiest houses he'd seen this year.

Placing the baseball bat on the icy ground, he blew his warm breath over his hands as he kept watching the garage door until it opened. The Green family was going to the Pinewood Springs Community Center to watch nine-year-old Abigail clunk across the auditorium's stage in a musical rendition of *The Night Before Christmas*. Most of the town would be squeezed together watching the annual Christmas show that featured kids from ages three to seventeen. He'd gone the previous year and had to leave because it was too kitschy.

As the red taillights from the Suburban disappeared into the swirling snow, he stepped out from his hiding place, baseball bat tucked under his arm. Plunging his hands in his pockets, he looked around cautiously, and after seeing no one around, he crossed the street quickly and headed to the back of the house.

To his amazement, the back door was unlocked. He paused before entering, making sure a snarling dog didn't rush toward him. He'd brought dog treats laced with sleeping pills just in case, but after a couple of minutes, he stepped fully into the mudroom and closed the door behind him.

Without wasting any time, he went into the living room, raised the bat, and swung full force at the Christmas tree. The shattered ornaments, cascading pine needles, and mangled garland made him grin for the first time since he'd driven to the neighborhood. Shrugging off his jacket, he tossed it on a nearby chair, then continued the destruction of Christmas in the Green household.

The brown-eyed man stomped, smashed, and ripped anything that looked remotely like a holiday decoration. The brightly wrapped presents under the tree were demolished—he used the family's kitchen knives to shred ties, scarves, and clothing. When he opened the larger boxes, he took special delight in demolishing the toys. Like a crazed Grinch, he dashed around the house, attacking the vintage snowmen and angels in the upstairs windows. After he'd destroyed the inside of the house, he went on the front porch and thrashed Mr. and Mrs. Claus. Breathing heavily, he leaned against the cold brick wall and laughed hysterically as he stared at the cracked faces of the figurines.

He straightened up and held his breath when he saw a car slowing down in front of the house, then stopping. The passenger window rolled down, and a woman's voice broke the quiet of the neighborhood.

"You have my vote for the best Christmas decorations in town. Great job!" She waved, and he waved back. Then the car drove on.

A sneer replaced the Grinch's panicked look from a few seconds earlier. He went back inside and headed into the garage in search of the breaker box. Finding it in one of the cupboards, he switched off all the circuits so darkness enveloped the residence, turning off the blinking and racing lights that littered the front yard.

Satisfied, he slipped away and walked to his car parked a few blocks away. Taking out a notebook, he switched on his phone's flashlight and leafed through the pages. When he came to a page with numerous names and addresses, he located the Green family and marked a large *X* beside their name.

Another one down. Switching on the ignition, he pulled away from the curb and drove around different neighborhoods, writing down addresses of houses he would go back to. His habit was to look up the address on the county website to find out the name of the owners, and then he'd dig deeper. He normally settled on houses that had children because those homes were the best to destroy. Watching a child cry when she saw her presents destroyed, or the Christmas tree smashed and lying on the ground, was what excited him. It gave him an indescribable rush of adrenaline that lit his body up.

Cranking the heater higher, he rode around, biding his time until the Green family came home. He'd make sure to watch them from across the street with binoculars glued to his eyes so he could see each expression of shock, anger, and sadness spreading across their faces. The man would be honing in on Abigail and her seven-year-old brother, Connor. The scene would wipe all the joy and pride from the Christmas show off their faces, especially when they saw their foil-wrapped presents mangled and broken. They'd sink to the floor, picking up the broken pieces and crying sweet tears of anguish.

And that was what he lived for.

CHAPTER ONE

CHAS

C HAS WOKE TO the soft rattle of the wind against the bedroom windows. From the dimness of the outside light, he figured it would be another gray, wintry day. He draped his arm around Addie as she slept and pressed himself closer to her back. His dick was hard and his hand slipped easily under her fleece nightshirt. Visions of them kissing, touching, and loving each other the night before made his dick ache more.

"Are you asleep?" he asked as he flicked his fingertip over her nipple, satisfaction coursing through him as it hardened under his touch.

"Mmmm... I was," she said in a sleepy voice.

"I need you, precious," he murmured against her neck as he nipped at it.

"What time is it?"

"Early. We got time before the kids wake up." He ran his hand down past her belly. "Open your legs."

She reached behind her and curled her fingers around his hardness. With a smile in her voice, she said, "You're always ready."

"That's because you drive me crazy all the time." He raised her top leg, then shifted his lower body into a half-kneeling position, entering her from behind. As he moved he played with her tits and nipples, then slipped his hand down to rub her nub while he buried his cock deeper into her. As he held her tighter, he kept his hands busy, touching and caressing her, and when she reached behind and fondled his balls, he thought he would lose it.

"That feels real good, babe," he said hoarsely as he plunged deep into her, hitting her in the spot she loved the most.

"Oh shit. Don't stop. Keep doing what you're doing," she said between pants.

As he thrust harder, she moved her hand to his ass and dug her nails into his cheek. "Yes, that feels so good," she groaned. Then she gasped and her hand flew to her mouth as if to stifle her scream. Low, guttural sounds came from her throat, making the pressure that had been building deep inside him explode and rush to a single point of exit. Grunting as he filled her, he squeezed her tits and then fell back with his arms wrapped snugly around her. She placed her hands on top of his and he drifted off to sleep.

A soft rapping on the door woke him up, and before he could say anything, Jack opened it.

"I don't feel so good," he said as he walked into the bedroom.

Pulling away from Chas, Addie got out of bed and went over to him. "What's wrong, honey?" she asked as she placed her hand on his forehead. "You don't feel warm."

"So what? I still don't feel good."

"Hey, watch your mouth," Chas said as he grabbed a long-sleeved T-shirt from the nightstand drawer and slipped it over his head.

"Are you sure you're not feeling well, or you just don't want to go to school?" Addie put her arm around Jack's shoulder but he shrugged it off.

"I'm sick! Why're you giving me the fucking third degree?" Jack stormed out of the room and Addie stood still, her hand over her mouth.

"Get your butt back in here and apologize to your mom!" Chas's blood pressure spiked as he quickly pulled on a pair of jeans and started after Jack, but Addie pulled him back. "What the fuck? I'm not letting him get away with talking to you that way."

Addie shook her head. "Listen to the way you cuss. He's learning from you. Besides, I think something's bothering him."

"I can tell you that I never spoke to my mom the way he just did to you, and my dad cussed up a storm when I was growing up. Respect dictates the way you speak to your parents. We aren't his goddamn friends. I'm not letting him get away with that."

"Chas, wait. I think he's having a problem at school. This is the fourth time in two weeks he's said he's too sick to go."

Chas stopped dead in his tracks and his body tensed as his mouth went dry. *Someone's messin' with Jack.* "Why didn't you tell me about this?"

Addie placed two hands on his shoulders and softly kissed the side of his face. "I wasn't sure if it was a problem or not. There's been a lot of colds and flu going around the school."

"This doesn't have anything to do with that. I'm gonna talk to him."

"Be gentle. Jack's a sensitive boy. I better get Hope ready for school. I can only imagine what she's picked out to wear." Addie laughed and went into her room just as Chas rapped on Jack's door.

"I'm trying to rest," Jack said through the door.

"Open the door or I'll break it down," Chas answered. In less than ten seconds, he heard the door unlock. He turned the knob and walked into Jack's room, making sure to close the door behind him.

"I know I was rude to Mom. I'll go and apologize," he mumbled as he sat on the edge of the bed with his head down.

"Yeah, you were. I don't ever wanna hear you speak to your mom like that again. I don't give a damn if you're fifty years old, you'll *always* be respectful to your mom. You got that?"

Jack nodded but his gaze was still focused on the floor. Chas sat next to him on the bed. "You wanna tell me what's going on with you and school?"

Jack wiped his nose with the back of his hand. "Nothing."

"Then why have you been BSing about not feeling good the last couple of weeks?"

His thin shoulders went up and down. "I guess 'cause I don't."

"Do you need to go to the doctor?"

"Maybe."

"Is someone messin' with you at school?"

Jack whipped his head up and stared into Chas's eyes. "No. Why did you ask me that?"

"Just got a vibe that may be the problem. You can tell me."

Shaking his head vigorously, Jack pushed up from the bed and went to the window. "It's not that. I just don't feel good. My stomach's queasy and I feel kinda dizzy."

Chas stared at his back, his insides twisting. He saw Jack was afraid, so he didn't want to push him. *Some punk is making his life miserable.* The urge to go to school, find out who it was, and teach the brat a lesson was strong, but he wouldn't do it. Jack had to learn to fight his own battles, but he could help his son be better prepared for the assholes who were going to be a constant in his life.

Jack looked over his shoulder, the color drained out of his face. "Are you gonna make me go to school?"

Chas's heart lurched, and he slowly shook his head. "No. If you don't feel good, then you shouldn't be at school." The relief that spread over his twelve-year-old son's face pained him. "When you get to feeling better, what would you say to me teaching you how to fight? You're at the age where you should know this stuff."

Jack's eyes widened. "Would you? That'd be real cool, Dad."

"If you're better by the weekend, I'll show you some moves."

The color returned to Jack's face as he pulled out a chair and plopped down on it. "I'm sure I'll be better by the weekend."

"Good. Take it easy today. I'm gonna take your sister to school. Be good to your mom. I don't want her to tell me you were rude to her. And make sure you tell her you're sorry. She was hurt by what you said to her."

"I didn't mean it. Honest."

Chas stood up. "I know, but words can really hurt, so you gotta be sure you watch what you say. And no video games for the rest of the week."

"Come on, Dad."

"If you argue about it, I'll make it two weeks. It's your call."

Jack grumbled something under his breath as Chas picked up a basket full of controllers. "You want some breakfast?" Jack shook his head without looking at him. "Okay. Probably a good decision since your stomach's hurting. But if you start feeling better, let your mom know and she'll fix you something. I gotta go." With the basket in his hands, he walked out of the room just as Hope came dashing down the hall.

"Daddy!" she said, then giggled as he swooped her up with one arm.

"Where're you going dressed so pretty?"

"School. You know that." She wrapped her arms around his neck. "You smell good."

He laughed. "I'll take her to school. Jack may want something to eat after I leave," he said to Addie as he handed her the controllers. "I took away video games for the next four days."

"Don't you think that's too harsh?"

"Hell no. If I would've spoken to my mom like that, my dad would've grounded me for two weeks and had me on pots and pans duty for a month, so he got off pretty easy."

"Well, I think a couple of days would've been enough. With a huge snowstorm in the forecast, it's going to be a long weekend for him," Addie said as she grabbed the basket from his hand.

"I'll keep him busy. Besides, he doesn't have to be in front of a screen all day. There's plenty to do."

"Maybe we can ask Banger to bring Ethan over for the weekend."

Chas shook his head and then pressed his lips on hers. "Sort of fucks up the punishment if he gets a sleepover, precious," he said against her mouth. Hope squirmed in his arm and he pulled away. "Is cereal good for her breakfast?"

"Yes. The Cream of Wheat's on the stove. Just give her half a cup with a splash of milk and a little bit of banana in it. I'll be down in a minute."

After Hope ate a few bites of her hot cereal and drank some of her juice, she was ready to go to school. As he was putting on her jacket, his phone rang. Glancing down, he saw Banger's name light up on the screen.

"Hold on, honey." He placed the phone to his ear. "What's up?" he asked.

"I'm just letting everyone know that we have an emergency church this morning at ten thirty."

"I'll be there. I just need to drop Hope off at preschool, and then I'll come to the club and hang until church. Uh… has Ethan mentioned anything about Jack getting picked on at school?"

"No, but that don't mean shit with kids. So your boy's getting bullied?"

"I think so. I mean, the signs are there, especially making excuses not to go to school. I just wondered if Ethan said anything. Can you ask him?"

"I'll talk to him and let you know. What're you going to do about it?"

"Teach Jack to beat the shit out of the brat."

Banger's laugh rumbled through the phone. "Sounds like the best plan. They gotta learn now so they can hold their own later in life. I taught Ethan some stuff and it made him feel a whole lot more confident. It's about time your boy learned to defend himself."

"My thinking exactly, although I know Addie would fuckin' freak out if she knew about it."

"Women are like that. They don't need to know everything that goes on. I'll see you later at church."

Chas slipped the phone into his pocket and shrugged on his leather jacket. "Come on, Hope, we gotta get going." Hope walked behind him as he made his way to the garage.

"Who were you talking to?" Addie asked as she came into the kitchen.

"Banger. The club's got an emergency church this morning."

"Sounds serious. What do you think it's about?"

He stopped and kissed her on the cheek. "Good one, but I'm not divulging shit." Hope tilted her chin up when Addie bent down to kiss her goodbye. "I'll see you later tonight." He grasped Hope's hand and went into the garage.

In less than thirty minutes, he walked into the clubhouse, greeting the brothers as he took a seat at one of the tables. After he'd dropped Hope off at school, he thought about Jack the whole time he drove to the club. Just the thought of someone hitting his kid made his blood boil. He'd spend the weekend teaching Jack to defend himself, and if that didn't solve the problem, then he'd intervene.

There was no way in hell he was allowing this shit to continue. The faculty at the school seemed to be turning a blind eye to the problem, so he'd have to take matters into his own hands.

This shit stops now.

CHAPTER TWO

HAWK

THE DIN OF angry voices ricocheted around the cramped room as Banger pounded the gavel on the wooden block. Hawk pushed off from the concrete wall and put two fingers in his mouth, letting out a high-pitched whistle. Slicing through the cacophony of shouts, several members of the Insurgents MC turned their attention to the front of the room and locked eyes with the vice president.

"Give me the damn gavel," he said to Banger. He threw it across the room and Wheelie and Rock leapt up, glaring at Hawk as their nostrils flared and their muscles flexed.

"What the fuck?" Rock said as he pushed hard against the table, moving it forward a few inches.

"You got a problem?" Wheelie said as he started walking toward the front of the room.

Hawk crossed his arms. "Come get it, fuckers."

Banger blocked Wheelie's path. "Sit your ass back down."

"You should've been respecting your prez instead of yapping away like a goddamn chick," Hawk said.

Pointing at the vice president, Wheelie breathed heavily. "You better watch your back, brother, 'cause this shit isn't over."

"Any time, asshole. I've been wanting to kick your ass for a while." Hawk glared at Wheelie as he retreated and headed to his seat.

"Don't make things worse," Banger whispered to Hawk. "We got shit we need to figure out."

"I don't like his fuckin' attitude." Hawk pursed his lips and leaned

12

back against the wall, his gaze still focused on Wheelie.

Silence fell over the room as the members fixed their eyes on their president. Banger scrubbed his face with his fist, then cleared his throat. "I know you're all pissed about the recent shit Reaper's been pulling in our territory," he said.

"Enraged is more like it," Chas said. Axe and Throttle grumbled their agreement.

"Okay, pissed as fuck, then, but we gotta keep our heads level to figure out what's really going on and what's damn rumor." Banger picked up his beer and took a long drink.

"Steel told me his sources are good. I knew the fuckin' Deadly Demons weren't going to honor the truce," Hawk said.

"You can never trust a damn Demon," Rock said. Soon the brothers were cussing and yelling about the Deadly Demons, and Banger just rocked back on his boots, shaking his head.

"Shut the fuck up!" Hawk's voice filled the room. Once again, silence settled over the meeting room. "We have shit to discuss. I know they're hooking up with some punk gang in Pueblo." Looking down at a notebook on the table, he searched for the name. "What the hell's the name of the asshole gang?"

"The 39th Street Gang," Rock said as he stood up. "According to Diablo, they work out of Pueblo, but they've been making some noise with another punk gang in Silverado. Fallen Slayers have been dealing with them for the past several months. The Night Rebels helped the brothers get guns and shit from Liam a while back."

"Aren't Satan's Pistons involved with the 39th Street Gang?" Axe asked.

Rock nodded. "And they've been tied to the wannabe gangsters in Silverado. I told Diablo we should join forces and stamp out these damn punk gangs."

"We should kick their asses just for having a stupid-as-shit name," Throttle said.

Several brothers guffawed, and Rags slapped Throttle on the back.

"Good one, dude. And you're so right. I mean, how much time did it take for them to come up with 39th Street Gang? Total pussies. Fuckin' lame."

"What the hell's the name of the other punk gang in Silverado?" Jerry asked.

"I don't know. Diablo just ranted about these 39th pussies," Rock answered.

"West Avenue Bandits," Bear said, and all eyes turned to him. He leaned back in his chair. "Tattoo Mike told me. He said the Fallen Slayers are having a helluva time with them. Steel's ready to have the Night Rebels jump in and give them a hand."

"Did Tattoo Mike say anything 'bout the Deadly Demons being involved with these punk gangs?" Banger asked.

"He said they don't know who the hell's helping them out. Satan's Pistons are bent on revenge after what the Night Rebels did to their clubhouse in Arizona, but he said the brothers don't think they have the money or manpower to fund two punk gangs."

"This shit has Deadly Demons written all over it," Jax said, pounding his fist on the table. The brothers joined in, pounding their fists and yelling out death epithets.

Hawk hung back and watched as anger filled the room. Neither he nor Banger stopped it, and from the hard look on Banger's face, Hawk was pretty sure he was feeling the same rage that was coursing through each of the brothers, including himself. The Deadly Demons had been trying to spread the drug, arms, and trafficking trade into Colorado—Insurgents territory ever since the club was formed thirty years before. During that time, the club wars had been fierce and rivaled any war zone in Afghanistan. After years of killing and bloodshed, a truce had been formed between the two clubs. It had held strong for the past eight years, but the outlaw grapevine had been reporting that Reaper was pissed as fuck that the Insurgents were making a shitload of money on legal weed while they struggled with constant harassment from the badges.

Hawk balled his fists. *I wouldn't put it past these fuckers to snake their way into our territory by using non-biker gangs as their damn smokescreen.* He glanced at the clock on the back wall. He'd promised Cara that he'd pick up Braxton from preschool in an hour. Turning to Banger, he said, "This shit could go on for hours. Pound the gavel and let's move on."

Banger picked up another gavel and slammed it down on the block of wood. Voices lowered to a hush. "We're all fuckin' pissed, and Hawk and I are gonna keep monitoring this."

"I'll keep digging to see what I can come up with," Blade said.

"If anyone can find shit through the internet, it's you," Chas said. Blade was a whiz when it came to computers, hacking, and anything else internet and computer related. He'd been a full member for the past few years and was proving to be a huge asset to the club.

"And keep the conversation going with the Night Rebels. They're closer to what's going on since all this shit is in their neck of the woods. I guess that wraps it up. What do you say?" Hawk glanced at Banger.

"That'll do it. Church is over." Banger brought the gavel down again, and the scraping of chairs against the concrete floor bounced off the walls as the brothers made their way out of the room and headed to the great room.

When Hawk walked into the great room, hard rock beats blasted from the overhead speakers while voices strained to compete with the music. Hawk went over to the jukebox and lowered the volume.

"That's a lot better, honey," a sultry voice said behind him. The scent of sweet roses curled around him as soft fingers ran up his forearm.

He straightened up and turned around. A young woman with long light-brown hair and big blue eyes smiled at him. She looked like she was barely twenty-one.

"Do I know you?" he asked as he took a step away from her.

"I'm Heather. I've seen you around the club, but you always seem too busy to notice me. I'm one of the new girls." She ran her eyes over his physique.

"How new?"

"A month. I was a hoodrat before, but now I'm a club girl." She stepped closer to him. "I was hoping you were going to be here when I was initiated."

When a woman wanted to become a club girl, she had to go through an initiation where all the members had sex with her. If she passed, she donned the Insurgents patch as property of the club. It earned her free room and board and the protection of the club.

Hawk placed his hands on her shoulders and pushed her back gently. "You're wasting your time with me. I've got an old lady."

"I heard that, but what happens in the clubhouse stays in the clubhouse. Plus, variety is a lot more fun." She reached out and traced her finger down his throat.

Grabbing her hand, he pushed it away. "When a brother tells you to back off, you fuckin' listen. I'm not interested. Find another brother who wants your pussy."

"You're a hard one." She pushed out her lower lip.

"Only when people don't listen." Spotting Throttle at the bar, he walked away and went over to him.

"What the fuck were you doing with the new girl, what the hell's her name?"

Hawk closed his eyes and tilted his head back. "Fuck. I don't remember, and she just told me."

"You're getting old, dude." Throttle laughed.

"I hate that shit. Let's see… it was something with an H, like Heidi. Yeah… it's Heidi."

"Who're you talking about?" Wheelie asked as he leaned over to scoop up a handful of nuts.

"The new club girl. Throttle was asking what her name was."

"Heather, and she's damn good with her mouth," Wheelie said.

Throttle glanced at Hawk. "Heidi, my ass. Like I said, dude, you're getting old."

"It's more like I don't give a shit."

"She's sure giving Tigger a good time even though she's looking at you." Throttle lightly punched Hawk on his arm.

Hawk turned toward the couches against the wall and saw Tigger lying back, his knees spread open, his head tilted back and his dick in Heather's mouth. As she sucked him, she fixed her gaze on Hawk. He shook his head laughing and turned back to his friends. "The new ones always want to fuck the prez and the VP. It's so damn predictable."

"At least you guys respect your old ladies, not like that sonofabitch Tigger." Wheelie glared over at Tigger and Heather.

"You know that's his business, dude," Throttle answered.

"Sofia deserves better than that asshole. He's always using her as a punching bag, and he fucks every chick that comes through this door. He never fucking misses a party."

Hawk saw the vein in Wheelie's temple throbbing. "Get a grip, man. What happens between Tigger and Sofia is their deal. Has she filed a complaint with Banger about the way Tigger treats her?"

Wheelie shook his head. "She's too scared of him."

"Has she told you that?" Hawk glanced over his shoulder at Tigger. Heather winked at him and he turned away.

"She doesn't have to say a damn word. She's always wearing sunglasses and long sleeves. Whenever he says something to her, it's like she shrivels up."

"Until she files something, we can't butt into another brother's personal life. You know that." Hawk brought the beer bottle to his lips.

"And you better focus your attention on another woman. You're asking for a whole lot of trouble sniffing around Sofia." Throttle's fingers wrapped around the beer bottle, but before he could bring it to his lips, Wheelie's fist landed on his jaw. "What the fuck?" Throttle spun around and threw a punch at Wheelie.

"I'm not sniffing around her." Another jab at Throttle, then one back at Wheelie.

Hawk stood watching as he finished his beer. Glancing at the clock, he grabbed Wheelie by the neck and pulled him away, then stepped in front of him.

"Let me at him," Throttled huffed.

"Enough of this shit," Hawk said. Wheelie jerked out of Hawk's grasp. "I'd say you overreacted to what Throttle said to you. Watch yourself. You know messin' with a brother's old lady will get your ass thrown out of the club."

"I'm not messin' with anyone's woman." Glaring at Throttle, his chest heaved in and out. "And don't ever suggest that I'm making moves on her again. Have some goddamned respect for her." He spun around and stormed out of the clubhouse.

Bringing the beer bottle to his reddened jaw, he shook his head. "He so fuckin' wants to get into Sofia's pants." He laughed.

A tight feeling seized Hawk in the chest. "You're right, but I'm hoping he doesn't act on it. We have enough shit going on with the Deadly Demons. Wheelie's a good guy." He looked at the clock once more. "Fuck! I've got to pick Braxton up at school. I'm outta here."

As he drove to the preschool, he thought about Wheelie, and heaviness filled him. The way his brother looked at Sofia didn't escape him, Banger, or several of the other members. He wasn't sure if Tigger had noticed it, but the brother had seemed so preoccupied with banging anyone with tits that Hawk doubted if Tigger had picked up the attraction Wheelie had for his wife.

Hawk couldn't deny that Tigger treated Sofia badly. He was always at the clubhouse, leaving her alone most of the time. The few times she came looking for him, he'd been so rude and condescending to her that it took all of Hawk's strength to keep his mouth shut and his fists inside the pockets of his leather jacket. But as long as Sofia didn't complain about Tigger, there was nothing the club could do. Her loyalty to her husband was solid, and she never said a bad word about him.

Hawk turned into the parking lot and jumped out of the SUV. Each time he entered the quiet hallways, he'd smile to himself over the looks he got from some of the teachers and parents at the expensive and prestigious school. He let Cara handle which schools their kids would go to. Braxton had been on the waiting list since he was a little over a year old, and Cara had just placed their eighteen-month-old daughter, Isabella, on the list. The whole thing seemed ridiculous to him, but Cara had insisted St. Rosa's Academy was one of the best elementary schools in Pinewood Springs.

The ringing bells echoed down the long hallways and several doors opened at once as children spilled out of classrooms. Leaning against the wall, Hawk smiled when he spotted his dark-haired son. When Braxton's blue eyes locked on to his, the boy grinned widely and ran over to him. Hawk picked his son up and looked at the blue construction paper he shoved in his face.

"Look, Daddy. I made a picture of my hands."

Hawk took the paper from him and saw the small handprints painted in red, purple, and yellow. "Totally awesome," he said against Braxton's cheek.

After securing Braxton in the car seat, he slipped into the driver seat and switched on the ignition. "Did you have fun at school?" he asked as he drove toward their house. The four-year-old chattered on about everything he'd done that morning, and Hawk kept glancing in the rearview mirror at him the whole drive home. He still couldn't believe he had a son and a daughter. He never thought he'd have a family, especially since his childhood had been wrecked with so much violence and betrayal, but there he was, with an adorable son, a precious daughter, and a wife who still made him hard just by looking at her.

"When are we going to see Santa Claus, Daddy?"

Focusing back on what Braxton was saying, he laughed. "I think we're planning to do that next week, little buddy."

"Everyone in class has gone already."

"You sure about that? I mean, *everyone* is a lot of people." When Braxton's brow creased in concentration, he chuckled to himself. "We'll get there. I promise. It's just that Mommy's been real busy."

"Isa wants to go too, but she might cry."

"Why's that?"

"'Cause that's what babies do when they see Santa. Mommy said I did it when I was a baby."

"Yeah, you did, but you'll be there with Isa, so she'll probably be good. You're her big brother and you have to always watch out for her."

"I know." Braxton fell silent and stared out the window as Hawk turned into their neighborhood.

"Some of the neighbors really went all out," he said as he passed a few homes with a ton of inflatables covering their front lawns. "Would you like to ride around at night and see all the lights?"

"Yep. Mommy said you were gonna take us to do that."

"She did? Good to know."

Twenty minutes later, Braxton was sitting on the couch watching cartoons while Hawk warmed up some leftover spaghetti and meatballs for lunch. Outside, snowflakes had begun to twirl down from the gray sky. He placed two plates on the table and called Braxton to come eat. The boy dashed into the kitchen and climbed up on the chair.

When they were almost finished with their food, he heard the garage door open, and anticipation of seeing Cara squeezed his insides. After all the years they'd been together, he still couldn't get enough of her. It was true when they said love was a drug, and he was addicted to the max.

Braxton's eyes lit up when Cara came into the kitchen with Isa in her arms. "Mommy!" He tried to push back his chair, but Cara went over to him instead and he wrapped his small arms around her neck, giving her a kiss on the cheek. He laughed. "I put spaghetti sauce on your face."

"That's okay, sweetie." She turned to Hawk and smiled at him. A rush of desire bolted through him and, for a split second, he wished the kids were at their grandparents'.

"Come over here, babe, and I'll clean you up," he said as he rose to his feet.

Putting Isa down, Cara headed to Hawk and he leaned in close. "You smell awesome," he whispered in her ear before he licked her cheek and then her lips. Heat stirred within him as she pressed close to him, and the warm and sensual mix of vanilla and apricot and Cara consumed him.

"Don't the kids have to take a nap or something," he murmured against her mouth.

"They do," she answered as she ran her hand over his arm, squeezing his bicep.

"Daddy said we can see Santa next week," Braxton said as he pushed away from the table.

Unfurling herself from Hawk's arms, Cara went over to Braxton and helped him out of the chair. "That sounds like a great plan. Let me wash your face." She took his hand and guided him over to the sink. Hawk watched her hips sway in her tight-as-hell jeans, readjusting his pants as his cock grew hard.

Bending down, he picked Isa up and ran his hand through her soft light-brown hair, then kissed her soft cheeks. "How's my sweet girl?" She giggled and burrowed her head into his neck.

Yawning, Braxton rubbed his eyes and curled his arms around Cara's legs. "Are you tired, sweetie?" she asked as she wiped his face with a warm cloth. He nodded.

Hawk carried Isa into her room and laid her in the crib, then stroked her head until she closed her eyes and her lips parted. He bent down and kissed her softly before making his way to his and Cara's room, where she was brushing her hair.

"Braxton must've been exhausted," he said as he quietly shut the door.

"He still loves his naps. He's worn out on school days." She came over to him and hooked her arms around his neck. "I've been missing you all morning," she said, her warm breath tickling his neck.

He ran his hands down her back and cupped her ass. "You look sexy as fuck in your jeans. You been on my mind too, baby." Tangling her hair in his hand, he jerked her head back, then crushed his mouth against hers. The small whimpers from her throat drove him crazy, and he slipped his hand between them and placed it on her breast, kneading it and grazing her hardening nipple with his finger. "You fuckin' kill me, babe."

She slid her hands under his T-shirt and scratched his chest with her fingernails, tugging at his nipple piercing. Fire rushed through him, and he picked her up and eased her on the bed. He tugged off his shirt, left his jeans and boxers in a pile next to the bed, and then he undressed her. Usually he liked taking his time peeling her clothes off her, but he had a bad burning inside him that needed relief real fast.

Grasping her breasts, he squeezed and sucked them until red love bites covered them like a blanket; he loved seeing his mark all over his woman's creamy tits. "Get on your knees," he rasped.

Cara turned over and rose up on her knees. He leaned back and took in her firm, shapely ass, her sweet puckered hole, and the glimpse of glistening pink between her legs. He licked his lips and leaned forward, spreading her knees farther apart. Pushing her tits into the mattress, he ran his finger through her wetness and she moaned. Flipping over on his back, he scooted between her legs and pulled her down a bit until his tongue reached her dripping pussy. Over and over his tongue laved her folds as his finger moved in and out, her warm walls tightening around it as she squirmed and moaned above him.

He knew she was close to exploding, so he slid out from under her, then entered her hard and fast from behind. While he pumped his cock in and out of her, he rubbed her sweet spot. When her walls squeezed him hard and her muffled moans increased in intensity, he knew she was going over the edge. He kept pummeling until he felt his balls tightening, pulling up inside him. And then the knot at the base of his cock dissolved in fire, melting.

"Fuck, Cara. Fuck!" Panting, he collapsed on top of her and lay still, his heart beating wildly against his rib cage. After a long while, he rolled off her and pulled her close to him.

She ran her nails up and down his chest. "I love you so much. That was awesome."

"Fuckin' awesome, babe. I love you too." He kissed the top of her head and nestled her closer, glancing out the window, watching the falling snow. "It's really coming down hard."

"You don't have to go back out, do you?"

"I've got to go to the shop for a few hours." He tilted her head back and looked deeply into her eyes. "You make me feel real good, woman." Bending down, he kissed her passionately.

And then Isa's cry came over the monitor.

"She's up," Cara said as she began to pull away from him. "She's not into long naps like Braxton was at that age."

Hawk pushed her back down and kissed her gently. "You relax. I'll get her. I have some time before I go to the shop. Kimber's there, so I don't have to worry."

He pulled on his boxers and jeans and walked out of the room. Picking Isa up, he held her close as he walked over to the changing table, grinning as he changed her diaper. She looked so much like Cara. With Isa in his arms once more, he peeked into the master bedroom and saw Cara sleeping.

"It's just you and me, princess," he said against Isa's cheek, and then he walked down the stairs.

CHAPTER THREE

BAYLEE

STARING INTO THE refrigerator, Baylee scanned the shelves for the diet ginger ale she was sure she'd seen the day before. Doubting Axe would drink it, she moved jars of olives, pickles, and cherry peppers out of the way. A wave of nausea seized her, and she straightened up and shuffled over to the kitchen chair. *I feel like shit.*

"What's wrong, babe?" Axe asked as he walked into the kitchen. He came over to her and placed his hand on her shoulder, kneading it gently.

"I think I have the flu. I feel like shit. Did you drink the ginger ale that was in the fridge?"

He chuckled. "No. It's not really my kind of drink." He walked over and opened the refrigerator. "Here it is. Do you want ice in it?"

"Yeah. I didn't see it. Where was it?"

"In the door. You've been under the weather for the last week. Maybe you should see a doctor."

The clink of ice against glass and the pop of the can deafened her. Her head swam and her stomach gurgled and heaved. Grasping the edge of the table, she pulled herself up and dashed to the guest bathroom, barely making it before she threw up. Clinging to the sides of the toilet bowl, she breathed heavily, waiting for the next bout of nausea to attack.

"I'm calling Doc," Axe's deep voice said from behind her.

"The one who patches all of you guys up when you slip into your caveman mode? Oh… shit." Another hurl into the toilet.

"He's a doctor and a damn good one. He's been part of the club for years, since way before I joined. Maybe he can give you something to make you feel better." He knelt down beside her and swept her hair back from her damp forehead.

"Nothing can help the flu but rest and seeing it through. I don't have time to be sick."

"Isn't chicken soup supposed to help? I'm sure we got a can of it."

"Just the thought of soup in a can makes me sick."

"If you tell me what to do, maybe I can make it for you."

"Are you serious? When's the last time I cooked for you since we've been together?"

"A year ago."

"And how was it? I won't be insulted."

He laughed. "Shitty as hell. Okay, I can run over to Weiner's Deli and get you a quart of their chicken soup."

"I can't even think of eating right now. Maybe for tonight. I'll let you know. I think the worst of it is over."

Axe helped her up and rubbed her back while she rinsed and brushed her teeth. Looking in the mirror, she groaned. "I look like a mess." Redness lined her hazel eyes, her face was white as a sheet, and a sheen of sweat shone on her skin.

"You always look beautiful to me," he said as he kissed the top of her disheveled hair.

"Thanks for that, but I know what I look like. How in the hell am I going to make it to the meeting the old ladies are having at the club-house?"

"You're not. I'll just call Banger and tell him you're sick. Belle and the others can manage just fine without you."

"But I canceled the last two meetings because of work. They'll think I'm not interested in helping out with the Christmas charity event."

"No they won't. They'll understand. They're busy too. Belle, Cara, and Kimber have a special obligation because their men are officers. I'm not, so you're good. And there's no way I'm letting you out of the house being this sick. Are you okay to go back to the kitchen, or do you want to go to bed?"

"The couch is good. I need that ginger ale. When I was a kid, my mom always gave me ginger ale with soda crackers, and I remember it always helped. After she was killed, I kept the tradition up."

"My mom never knew if I was sick or not. I can look to see if I have any crackers." Axe wrapped his arm around her shoulders and led her into the family room, helping her down on the couch.

"They're in the pantry. I'm actually feeling a bit better."

"I'm calling Banger."

"Hold off on it. The meeting isn't until this afternoon, and I may feel a lot better by then. It may have been something I ate. I thought the leftovers tasted funny last night."

"Yeah, you mentioned that." The ice cubes clinked as Axe set the glass down on the coffee table. He sat next to her and placed her head in his lap, raking his fingers through her hair.

After an hour of lying down, the nausea had lessened, so Baylee sat up and ripped open the cracker wrapper. Nibbling on one, she leaned against Axe and placed her hand on his jean-clad thigh.

He brushed a kiss on her left temple. "Feeling better?"

She nodded. "I think I'm good enough to go to the meeting." She held up her hand as Axe opened his mouth. "I know what you're going to say, but I promise I won't stay longer than a couple of hours, and when I get home, I'm in for the rest of the day. I'm also going to take tomorrow off work. And I would love for you to bring me chicken soup for dinner. You can get yourself a Rueben sandwich. I know how you love the way Weiner's Deli makes them."

At the thought of corned beef and sauerkraut, her stomach rolled over once again, and she placed her hand over it to calm it down. She hoped he didn't notice or he'd make her stay home regardless of what she said.

"Okay, but if you're not better in a couple of days, I'm calling Doc. And I don't want any fucking arguments about it."

"Okay, honey." She bent her head back and he kissed her softly on the lips. "You may not want to do that for a while. You don't want to get the flu."

"Fuck that. I haven't been sick since I was a kid. And there's no damn way I'm not going to kiss you." He kissed her again, harder and deeper.

She pulled away and laughed. "I don't want you blaming me when you get sick."

"Never." He leaned over and kissed her quickly, then rose to his feet. "I gotta get over to Rocky's to see what's going on with the ordering. Banger said the manager we just canned had it all fucked up. If we find out he'd been stealing food, he's not going to like the way we deal with it."

"If he was stealing inventory, just call the cops."

His dark eyes narrowed. "We like to handle things internally. We don't need help from the fuckin' badges."

A shiver ran up her spine as it always did when she heard Axe say things like that. Most of the time, she forgot he was an outlaw biker, considering his world didn't really collide with hers very often. The family get-togethers were fun times with the members, the old ladies, and the children. Those times didn't depict the dark, gritty, and violent side of the club. For her, it was best to push that part to the far reaches of her mind.

"I'm going to take another shower. You don't have to babysit me, honey."

Looping his arms around her waist, he pulled her back against him. "I want to. I wanna make sure you're okay. We can walk out together. Take your time. The restaurant's not going anywhere."

She brought his hands to her mouth and kissed them. "I love you."

"Me too, babe."

An hour later, Baylee cruised down the desolate road that led to the clubhouse. The snow sparkled under the brightness of the sun, and the frost on the evergreens glistened beneath clear blue skies. The mountain peaks, covered in snow, looked like upside-down snow cones, only more jagged.

She stopped at the iron gate and smiled when Rusty, the newest prospect, came up to her car. Rolling down the window, she gave the tall, lanky biker her driver's license. Even though he knew her from the numerous times she'd been at the club with Axe, he acted like he'd never seen her before.

"Hi, Rusty. How's life treating you?"

"Good." He handed back her ID.

Laughing to herself, she drove through the checkpoint. She knew Rusty wouldn't engage in conversation with her. He knew his duties as a prospect were to do whatever club members asked him to do and to keep his mouth shut unless he was spoken to by a club member or an old lady. A prospect never initiated any communication unless it was an emergency, and then he'd convey that to a member only. Baylee was surprised at the number of men who wanted to prospect for the Insurgents. She couldn't imagine jumping on command as a life she'd want, but each of the brothers had gone through a couple of years of prospecting before they donned their full patches.

When she walked into the clubhouse, the first thing she saw was a young club girl wrapped around Tigger. *Doesn't that asshole ever work?* To say she couldn't stand Tigger was an understatement. He epitomized everything she despised in a man, and the way he treated Sofia broke her heart. But if she was being totally honest with herself, she also despised the way Sofia allowed Tigger to treat her. She knew she was being unfair, and that Sofia had come from a background laden with abuse and neglect, but the strong feminist strain inside her made her want to grab the thin woman by her shoulders and shake some sense into her.

"Baylee," Belle called out, and she made her way over to a large round table near the pool tables.

"I'm glad you could make it," Cara said as she glanced in the direction of Tigger and the woman.

Baylee shook her head. "I can't believe he has the fucking nerve to be so open about his cheating, especially with Sofia coming to the meeting."

"Sofia's not coming," Cherri said. "And Tigger's a fuckin' idiot." The women burst into laughter, and a jolt of satisfaction rushed through Baylee as she saw Tigger turn and glare at the women.

"We're all here. Are you feeling okay? You look peaked," Belle said.

"Actually, I've been feeling like crap for the last few weeks. I didn't think I was going to make it today because I was so nauseous this morning. I think I may have the flu, but it comes and goes, which is weird."

"Do you throw up?" Addie asked.

"Sometimes."

"Do certain smells really bother you?" Cara said.

Baylee nodded.

"What about heartburn?" Clotille said.

"Not really."

Cherri leaned forward. "Does the nausea last all day some days and only a little on others?"

"Yeah, or sometimes I'm not nauseous at all. Why all the questions? Is that what the flu symptoms are like this season?"

"Sounds like you're pregnant," Belle said, and the others voiced their agreement.

"Pregnant? No way. Impossible. I'm on birth control."

"Classic signs of morning sickness," Cara said.

Morning sickness? Pregnant? I can't be fucking pregnant. I'm in the middle of opening another office in Aspen. And Axe doesn't want kids. We both decided if we changed our minds, it'd be years from now. I can't be. No. Impossible.

Clotille placed her hand over Baylee's and squeezed it. "This is so exciting. You have to go to a doctor right away. Dr. Neely is the best. I got her name from Cara when I was pregnant with James."

Baylee pulled her hand away. "Wait. Stop. I'm not pregnant. Axe and I don't want kids."

"Who doesn't want kids? I'm so happy my Paisey's in my life,"

Cherri said softly.

"Paisley's adorable, and so are Harley, Braxton, Isa, James, and all the other kids, but we just don't want them. Maybe when we're in our late thirties we may change our minds, but we're good the way we are."

"Just because you don't want kids doesn't mean you're not pregnant," Belle said.

"And the pill isn't foolproof. You're one of the two percent like I was," Addie added.

All of a sudden, a wave of nausea washed over Baylee. She covered her mouth and ran to the bathroom, hoping she could make it in time and not embarrass the hell out of herself.

Twenty minutes later, she splashed cold water on her face and finger-combed her hair. Dread wove through her as she tried to remember the last time she'd had her period. It seemed that she was a little late, but she was never regular like most of her friends were.

"I've just got the flu. That's all," she said to her reflection. Drying her face, she fought down the nausea as she decided to call it quits and go home to get under the covers.

The knowing looks on the old ladies' faces irked her. "I guess I shouldn't have tried to come today. I'm going to go home and get into bed. This flu is the shits. Call me and update me about the fundraiser, Belle. I'll talk to you all later."

"If you need Dr. Neely's phone number, let me know," Clotille said as she left.

Baylee looked over her shoulder and mustered a smile. "Thanks, but a few days of rest, soda crackers, and chicken soup will do wonders."

I can't be pregnant.

And with that thought in her mind, she stepped out into the sunshine and breathed in the frosty air.

CHAPTER FOUR

SOFIA

S OFIA SWAYED OVER to the bathroom and turned on the faucet. Cupping the cool water in her hands, she rinsed her beaten face, wincing when her fingers touched the skin. Drying the water gently from her face with a towel, dread wove through her as she assessed what Tigger's recent tantrum had done to her. There was a cut above her right eye, the blood already dried and brown, and bruises were beginning to form on both cheeks. She glanced down, noting the grip marks on her arms were pronounced; he loved to keep her from running as he raged and screamed.

She hung the towel up and walked slowly to the couch in the living room. When she sat down, a small yelp escaped her lips. She placed her hands on her belly and pressed down, hoping the pain would subside. It felt like her guts were on fire.

She glanced over at the small china cabinet they'd purchased together when Tigger had first been released from prison. How happy she'd been back then. She'd waited four long years for his release, marking each day off her calendar with a black marker. Twice a month, she'd drive two hundred miles to Canon City to see him, then turn around and drive back to Pinewood Springs. Back then, she'd thought she'd die from missing him so much. The whole reason he had done time was because he was protecting her from some jerk who was coming on to her and saying nasty things. Tigger flipped out and had practically beaten the man to death. *He wouldn't have done that if he didn't love me, would he?* She asked herself that question a lot.

The first six months after Tigger had been released on parole, they couldn't get enough of each other. They fucked, made love, watched silly movies, went for long rides on his Harley, and ate tons of pizza. It had been romantic and magical, and she couldn't remember a time in her life that she'd been happier.

And then it had ended.

If she had to pinpoint the exact time it'd stopped, it was when they went to Steelers with the rest of the Insurgents and she was sitting with Cara, Addie, Cherri, and Kimber, laughing and talking with them. Tigger was with his brothers, but she'd noticed he kept looking at her, and each time she'd glanced at him, his gaze grew more hostile and ominous. Not knowing what was going on with him, she presumed something had come up with one of the rival clubs and he was super pissed about it. A lot of the Insurgent men wore perpetual scowls or menacing looks on their faces, so she'd grown used to it.

When they'd said their goodbyes and went to the parking lot, he turned her toward him and smacked her full force across the face. Her teeth had rattled and she'd been so surprised by it that she simply stood there gaping. He then grabbed her by the neck and pushed her against his Harley. People had started milling out of the bar by that point, so he walked her over to the bushes and threw her into them, then started choking her. She'd clawed at his hands, but the rage and anger flashing in his eyes made her think she was going to die. Not sure what had provoked such a reaction in him, she helplessly tried to push him away. And then he'd let go.

"Find your own fuckin' way home. Next time you ignore me or look at another man, I'll beat the shit outta you!" He'd stomped away, leaving a sobbing, confused woman to fend for herself.

From that day on, he lived with anger in his heart. Of course, she'd been too ashamed to ask Cara or Cherri for help, so she waited in the bushes until they'd all left, then walked the four miles to her home. By the time she'd arrived at the house, the rage had been replaced by professions of love in his quiet moments of regret. She'd forgiven him, believing his words that it would never happen again. And now, three years later, he still professed love and his regret, but the abuse had become more frequent.

I've become my mother. The irony touched her deeply as she remembered how she'd sworn to herself that she'd never let a man place an angry hand on her like her mother had.

Sofia swung her legs up and leaned back, her head on the couch arm, her legs stretched out. The bruises would slowly vanish and the broken bones would heal, but what about her battered emotions? She was torn inside and those tears remained open wounds, never healing or scarring. The man she loved did that to her, and how could he? He left her a ghost of a person, living but not alive. She stifled a sob with the scuffed palm of her hand and turned her face into the pillow, her salty tears clinging to the cracks on her lips.

The chime of the doorbell made her heart race. *What time is it? I haven't made dinner or anything. Don't let it be him. Not yet.* She pushed herself up and shuffled over to the door while smoothing her hair down. *He's going to be mad that I don't have any makeup on. I didn't know it was so late!* With trembling fingers, she undid the locks and opened the door, her stomach in knots and her heart in her throat.

"Hiya, Sofia. I was in the neighborhood." Wheelie's gray eyes smiled.

"Uh… what time is it?" she whispered.

"Two o'clock."

Relief washed over her and she giggled from giddiness. She had time to clean up, put herself together, and get dinner on the table before he came home. *If he's coming home.* The thought of him with one of the club girls made her eyes water, but she wouldn't call or text him to see if he'd be home. That would only make him angry, and she couldn't withstand another of his rages in the same day.

"Can I come in?"

She darted her eyes around the street, making sure no one was watching. She was positive Tigger had people informing him of everything she did.

"I don't think that's a good idea."

"Just for a minute? Tigger's at the club. He'll be there for a while. The club's got some shit going on that we have to figure out."

Wanting the company, but afraid Tigger would find out she had a man in the house, she started to close the door. "I don't think Tigger would want you in here without him being home."

"We're brothers. It's cool. Besides, he didn't mind when I'd take you to the pen to see him when your car broke down."

She smiled, then winced from the pain. Wheelie had been a good friend to Tigger and to her while he was locked up. He'd been at the biker bar the night Tigger had gone ballistic and been arrested. A bond had formed between the three of them that night, only to grow stronger when Wheelie had helped her out so many times during Tigger's incarceration.

Moving aside, she opened the door wider, trying to hide her face behind her hair as he slid past her. "Have a seat. Do you want a beer?"

Wheelie sank down on the couch. "Sure. Do you think you can open some of these drapes? It's dark as hell in here."

"I like it dark. The light gives me a headache, and I feel one coming on." She took out a can of Coors for Wheelie and a Pepsi for her. "Here you go." She handed it to him.

He popped open the top and took a long drink, tilting his head back. His dark brown hair fell just below his collar and the silver earring he wore in his right ear dangled. Placing the beer down on the table, he smiled at her and she turned away.

When she'd first met Wheelie, she'd thought he was a heartbreaker in leather. He was good-looking and he knew it, but he wasn't stuck-up about it; he just knew he was handsome the way a person knew he had two ears, a nose, and a mouth. His square jaw, full lips, and perfectly shaped brows over gray eyes the same color of the ocean during a storm made her give him a once-over. Tigger was nice-looking, but Wheelie was ruggedly gorgeous in a way that drove women wild. He was buff, though not like Tigger's body builder's physique; Wheelie's body was toned, taut, and perfection. And the perpetual scruff he wore made her want to touch his face. When Tigger had scruff, he'd always shave it when she told him she liked it. That was his way of showing her that her opinions, likes, and dislikes didn't mean shit to him. It was his way of controlling her. One of many.

"The women missed you at the meeting today."

She crossed and uncrossed her legs. "I wasn't feeling well." *He must see the shape my face is in.* She pulled her hair over the right side, trying to cover what she could. "How've you been?"

"Good. You don't have to hide your face. I've already seen what that sonofabitch did to you. I saw it when you opened the door. Is that the real reason you didn't come?"

Looking down, her insides quivered and her eyelid twitched. "You know it is. I don't want to hear anything about it. I already know how you feel about it. You've made all that perfectly clear before. I'm just not in the mood, okay?"

Wheelie stared at her, his eyes soft and kind, and then he nodded and picked up his beer. "You wanna go out for dinner when Tigger goes on the poker run over the weekend?"

Fear that they'd be spotted assaulted her. "No. I can't. Please don't ask again."

He ran his eyes over her. "Okay. What about me bringing dinner to you? We can eat here, talk, and watch a movie."

Excitement coursed through her as she pictured them having a pleasant night without any fear, incriminations, or insults. She missed companionship with other people. Tigger had made sure that her friends and family didn't call or come over anymore, and the contact she had with the old ladies was only for club purposes. After she kept telling them no for happy hour get-togethers, dinners, and movies, they'd stopped asking. She missed having a friend. *But what if Tigger finds out? He'd kill me for sure.*

"It wouldn't be a big deal. We're friends, right?"

We are friends and it shouldn't be a big deal. She rubbed her cheek and winced, forgetting it was sore from her earlier beating. If Tigger had hurt her just for not washing his favorite pair of jeans, she could only imagine what he'd do if she had Wheelie over for dinner when he was out of town. Back and forth she wrestled with what she should do, her mind a scramble of fear, excitement, disgust, and defiance. *I'm so fucking tired of being afraid. I'm even more tired of being isolated.* She couldn't remember when she'd spent time with someone other than Tigger. She was desperate for a pleasant interaction with someone.

"So what do you say?" Wheelie asked.

I want to. Can I do this? Am I willing to suffer the consequences if Tigger finds out? "I'm not sure. I'd like to, but I don't know," she said softly.

He put his hand on hers, and his cool touch calmed her, parting the reeling emotions and chaotic thoughts. She glanced up at him and his kind eyes pulled her in, and an inner strength surged inside her. Enough was enough. She'd deal with the fallout when it came, but she wanted to spend time with Wheelie. He'd always been a good friend to her. She breathed out a ragged breath. "You coming over would be good."

"Then it's a plan. Saturday night good?"

Any night would be fine since she never had any plans. She nodded. "I can't have Tigger find out."

"Tigger actually suggested that me, Bear, Chas, and Jax look in on you while he's gone to make sure you're safe."

"Oh."

"I told the others I'd keep an eye on you, so we have the whole weekend. If the roads aren't too icy, we can go for a short ride on Sunday if you like."

Sofia loved being on the back of a motorcycle. It was freeing and it felt like she was soaring high in the sky. Tigger knew how much she loved it, so he took it away from her. They hadn't gone on bike rides for the past two years, but what really hurt her was knowing he'd taken some of the club girls and a couple of hoodrats on the rides she'd loved so much.

"I'd really love that. It's been a while since I was on a Harley." It'd been a long time since she'd looked forward to anything, but anticipation weaved around her nerves and spine at the idea of riding once more, and she had to will herself to calm down. Tigger had taught her that the more she wanted something, longed for it, the less she'd get it. She wouldn't put it past him to fuck this up for her.

An icy fear grabbed hold of her spine. *What if Tigger's setting me up? What if this is a test?*

"What's wrong?"

"Nothing. Are you sure Tigger told you this was cool?"

"He said to keep my eye on you. I didn't tell him how I was going to do that. Pizza, a movie, and a bike ride can just be between us. You know how he overreacts."

Thrumming her fingers against her mouth, she nodded.

"Then I'll come by at around six on Saturday. I better get going."

"Yeah, I should get this place cleaned up and get dinner going."

"Do you need help cleaning up?" He placed his hand on her forearm.

She jerked it away as though it were on fire. "No, I'm good. The place is clean. I mean, that's all I do is clean it every day. I just need to straighten out the clutter."

Looking around, he said, "There's no clutter."

"Yeah… well, Tigger likes things to be in their own place. Like the magazine on the table. He'll go ballistic if he sees it. It needs to go in the magazine rack. I mean, I can see his point. He bought the magazine rack for a reason and that's where magazines are supposed to go, so I can see why he'd be mad about that." She ran her hands up and down her arms. *He thinks I'm a nut. I can see the way he's looking at me, but he doesn't live with Tigger. Everything has to be in its place.*

Wheelie cupped her chin and tilted her head back, his gaze locking with hers. "If you need me, call me. You remember my number, right?" She blinked rapidly. "I mean it. You don't need to put up with this shit from him. You deserve a whole lot better. If I knew you were ready to walk out on this fucker, I'd go to the club right now and beat the shit outta him for what he's done to you." Tears slid down her swollen cheeks and over his fingers. "I care what happens to you." Then he bent down and softly brushed his lips over hers. "Watch yourself."

The lump in her throat grew larger as she watched him ride away. She closed the door, then picked up the magazine from the table. Hugging it to her, she let out all the anguish she'd felt for the past several years, her wails and sobs filling the small house.

Chapter Five

Throttle

"DID YOU READ this article in the paper?" Kimber asked as she thumbed through the *Pinewood Springs Tribune.*

Throttle came up behind her and gave her ass a quick smack. "Which one?"

"It's the most bizarre thing I've ever heard of. Someone's breaking into people's houses and destroying their Christmas decorations. What the fuck's up with that? And the paper's coined him 'The Crazed Grinch.'"

Throttle laughed and poured himself another cup of coffee. "Is that all that's going on around here?"

"It's serious. I mean, the person does a lot of damage like breaking toys, taking expensive gifts, and cutting wires. He's done several thousands of dollars in damages, and he's hit ten houses so far. What a fucking lunatic. This town seems to be filled with them."

"You being the biggest nut of all, but I love you." He spun her around and kissed her, slipping his hand inside her panties. "You feel nice and wet."

"It's probably from early this morning." She laughed when he nuzzled her neck.

"What can I say, babe? I can't get enough of you." He picked her up and placed her on top of the table. Glancing down, he saw a picture of a destroyed Christmas tree and shoved the newspaper off the table.

"I have to get to the shop," she murmured. "Hawk's in Silverton buying parts and I have to open up."

"No one's gonna be lining up to get their Harleys fixed in this damn cold." He pulled down her black panties and unzipped his jeans, then bent down and captured her lips. He was so addicted to the way she tasted, smelled, looked, and fucked. Everything about her always kept his dick on high alert, and he could never get his fill. He loved her more than he ever thought it possible for a man to love a woman; he was intoxicated by her very essence.

Spreading her legs farther apart, he swiped his tongue across her clit, and her ass jumped off the table. He chuckled and continued licking her, locking his gaze on hers as he sucked her sweet nub into his mouth, savoring her juices. A moan broke from her and her breath came in rapid pants.

"Kiss me," she rasped as she gripped his hair and pulled hard.

He slid up her body, forging a wet trail along the way until he covered her mouth. His lips were glistening as he kissed her hard. "Do you like the way you taste?" he said against her mouth before plunging his tongue inside. She writhed beneath him, pulling even harder on his free-flowing hair while her tongue twirled around his in a sensuous dance.

Grabbing his cock, he pushed into her while his mouth still covered hers. He pushed in deeper, harder, and whimpers rose from her throat. He pulled away, pinched her nipples hard, and then thrust into her again and again. Her ass smacked against the table as he kept pumping into her, and he felt her ready to come—all tight and swollen. He wanted her pussy squeezing his cock as he exploded in her. Faster. Harder. She cried out and her warm walls gripped and tightened around his dick, driving him to climax. Then he shot into her, his seed filling her up.

"Fuck, Kimber."

Her gaze was glassy and unfocused, a slow smile spreading across her face as she pulled him close to her. Their rapid heartbeats pounded against each other's chests, and they stayed fused together for a few minutes before Throttle pulled out of her. Grabbing a napkin, he wiped his dick and then shoved it into his jeans. Dipping his head down, he kissed her passionately.

"Great way to start the day," he muttered on her lips.

Laughing, she took his hands and he helped her sit up. "If Hawk gets on my ass about being late, you're going down for it." She squeezed his butt and kissed him quickly. "It was awesome."

He watched as her hips swayed while she walked to the bedroom, her robe and panties in her hand. *Fuck, she's beautiful.* He never got tired of seeing her naked. She stirred deep emotions and desire in him, and they grew stronger each day.

"What're you going to do today?" she asked when she came back, fully clothed with her jacket and hat on.

"I'm gonna check on how the crew did shoveling the contracts we have, and then I got some errands to run." Throttle's landscape business in the winter consisted mostly of snow removal. Sometimes he'd help out and drive the snow plow, but mostly his partner, Rags, liked doing it, leaving Throttle to handle quality control on the numerous contracts their business had.

She gave him a quick kiss on the lips. "I've got to go. How's chili sound for dinner?"

"Good as long as you make some cornbread to go along with it."

"Yes, sir." She saluted him.

"Smartass." He smacked her butt. She giggled, blew him a kiss, and went into the garage.

Throttle put the coffee cups in the dishwasher, then took out his phone and called Rags.

"Yo. How'd the crew do with the snow removal early this morning? I got a complaint from one of our contracts. She said the guys didn't do a good job."

"Was it from Mrs. Christiansen?"

"Yeah, that's the name. Do you already know about it?"

"I went to check it out and it looked good to me. She insisted that she wanted you to come by and discuss it with her," Rags said.

"What the fuck's up with that? Did you tell her you're one of the owners?"

"Yep. She didn't give a damn."

Throttle scrubbed his face. "I don't have time for this shit. I'll give her a call. We got a lot more important contracts we have to take care of. If she drops us, it won't make a difference to the business income since I think we're gonna get Allard Food Mart."

"That'd rock. When are they gonna let you know?"

"Tomorrow, but I'm pretty sure we've got it."

"Fuckin' sweet. You wanna join me and Wheelie for some chow at Ruthie's?"

"What time?"

"We're gonna head over there now."

"I'm on my way."

Throttle slipped the phone into his pocket, threw on his leather jacket, and picked up the keys to his Harley. He'd missed being on it. For the past couple of weeks, the snow had been too heavy to ride safely on his bike. When he was younger, he didn't give a shit about what condition the roads were in; he just cared about the ride. But now that he was thirty-seven and had Kimber in his life, he wasn't into taking stupid chances. He backed out of the garage and headed toward town, the rush of cold air dancing around him and whipping against his cheeks.

When he walked into the diner, a blast of heat enveloped him as he scanned the packed room for Rags and Wheelie. Sparkling silver and gold miniature trees lined the shelves behind the lunch counter, and multicolored strands of lights framed the windows, cash register, and pass-through counter. The clatter of dishes, the waitstaff calling out their orders, and the lively beats of "Jingle Bell Rock" cooing from the speakers filled the place.

"Hiya, handsome," Ruthie said as she placed a slice of pie in front of an older gentleman sitting at the counter.

Throttle lifted his chin to her as he took off his leather gloves.

"Your two friends are at the last booth next to the window. Coffee as usual?"

"Yeah. Thanks," he said as he made his way to the table.

He slid in next to Rags and picked up the menu. "Did you two order already?"

"We waited for you," Rags said as he waved the waitress over.

Stella had been working at Ruthie's for the past twelve years and was one of the Insurgents' favorite waitresses. She placed a glass of water and a steaming cup of coffee in front of Throttle.

"Thanks, Stella. How's life been treating you?" he asked as he stirred sugar into his coffee.

"This week? Shitty as all hell. Last week? Not bad."

The guys laughed and placed their orders of chicken fried steak, eggs, and cottage fried potatoes.

"Damn, it's cold outside," Wheelie said as he picked up a glass of orange juice.

"I thought my balls were gonna freeze off when I rode over here, but I was going fuckin' crazy without riding." Throttle wrapped his hands around the warm cup.

"I know what you mean. It's been so damn snowy and icy the last couple of weeks. I'm getting restless too. How were the roads?"

"Icy as hell, but it felt good being on my bike." Throttle took a sip of coffee.

"I'm leaving the icy rides to guys like Jerry, Axe, Chas, and the other younger members. Remember how we used to go on the back roads and do wheelies in the snow?" Rags asked.

Wheelie laughed. He was known for taking crazy chances with his Harley, and his freestyle and complex wheelies earned him his road name. "Hell, I still go out and do that shit."

Stella placed three piping-hot plates in front of them and a basket of warm biscuits in the center of the table. "Except for refills, is there anything else you need?"

"That should do it, darlin'," Rags said as he reached over and took a biscuit.

"I heard Mrs. Christiansen is being a pain in your ass," Wheelie said before he shoved a big bite into his mouth.

Throttle nodded as he chewed.

"I told the bitch she could tell me what the problem was, but she just told me the shoveling wasn't to her liking and she needed to speak to you and you only," Rags said.

"She's a horny one. I guess her old man isn't giving her want she needs," Wheelie said.

"Whaddaya mean?" Throttle asked.

"She's always hitting on guys who work for her. A buddy of mine cleans carpets, and he told me that when he was doing a job over at her place, she kept staring at him the whole time. And when he was getting ready to leave, she patted his ass and gave him her cell number." Wheelie shook his head, laughing.

"Did he fuck her?" Throttle asked.

"Yeah. He got a lot of referrals from her."

"Is he still fucking her?" Rags buttered a biscuit.

"Nah, it was only for a month or so, but he got a lot of lasting business from it, so he's happy."

"I bet he is," Throttle said. "If that's what she wants from me, she's gonna be disappointed 'cause I'm outta commission."

"I should be insulted the bitch didn't want me," Rags said.

"I told you you're too damn skinny." Throttle chuckled.

"I heard she's a real looker too." Wheelie pushed his empty plate away.

"I know her name. Did we do her yard this past summer?" Throttle asked Rags.

Rags slowly shook his head. "No, she's a new contract, but she called because she said Lara Mayfield recommended us. More specifically, she recommended you."

"That's right. Damn, Lara was a pain in the ass. If her old man didn't have all those rental properties, I would've dropped her account," Throttle said as he leaned back against the booth.

"She wanted your cock so bad." Rags laughed.

"Figures they're friends. Damn. We need to tell these women's husbands how to perform before we take the contracts," Throttle joked, and the other men laughed.

"You guys want any more coffee?" Stella asked as she cleared off the table.

"I could go for a cinnamon bear claw and a bit more coffee," Rags said while the other two shook their heads.

"Be right back." Stella walked away.

"Where the hell do you put it?" Throttle asked Rags, who shrugged.

A loud rumble outside had the three men looking out the window. Tigger, Bones, and Cruiser killed the engines on their Harleys and walked toward the front glass doors.

"I thought they were on a poker run," Rags said.

"They leave on Friday," Wheelie replied.

"Hey, brothers. How's it goin'?" Bones asked as the three men approached the table.

"Not too bad," Throttle said as he scooted over. Tigger slid in beside him, and Bones and Cruiser slipped in next to Wheelie. "The chicken fried steak and eggs rocks."

"I'll have to try it. Did you see Brenda?" Tigger asked as his eyes darted around the room.

"Brenda?" Throttle asked.

"The hot waitress with big-as-hell tits and hair down to her sweet ass." Tigger continued to look around while Bones and Cruiser sniggered.

"I'd love to sink my cock into her," Cruiser said.

While Rags chuckled and Throttle laughed, he noticed Wheelie staring at Tigger with cold eyes. *He's got it bad for Sofia. Fuck.* He cleared his throat and looked at Rags. "You about done here?"

With a puzzled look on his face, Rags wiped his mouth. "Yeah. You in a hurry?"

"Yeah. I gotta get something."

"I've got to get going too," Wheelie said as Bones and Cruiser got up to let him out. He pulled out some money and picked up the bill.

"I'm going with you guys." Rags slipped out of the booth, and after he and Throttle said goodbye to their brothers, they joined Wheelie at the cash register and threw in their share of the bill.

Outside, the icy wind lashed around them as they walked bent over against the cold to the parking lot. Clumps of wet flakes drifted down, the pavement mushy beneath their black boots.

"Are you headed to Christiansen's house?" Rags asked, his breath forming pale clouds.

"No. I'll call her tonight. I'm headed to Trinity Jewelers." Throttle pulled his gloves on.

"Whatcha got going at the jewelers?" Wheelie cupped his hands together and blew into them.

"I'm getting something for Kimber. You guys wanna come along? I could use some help in deciding."

"I got nothing to do," Wheelie said.

"Count me in. Do you wanna put your bike on the bed and ride back with us? Looks like it's gonna snow for a while." Rags opened the door to his pickup.

"That'll work," he said as he rolled his bike over to the truck. He glanced inside the diner and saw Tigger and Cruiser shaking their heads and laughing while they watched Rags cover his Harley with a tarp. If he were their age, he wouldn't be caught dead doing what he was doing, but age brought wisdom and love toned down the urge to be stupidly macho. He lifted himself up and slid into the passenger seat of the truck.

Rags found parking right in front of the store, and when they went inside, a well-groomed man with graying hair at his temples came up to them, his shoulders drawn up tight around him. Several of the patrons took a few steps backward as if to distance themselves from the three men clad in leather and denim, chains dangling down their pant legs, and earrings catching the overhead lights.

"Is there something I can do for you?" the man asked as he gripped the corner of one of the cases.

Throttle chuckled. "I'm looking to buy a ring."

"What kind of ring? Engagement, wedding, or any occasion?" The man tugged at his ear.

"We're not planning on robbing you," Wheelie said. "If we were, we would've already been done with it and gone. So you can all fuckin' relax."

Gasps from behind him as well as the salesman's skin turning ashen made Throttle laugh and clap Wheelie on the back. "You crack me up, dude." Rags joined in. The more people cringed away from them, the harder they laughed until the salesman cracked a smile and chuckled.

Throttle cleared his throat. "I'm looking for an engagement ring."

"What the fuck?" Rags said as he followed Throttle to one of the cases lining the back wall.

Rings of all shapes and sizes sparkled under the soft lights, and the man took out a key and unlocked one of the cases. He pulled out a large solitaire on a white gold band.

"This is one of our most popular engagement rings," he said as he set the ring on a very small black velvet pillow.

"Dude, is this for real?" Rags leaned over and looked at the ring.

"Yeah. I'm gonna ask her if she wants to get hitched. I don't want you guys saying shit to anyone until I do. If you blow this, I'll beat your asses."

"Why do you wanna get married? She's already your old lady," Wheelie said.

Throttle picked up the ring and held it up, turning it from side to side. "I don't know. I just do. Whaddaya think of this one?"

Rags and Wheelie looked at the ring in Throttle's hand. "It looks like a ring with a diamond. It's okay, I guess," Rags said.

"Exactly. It's too ordinary."

After the salesman showed him dozens of rings, an incredulous look spread across his face when Throttle pointed to a ring and said, "Fuck. That's it." At that point, Wheelie and Rags were both sitting on chairs the salesman had brought out for them, fiddling with their phones.

"This one?" he asked as he took out a ring with a black diamond solitaire.

"Yeah. It's totally Kimber. All pink and beautiful with a wicked dark side to her. This totally rocks."

"The princess-cut stone is three carats, and the surrounding pink sapphires are a total weight of another carat. The rest of the wide band is black diamonds, set in fourteen-karat white gold. You have good taste. It's pretty expensive." The man looked fixedly at him.

"How much?"

"Thirty-nine-hundred dollars. I can give you fifteen percent off since we're having a Christmas special." The man put the ring back in the case and locked it. The small smile he offered Throttle said that he'd just wasted a couple of hours on a guy in leather who could never begin to afford the ring.

"I'll take it," Throttle said.

"What? Are you sure you have the mon—I mean, we'll have to run the amount on your card to make sure it goes through."

He sneered. Looking behind him, he said, "Get your asses over here. I want you to see the ring I picked out."

"'Bout fuckin' time," Rags grumbled as he and Wheelie shuffled over.

"It's kickass, yeah?"

"It's great. Are we ready to go?" Rags said.

"Kimber's gonna love it. It's not the usual clear diamond ring. And I'm with Rags... are we ready to blow this joint? I can't believe how damn long it took you to pick out a ring."

"Quit bitchin' and tell me how much money you got on you. This ring costs four grand. I only have three on me. You got a thousand between the two of you? I'll pay you back when we get to my place."

They nodded and handed over the money, the salesclerk watching with bulging eyes as Throttle laid the bills down on the counter.

A half hour later, they were downing beers in front of a crackling fire, their feet up on the coffee table. Outside, the snow fell like confetti from the grayish-white sky, blanketing everything in shimmering white.

As Throttle brought the beer bottle to his lips, he glanced over at Wheelie. "What's up with you and Tigger?"

Wheelie's eyes narrowed and he stiffened. "Nothing."

"Bullshit," said Rags.

Throttle reached over and put his beer on the side table. "Now don't go taking a swing at me like you did at the club last week, but you gotta leave this shit alone, dude. Sofia's with Tigger. She wants to be with him."

"You're not telling me something I don't know. Fuckin' leave it alone." Wheelie grabbed his bottle and guzzled it down.

"Throttle's just bringing it up because Jax said you told him you'd keep an eye on Sofia while Tigger's on the poker run."

"So? Tigger asked me to."

"Yeah, but he asked Bear, Chas, and Jax too."

"They have families. I don't. Fuckin' leave it alone. This is the last time I'll warn you."

Throttle pressed his lips together and a strained silence fell over the room.

Wheelie pushed up from the chair. "I gotta get going."

"Dude, I'm just telling you to be smart here. Tigger's a damn jerk, but he's a brother and Sofia's his old lady. You gotta respect that," Throttle said.

"Tell her to file a complaint with Banger. You know you can't mess around with a brother's woman." Rags stood up.

Throttle saw the vein in Wheelie's temple pulsing, his jaw rigid, and decided to change the subject. "You wanna come over Thursday night for poker? I'm hosting it this month. Kimber makes kickass guacamole and the best kickass burritos in town."

Wheelie's jaw visibly softened and he ran his hand through his hair. "Sure. Count me in."

"We all go way back," Rags said as he shrugged on his leather jacket.

"Let's not let shit get between us."

Throttle nodded, but he knew Rags was just trying to smooth things over. Wheelie was on a fucking slippery slope with Sofia, and Throttle knew how hard it was to resist the pull of a woman who touched you deeply. No matter how hard a guy resisted it or tried to talk himself out of it, it was inevitable that he'd end up with his cock buried deep inside her. He knew all about that firsthand. Of all the brothers, he never thought he'd end up with an old lady and buying an engagement ring. He'd resisted it like hell, but he'd been lost the minute Kimber's sexy rose and patchouli scent wrapped around him.

And that's what scared him about Wheelie. When he talked about Sofia, he had *that look* in his eyes, and there was nothing Banger, Hawk, or the entire membership could do to stop him from sliding down the slope. Throttle didn't want Wheelie thrown out of the club; the only hope was that the loyalty and love he had for the Insurgents had a bigger pull than Sofia.

Rags gripped Throttle's shoulder. "I'll make sure the crews are up and ready to plow once the storm dies down."

The wind howled, piling up snow in drifts, filling the air with icy dust.

Wheelie gave him a chin lift. "See you Thursday."

Heaviness weighed Throttle down as he watched his brothers walk to the truck and then vanish, swallowed by white.

He closed the door, went back to the family room, and stared at the flames as they curled around the burning logs.

CHAPTER SIX

BANGER

RUBBING HIS EYES with his callused fingers, Banger tipped the leather chair back and stretched out his legs. He'd been sitting at the desk most of the day, and the glare from the computer screen was playing havoc on his baby blues. He glanced out the window and stared at the falling snow. *Someone's messin' with us and I don't know who the fuck it is.* His chest tightened and the dull throb at the base of his skull indicated a doozy of a headache was on its way. Gripping the back of his neck, he rubbed it while he watched the snowflakes twirl and turn as they fell silently down.

As president of the Insurgents MC, Banger was the man the brothers depended on to make the right decisions for the club. He wasn't just the president of the MC in Pinewood Springs, but he was the national president as well, and that honor came with a huge burden. Decisions made in the national club carried over to all the chapters throughout Colorado, Wyoming, Nebraska, Utah, and Kansas. If he fucked up, it'd ripple to all three hundred and fifty brothers.

Glancing down at the papers on his desk again, he picked up a bottle of aspirin, shook out three tablets, and guzzled them down with a gulp of water. He thumbed through the various correspondences he'd received from Insurgent charters as well as affiliate clubs around the country. Something wasn't right. It seemed like the Deadly Demons were trying to move into Colorado and set up shop selling fucking smack, crack, and acid, but some of the reports coming in led Banger to question whether Reaper was behind the push, or some other club or organization was trying to mimic the Deadly Demons and start a war between the Insurgents and them.

Fuck! He pushed the papers away and closed his eyes, only opening them when a soft knock came at the door.

"Come in." A smile spread across his face when Kylie walked in. He hadn't seen her in over a month, and he missed his daughter terribly. "You're a nice sight for sore eyes. When did you get back to Pinewood?"

"Last night. The drive was a bitch." She walked over to him and kissed him on the cheek while wrapping her arm around his shoulders. "You look exhausted. I worry about you."

"Well don't. I'm fine. Anyway, Belle's doing enough worrying for the both of you." A frown settled on his forehead. "You made the drive from Crested Peak by yourself? Where the fuck was Jerry?"

"He drove me back. You're always on his case, Dad." She went around and sank into the chair in front of his desk.

"I just wanna make sure he's treatin' you right. I've told him I have zero tolerance for any shit he does that hurts you."

Shaking her head, Kylie's blue eyes sparkled. "Poor Jerry. You'll never ease up on him, will you?"

"No fuckin' way. I'm pretty sure it's gonna be that way until I die. You gonna stay for supper?"

"Yes. Jerry's playing poker with the brothers at Throttle's house. I'm surprised you're not over there."

"I have too much shit on my mind to concentrate on the game so I passed this time. Maybe next month."

"You getting one of your headaches?"

Banger nodded and she rose to her feet and moved behind him, placing her hands on his shoulders. Slowly she massaged the tight muscles, her fingers working wonders on the knots at the base of his neck. He closed his eyes and let himself relax as memories of a young Kylie flooded his mind.

"Does it feel better?"

"Yeah." He grasped her hands, brought them to his mouth, and kissed them. "You've still got the touch. I remember how you used to have to climb up on a chair to give your old dad a neck rub. You always knew when I needed one."

"I still do. You need to relax more. Belle told me you have something big worrying you. She said you're not sleeping well, and you bury yourself in here or at your office at the clubhouse. She's worried about you, and so am I."

"Sometimes shit happens and I've got to figure it out. That's what a president does."

Kylie came back around and plopped down in the chair again. "How much longer are you planning on being president?"

"What the fuck kind of question is that?"

"I mean, don't you want to slow down a bit? Go on trips with Belle? It's freezing cold outside, so wouldn't it be awesome to go to California, take Harley to the beach and to Disneyland?"

"You went to the beach and Disneyland when I was president. As a matter of fact, Harley has it better 'cause I'm older and at home more. I don't go to the parties unless I have to, and even then I only stay a few hours. I have no intention of stepping down. Did Belle put you up to this?" Kylie hung her head down. "I thought so. I knew this shit didn't come from you. You're the daughter of an Insurgent. You know what that means. You grew up with it. Belle still doesn't understand that this is in my blood and I can't fuckin' retire from it."

"Please don't be upset with her. She's only worried about you. Mom used to be too. You know our world is dangerous and can be deadly. Mom at least grew up in the life with Grandpa being in a biker club, but Belle is still trying to assimilate. And she's scared to death that Ethan and Harley will join the Insurgents."

Banger shook his head. "I don't think we gotta worry 'bout Harley since he just turned five and has a while yet to decide if he wants to join. Ethan's only thirteen, but if he wants to join when he's eighteen, he'll have to prospect like all of us did. A lot of guys can't handle prospecting."

"I think Belle just wants you to assure her that you'll talk him out of it if he decides to join."

"I'm not talkin' anyone out of joining. When parents start doing that shit, the kids join for sure. The chips will fall where they're supposed to. Now tell me how you're liking graduate school."

"I love it but Jerry hates it. We're back to commuting, so next semester I'm going to take all my classes online. He's still a little mad at me for going to grad school. I told him it was always in my plan. I think he's feeling neglected or something because I study so much. I don't know."

"Don't let him tell you what the fuck to do. He's a grown man. He needs to deal with it. There are times when he's gone for days for club business and you don't give him shit."

"I know. I shouldn't have said anything about it. I guess I'm still hyper from finals. I have a month off before next semester starts. I'm excited about doing the semester online. It'll be good to be home again. I miss Jerry a lot."

"Can't say that I'm not thrilled you'll be back home. I miss you, girl."

"Me too, Dad."

Banger pushed up from the chair. "Let's go to the family room. I'll get a fire going. The snow's really coming down hard."

While they were sitting on the couch, Banger's phone rang and he saw Hawk's name flash on the screen. He jumped up and went into the laundry room, closing the door behind him.

"You got something?" he asked Hawk.

"Maybe. Sketcher said he'd heard a shipment of crack was coming through soon. He's not sure exactly when."

"Fuckin' bastards! They've got balls to deal that shit in our county."

"It's bypassing Pinewood and going to Silverton," Hawk said.

"Did he say it was the fuckin' Deadly Demons?"

"Not exactly. He said he thought bikers are involved, but he isn't sure from which club yet."

"Tell Sketcher I wanna talk to him tomorrow at Belcroft's farm off the old highway. I'll meet him at ten in the morning."

"I'll come too."

"Sounds good. We gotta stop this shit before it gets too big. I wanna know everything I can about these two punk gangs in the Night Rebels' neck of the woods. Call Steel and Paco and set up a conference call for tomorrow afternoon around three."

"Will do. You playing poker tonight?"

"Nah."

"Me neither. It looks like Braxton's coming down with something, and this whole damn mess with the Deadly Demons is constantly in my head."

"Mine too, brother. We gotta crush 'em if they're involved in this shit. I'm not too sure they are, but we'll talk about that tomorrow."

When Banger exited the laundry room, Belle came up to him. He looped his arm around her waist and pulled her close, kissing her on the lips. "You smell amazing, woman."

Her electric blue eyes sparkled. "It's flour, onions, and garlic you're smelling. I made pot roast and it's on the table." She squeezed him hard. "Take the rest of the night off. We can watch a movie with the kids. I'll make caramel corn."

He laughed. "You know me well, woman." Since he'd been a kid, caramel corn had always been his favorite. He'd used to sneak under the fence when the carnival would come to town during the summers just to buy a bag of it. The other kids he'd go with snuck in for the rides or the games, but he was there just for the caramel corn.

After dinner, Banger sat on the couch, his feet propped up on the coffee table as he channel-surfed. Ethan came over and sat down on the cushy chair by the fireplace, staring at the television screen as images flashed by.

"That was a good dinner your mom fixed," Banger said, glancing sideways at him.

"Yeah. Pot roast is my favorite. Whaddaya trying to find on TV?"

"Nothing much. Just waiting for the women to get in here so we can watch the movie." Harley came over and climbed up on the couch. Banger tugged him close and nestled him under his arm.

"Is Emily gonna watch the movie too?"

"Seems like it." Emily had just come home the previous week from another stay at the alcohol rehab center. So far she seemed happier than she had for the past few years. She'd been excited to go Christmas shopping with Kylie, and Banger hoped that his nineteen-year-old stepdaughter had finally realized life was too short to spend it in and out of rehab.

"We're almost done," Belle said from the kitchen. The scent of freshly popped popcorn and sweet buttery caramel filled the room.

"Smells good, Mom," Ethan said.

"How's Jack doing?" Banger asked his stepson quietly.

"Good."

"Is he having trouble with someone at school?"

Ethan shook his head, but the way he diverted his gaze from Banger gave the real answer.

"You sure? It's important I know."

Ethan pulled at his flannel shirt and squirmed in the chair. "I promised I wouldn't say anything."

"I'm not gonna say shit to Jack."

"But he doesn't want anyone to know, especially his dad."

"Why not his dad?"

"'Cause he doesn't want his dad to think he's a pussy-ass."

"Ethan! Watch your language," Belle fumed as she brought in two huge bowls of steaming popcorn.

"Mom, I didn't say it. Jack did. I was just quoting."

"He's right," Banger said as he reached over and scooped up a handful of the caramel corn.

"You better not be protecting him. I don't want to hear you speak like that, Ethan." She pointed at Banger. "And you wait until I bring the individual bowls."

Banger watched her go back into the kitchen, then winked at Ethan. "So who's this fucker who's in Jack's face?"

"A new kid. He's in my class. He just came to school a month ago. I tried to protect Jack, but when I did, Owen just gave it to him worse. Jack told me not to interfere anymore." He glanced at the kitchen, then back to Banger. "You promised you wouldn't tell anyone."

"I promised I wouldn't tell Jack. His dad's got a right to know." Banger popped a few more bites of popcorn in his mouth, his gaze fixed on Ethan. "Don't look like you're gonna die on me. Chas won't say shit to Jack. He already suspects some shit was goin' on with his son. He just wanted to make sure. He's gonna teach Jack how to defend himself."

Ethan's eyes brightened. "That'll be great! Once he decks Owen, that'll stop what he's doing."

"I hope you're not saying that fighting is the way to resolve a problem," Belle said as she placed the bowls on the coffee table and scooped caramel corn in them.

"No, Mom. I was just talking hypothetically." He looked over at Banger, who winked at him.

Banger cleared his throat and took the bowl Belle gave him. "We were just kicking some what-ifs around. That's what guys do."

"Do they?" Belle threw him a suspicious look and he blew a kiss at her. She shook her head and finished doling out the bowls of popcorn.

Emily went over to the TV and popped *National Lampoon's Christmas Vacation* into the DVD player. She picked up her bowl of popcorn and settled into the overstuffed chair opposite of Ethan's.

"This is to die for," Kylie said as she popped a puffed corn into her mouth. "You're going to have to give me the recipe. Jerry will love it."

Harley yawned and snuggled closer to Banger as the movie started. Soon his blue eyes grew heavy and Banger watched him as he drifted off to sleep. Sitting with his family, eating the best caramel corn he'd ever had, and watching a funny-as-hell movie were the best antidotes to encroaching danger. And for a small slice of time, he could pretend all was well in his outlaw world.

CHAPTER SEVEN

THE CRAZED GRINCH

THE COMPUTER SCREEN glowed eerily in the dark basement. Clicking on a diamond and emerald–studded tennis bracelet, he leaned back in his chair and smiled broadly. The bracelets listed on various online stores were selling for three to four thousand dollars. All he had to do was list it and wait for the bids to come in. Glancing at the Christmas tag that read "To Glenda, with all my love, Phil," he took the jewelry out of the green velvet box and ran his smooth fingers over the stones. Grabbing his camera, he switched on the overhead light and positioned the item on a black cloth.

"It's almost one o'clock. You're going to be late." His wife's voice washed over him as he hunched over, trying to get the perfect shot. He glanced at the time on the computer. *Shit.* "Are you going in today? I thought you told me you were. I don't know why you volunteered to do this on your weekends. You're gone most of the time as it is."

Shut the fuck up, you stupid bitch! "I'm coming. I didn't forget."

His footsteps clumped on the stairs, and he brushed past his wife seated at the kitchen table, thumbing through a magazine, a cup of something in her hand. *Probably her favorite drink—tea spiked with scotch.*

They didn't say anything to each other. They rarely did; they merely coexisted in their home, picking fights on occasion when the silence and boredom became too stifling. That day, she wanted her booze and a magazine, and he wanted to get the hell away from her.

Picking up his keys from the counter, he trudged out to the garage and closed the door behind him. His wife never went into the basement, so the stash of gifts he'd stolen at the various homes he'd broken into were quite safe. He'd make a nice sum of money after he'd listed everything that night. When he'd first started destroying Christmas, he hadn't taken any of the presents, his only goal to destroy as many decorations as he could. But after he'd found a ten-thousand-dollar necklace in one of the brightly wrapped gifts, he'd decided that making a profit from his hatred of the holiday wasn't a bad idea. It was a double whammy for the victims, and he enjoyed that very much.

"Goddamn holiday," he cussed under his breath as he maneuvered his car up and down the lanes searching for a parking space. He hated that time of year with a passion, and he wished they would abolish it. If he had to hear another fucking Christmas carol again, he couldn't be held responsible for what he'd do.

Turning sharply, he nabbed a space, lifted a small suitcase on wheels out of the back of his car, and headed for the entrance of the Aspen Grove Mall. The stench of hot dogs, pine, and kids clobbered him in the face when he entered the shopping center. The place was packed and he moved through the wall of people, trying not to run into the pop-up kiosks that always invaded the mall during the holiday season. Vendors called out to him as he walked by ignoring them.

Up ahead, Santa's village loomed. He gripped the handle on his suitcase tighter and fought through the crowd until he was in the back of the makeshift mountain. In front of it, hordes of children stood in line as elves in all sizes and shapes handed out suckers to them. Parents stared vacantly ahead, several of them glancing at their watches as they waited for Santa to take his place again.

Opening the back door, he nodded to the employees on break and slipped into the dressing room. Several minutes later, he came out and took his seat on the golden throne, adjusting the long white beard hanging from his face. Children cheered and adults looked relieved when a petite elf unhooked the velour-covered rope and let the first group of children through.

When he'd seen the ad for a Santa position at the mall, he thought the irony of him playing Santa was too good to pass up, so he applied. The notion was quite ingenious, and he patted himself on the back when he actually landed the damn job. His wife couldn't believe he even wanted to do it knowing how much he detested the season, but he enjoyed whispering into the young children's ears that he knew they'd been really naughty all year, and he couldn't promise he'd stop by on Christmas Eve. The misanthrope made sure he didn't say it to every kid, just to a smattering of children. The real bonus was getting names from the sign-up list for coupons and free goodies, or from the credit card receipts. Later, when he returned home, he'd input the names and search if they owned any property in the county. If they did, he'd drive by, and nine times out of ten, their houses proved to be garish and had at least one inflatable something in the yard. He'd then add the names to his list. If he regretted anything, it was that there wasn't enough time to destroy all the homes he'd written down.

An hour into his shift, a cute blonde girl came over to him and he settled her on his lap. She waved at the crowd and he watched as a pretty blonde woman waved back. For a moment, he was taken with her beauty, and then he frowned when he saw a tall man in a leather jacket put his arm around her and kiss her quickly. The angry Santa hated men who wore leather jackets and the women who swooned over them. He bet if he approached the pretty woman, she'd never give him the time of day. *She's probably some cheapie.*

"Hi, Santa," the girl said, bringing him back to the task at hand.

"Have you been a good girl?"

The girl nodded. "Mommy and Daddy say I have."

"Are those your parents? Your dad in the leather jacket?"

"Yeah. He rides a big motorcycle and belongs to a club. He took me around the block once, but Mommy got real mad and he can't do that until I grow bigger."

So, he's one of those assholes who parade around town thinking they own it. The Insurgents. His wife's definitely a slut.

"What's your name?"

"Paisley, but Mommy calls me Paisey."

"What do you want for Christmas?"

"LuvaBella, the genie dream place, the kitchen with food and pots and pans, and that's it."

"Do you think you've been a good enough girl to get all that?"

Paisley nodded. "Mommy and Daddy told me I am."

"But they're not with you all the time, are they. Do you really think you've been good all year?"

The little girl hung her head down and shook it. "Can I get LuvaBella?" she whispered.

"I'll have to see. Do you know where you live?"

She jerked her head up. "You're supposed to. You're Santa Claus."

He laughed dryly. "Answering like that isn't nice, and it makes me not want to visit your home."

Her big blue eyes glistened and he smiled inwardly. "Sorry," she said through the fingers over her mouth. "My house is thirty-seven something Meadows Street."

He patted her knee. "That's very good. Don't tell your mommy or daddy, because I'm bringing you something real special and I want it to be a surprise for you and them. Okay?"

She bobbed her head up and down, her pigtails bouncing around her head.

He glanced over at the photographer, who pointed at her watch. He cleared his throat. "Now, smile big for the camera, Paisley." Helping her down, he leaned in close. "Remember our secret. I'm bringing you a very big surprise."

"I won't say anything." She jumped down and ran over to the man in the leather jacket. The pretty woman hugged Paisley, then grasped her hand. The man clutched her other one and they walked toward the booth to retrieve their photographs. The back of the man's jacket read "Insurgents MC."

Curling his lip, he had a sour taste in his mouth. He had every intention of paying a visit to Paisley's home. It would be his biggest challenge to date. *I'll have to watch the house and see what their pattern is.* The last thing he wanted was to run into the biker. If Paisley and her mother happened to be there, that would make it all the more exciting.

The Crazed Grinch couldn't wait to return home and start planning his next break-ins.

Chapter Eight

Cara

CARA WAVED AT Evan Christiansen when she entered the Brighter Lives building. Evan was the vice president of marketing and development with Brighter Lives charitable organization. Cara had been volunteering with the charity for the past five years. The Insurgents worked in conjunction with the organization for their annual Toys for Tots fundraiser. Some of the board members weren't too keen on Brighter Lives being associated with an outlaw biker group, but the amount of money they raised and the smiles on the children's faces at the event made them turn a blind eye to the club's sketchy lifestyle.

"Is everyone waiting for me?" Cara asked, unwrapping the scarf around her neck.

"Yes. Here, let me take that," Evan said, picking up the tray of sweet rolls she'd put on the receptionist's desk.

They rode up the elevator together, chatting about the upcoming fundraiser. Cara had worked with three vice presidents in the past five years, and Evan had been with Brighter Lives longer than the last two. She loved that the charity's sole purpose was to make children's lives better in any way they could. She was active with the food drives, back-to-school barbecues, and the many clothes drives they hosted throughout the year.

"Here she is," Addie said as Cara entered the conference room. Gathered around the large oval table were Belle, Addie, Clotille, and Kylie. Baylee had called Cara the day before saying she had to go to Aspen for a project, and she'd mentioned she was still feeling pretty lousy.

Doris, Marlena, and Bernie should've been at the meeting since all the old ladies were involved in the Insurgents' fundraiser, but they rarely got involved, especially with helping out. All they really did was show up at the event and drink a lot of beer. Cara had noticed they did that at the bike rallies as well. It seemed that the minute Cara became an old lady, they turned over a lot of the work to her, and once Belle and Banger married, they dropped out entirely. Belle told Cara she didn't care because she couldn't stand the way the women gossiped and acted like they were her friend. The truth was the three women resented Belle and Cara because they were in charge since Banger was president and Hawk was vice president. It seemed so silly to Cara, but it was the way they were.

"Where's Cherri?" Kylie asked as she stood up.

Belle took the platter of sweet rolls from Evan and placed them on a long table against the wall. "She had to help out at Paisley's school today," she said over her shoulder.

Scattered around the table were small red and white poinsettia plants. Trays of croissants, sliced fruit, and mini bagels along with tubs of cream cheese, apple butter, and various jams spread across the table. Kylie picked up a plate and speared a slice of cantaloupe.

"So sweet," she murmured as she popped a bite into her mouth.

"I'll have to try a slice," Cara said, picking up a plate.

"Kimber wanted to come, but Hawk told her she had to watch the shop because he had some club stuff to do." Kylie nabbed a blueberry sweet roll.

"Those are my favorites too. I love blueberry. And what can I say? Hawk does what Hawk wants," Cara replied.

"It's the same with all these guys," Clotille added.

"But we love them that way, don't we?" Addie placed a couple of bagels on her dish. "Did you make the apple butter, Belle?"

"I did. And you don't know the meaning of stubborn, rough, and independent until you've married a president of the club." Belle shook her head. "Sometimes I want to kill him, but then he does something so sweet and gentle and I turn into putty."

"I don't think you have to be a biker to be stubborn as all heck. You need to meet my husband," Torey said, pouring a glass of orange juice. "Mitch's head is made out of steel. He won't budge at all."

The women laughed, and Evan cleared his throat as if to remind the women that a man was in the room.

Torey Sinton was the Director of Children and Teen Services and had been working with Brighter Lives for the past ten years. She and Cara had gone to the same high school, and even though they hadn't been best friends, they stayed in contact through their social connections. Cara had dragged Hawk to Torey's wedding two years before. Her husband, Mitch, came off as a grumpy cynic, and from Torey's comment, it seemed like he wasn't improving with age. Each time Cara saw him at the social events he'd attend, he usually had a frown on his face and rarely spoke to anyone.

"Hello, ladies," a cheerful voice boomed.

Putting her plate down on the conference table, Cara looked up and smiled widely at Joseph Ross. At forty-seven years old, Joseph was CEO and President of Brighter Lives. He'd taken over the position when Dianna Wheaton, who'd been with the organization for over two decades, retired. He was a hands-on CEO and not only attended the fundraising events but put in hours at Brandon House, the residential program for homeless and runaway teens. Cara admired his dedication in helping minors have safe and better lives.

After Joseph called the meeting to order, Lindi Dixon, Vice President of Program Operations, confirmed that the community center would be decorated by the city for the charity event that was coming up in a couple of Saturdays. As they discussed the logistics of passing out the toys, setting up the tables, and where Santa would sit, among other things, Cara felt the flutter of excitement she normally did when all the hard work she and her committee had done was finally going to come to fruition.

She noticed how tired Lindi looked. She was only thirty-five years old but looked fifteen years older. *I'm being so catty.* But it was the truth. Lindi worked more than full time, had three little ones at home, and a husband who worked insane hours for a realtor. Dale was always at work, even at night. Cara couldn't help but wonder how many buyers really wanted to see homes in the late evening. He always seemed distant, rarely offering any gestures of intimacy with Lindi when she'd see them at functions together.

Maybe he's having an affair. She mentally chastised herself. *Stop being this way. Focus on the meeting.*

"Who's going to play Santa this year?" Cara asked, looking at Evan and Joseph.

Joseph shook his head. "I've done it for the past several years. I'd like a break. What about Dale doing it?"

"I'm not even sure he can be at the fundraiser," Lindi replied.

"I can ask Mitch, but he's so down on the holidays, I don't think he'll want to."

"Who doesn't love the holidays?" Addie said.

"My husband just isn't into them. I absolutely love this time of year, and I wanted to go all out, but he wouldn't have it. I had to fight to get a tree up."

"That may be a good thing, considering what's happening with that wacko who's breaking into people's homes," Lindi said.

"What does the paper call him?" Joseph asked.

"The Crazed Grinch," Cara and Evan said in unison.

Joseph's brow knitted together. "I can't believe we have someone like that in our town."

"We have a lot of nasty stuff going on in our town," Kylie said. "Jerry insisted we totally deck out our house this year. I think the macho in him wants the guy to come after our house so he can catch him." She giggled.

"I never thought about the crazy person who's roaming the streets looking for houses to hit. I guess I shouldn't be too upset with Mitch."

Torey leaned back in the chair.

"A lot of people hate all the commercialism that's defined the holiday. I read in the *Denver Post* that there's a backlash against commercialism this year," Cara said.

"Simpler is better," Evan said, the others nodding in agreement.

"But the kids love all the lights and decorations. If I had it my way, it'd be a small tree. It's so much work to put everything up, especially when I'm doing it alone," Lindi remarked.

"I just wanted a little bit more pizzazz since I'm hosting the Christmas party for the volunteers this year. Remember, the party's on the 22nd," Torey said as she rose from her chair.

Lindi, Evan, and Joseph also stood up.

"Ladies, if you want to stay and chat, the conference room is yours for the next hour, and then we have a financial meeting," Evan said before leaving the room.

The women said their goodbyes to the staff, then went back to the table for a second round of goodies. As Clotille walked around, refreshing everyone's coffee, she said, "I've been offered a job in Human Resources with Brighter Lives. I applied for it never thinking I'd get it. Now I don't know what to do. I want the job, but I know Rock will flip out. He thinks a mother should be home with the kids. I think it stems back from when he was a child and his mother had to work all the time because his dad blew all his earnings on drink and women. Rock hated seeing his mother so overworked, and he missed her in the home."

"Just because he has those ideas from his childhood doesn't mean they're yours," Addie replied.

"That's true. I have to admit that I'd love to see what it's like to work. I never really earned my own money, and I feel like I need something more than just taking care of the house and the kids. James is in preschool now, Andrew's in high school, and Rock's busy with the club. I need something too."

"I'll tell you, if you can afford to stay home, do it just until Andrew's out of high school. I think teenagers need their mom around if it's possible. All my problems with Emily started in high school, and I was too damn busy trying to earn a living to be around when she needed guidance and a firm hand. I didn't have a choice, but if I had, I would've stayed home until she graduated. Now with Ethan approaching high school, I'm glad I can be around for him."

Clotille rubbed the back of her neck. "We *are* having some problems with Andrew. It just started this school year when he went into his sophomore year. The school has called a couple of times saying he's skipped classes, and Rock's also caught him sneaking out the window at night."

"That's tough," Cara said as she threw her paper plate into the trash can. "I see a lot of teenagers getting into trouble. It's not always because the mother works, but sometimes having less free time or someone around to make sure the teen is home helps. Of course, teens can do things behind their parents' back too."

"I sure did, and my parents didn't have a clue," Addie said.

"I feel very torn on this. I guess I just have to think about it and talk with Rock. Are any of you free to come on Friday night for jambalaya and cornbread? I'm going to call Cherri, Baylee, and Kimber and see if they can come too."

"Count us in," Addie said.

"I'm sure we can, but let me check with Hawk." Cara took out her lipstick and reapplied it. Glancing at the time, she gathered her coat and scarf. "I have to get going. I'll call you," she said to Clotille as she slipped on her coat and then walked out of the room.

Cara had cut her law practice down to part time when Braxton was born. She'd thought she'd go back to full time once he went to full-day school, but then Isa came, and Hawk was planning on at least three more. She chuckled as she remembered how happy he was when she'd told him she was pregnant again. She'd be good with one, maybe two more, but three? *I don't think so.*

Spotting a parking space in front of the office building, she sped over to secure it, ignoring the honking horns. Before going in, she took out her phone and called her mom to make sure Isa was doing all right. Her mom would pick Braxton up at school later, and then Cara would swing by her parents' and take both kids home.

When she opened the door to her office, she saw a medium-sized man folded in one of the leather chairs. Straggly hair fell over his face, and light brown eyes stared at her through the strands. She went over to Asher and asked him in a low voice, "Do I have an appointment I forgot about?"

"No," he whispered back. "This dude came in about a half hour ago insisting on seeing you. He said his name was Garret. I told him you don't take walk-ins, but he was adamant that he had to talk to you. And he's been sitting there the whole time watching me. It's pretty creepy. Do you want me to throw him out?"

Shaking her head, she whirled around and went over to the man. She extended her hand and he clutched it, his palms cold and wet. As inconspicuously as she could muster, she pulled away from him, wishing she could find a discreet way to wipe her hand off. "What can I do for you?"

"I need to talk to you in private." His eyes were everywhere but on her.

"All right. Let's go into my office." As she passed Asher, he tilted his head to her as if to say he had her back. Stepping inside, she gestured to the man to sit down. When he started to close the door, she shook her head and grasped its edge. "The door always stays open. Have a seat."

The man stared at her, then at the door, and back at her. Slowly he turned around and walked to the chair. She noted he was a thin, wiry man with long, unkempt hair. He looked like he was in his late twenties or very early thirties.

Sitting behind her desk, she looked fixedly at him and he seemed to squirm under the intensity. "What brings you to my office? Are you in trouble?" The way he fidgeted in his seat, kept running his hand through his hair, and looking everywhere but at her told her something was amiss with him. She'd been a criminal defense attorney long enough to be able to read people when they came in to see her.

"Nah. I'm not in no trouble."

"Okay. What's your name?"

"Why do you need to know that fer?"

"Because you know mine. That doesn't seem fair, does it? Would you like some water, juice, or a Coke?"

"Coke's good."

She swiveled around and opened a mini fridge in the corner behind her. Handing him the can, she smiled and reached for a legal pad.

"Thanks," he said before popping the top. He took a long drink, then burped. "Name's Garret."

"Hi, Garret. What can I do for you?"

"I just wanted to ask a few questions, that's all." Another long drink. Another burp. "Uh… what's the punishment for breaking into someone's house?"

"It depends. Colorado has two degrees of burglary for breaking and entering into a home. If a person breaks in with the intent to commit a crime against another person or property inside, then that's second-degree. It's a felony and the max is four years in prison. First-degree has the same elements as second-degree except the one breaking in has to assault or menace a person during the burglary. That felony carries a maximum of twelve years in prison."

Garret crushed the can with his hands and wiped the corners of his mouth. Nodding, he stood up and paced back and forth for a few seconds, then sat down on the edge of the chair.

"I'd need more details if you want me to answer with more specificity." Cara's nerves began to tingle as Garret leaned forward, then slammed back against the chair.

"You don't need nothing more. Why're you asking me fer details? I didn't do nothing." Bouncing his knee, he bit at his lips.

Noticing he was jumpier than a jackrabbit, Cara pushed back a little from the desk. *I may have to make a dash for it.* "I didn't say you did anything. I just wanted to give you a more accurate answer, that's all."

"I'm thinking of writing a mystery book. That's all. Anyway, in the book, the guy goes into people's home to break things. You know, vernalize."

"Vandalize?"

He grinned, exposing crooked teeth. "Ya. That's it."

"If no one is hurt and—"

"No one's at home when it happens."

"It's second-degree burglary. So that would be four years and a hefty fine."

"But if he never done nothing before, he could get less, right?"

"Yes. A person may even receive probation and a few months in jail. The punishment isn't a mandatory sentence."

Cara jumped when, all of a sudden, he leapt to his feet. He paced back and forth three times, then stopped in front of her desk.

"Thanks. Thanks." He rushed out of the office.

When she heard the front door close, she slowly got up and went over to Asher, who stared at the door. "That was one of the strangest conversations I've had with a potential client in a long time," she said.

Asher laughed. "Face it, Cara... you're a magnet for nutty clients."

She sniggered. "True. I better get some work done. Five o'clock comes fast."

For the rest of the day, she worked up a few cases, her mind drifting back to Garret and his questions. For a split second she wondered if he might be the Crazed Grinch, but she quickly gave up that thought. *He didn't strike me as someone who could mastermind something so calculated. He seemed very high-strung.*

After a few hours, Asher poked his head in. "I'm taking off. You want to walk out together?"

Glancing at the clock, she nodded. "Give me a few seconds to finish this paragraph. Oh... did you get a copy of that weird guy's ID?" The policy in her office was to take a copy of any potential clients' IDs, as well as those clients who retained her services. Some bad experiences from her past taught her to make sure she knew up front with whom she was dealing.

"I did. I was pretty surprised he gave it to me. It didn't have his address or anything, just a picture ID with his name. It was an old one. He told me it used to be his ID at his job before he was laid off. It's real hard to make out his last name, though. When I asked for his last name, he started to freak, so I backed off."

"Please make me a copy."

Fifteen minutes later, she headed in the direction of her parents' house. After she spent some time talking to her mom, she strapped Isa and Braxton in their car seats and closed the door.

"Cara," her mother yelled as she ran outside, clutching a sweater around her. "I forgot to ask if you, Hawk, and the kids can come over for the family pre-Christmas dinner. I'm hosting it this year, but your Aunts Teresa, Lucille, Maryann, and Carmella are helping with the cooking."

"I can't believe you're hosting it. How did that happen?" It was a family tradition on her dad's side to bring the aunts, uncles, and cousins together for a pre-Christmas dinner. It had been part of her upbringing, and Cara looked forward to it each year. Sometimes it was the only time she saw her family who lived out of town. She knew her mother hated having all of her dad's relatives over for the big dinner and tried to find excuses to back out of doing it every time her turn came up.

"Your Aunt Carmella made some smart cracks to your dad, and we're having it here. I can't wait for it to be over."

"Considering you haven't done it for the past seven years, you got off pretty easy. I'll bring over some food. I'll call you and coordinate it. I'm thinking of doing it next year at my house."

"Unless you're pregnant."

Cara rolled her eyes. "You're just as bad as Hawk. Count us in, and see you soon."

As she drove home, Braxton pounded on the back window. "Mommy, look how pretty that house is. It has so many lights."

Cara glanced to her right, then turned the corner and slowed down.

The whole street was lit up like a Las Vegas casino. She smiled as Braxton excitedly pointed out reindeer, elves, snowmen, and a slew of other characters. As she drove around the neighborhoods, a few of the houses were over the top, and she wondered if the Crazed Grinch had targeted the homes. As the thought went through her mind, a patrol car slowly drove past the houses.

Taking the next left, she headed home, glad they lived in a guarded and gated community.

CHAPTER NINE

ROCK

ROCK STARED AT the slumped-over body tied around a tree trunk: sitting down, tied at the waist, legs spread. A large amount of blood pooled under the body, staining the snow a dark crimson. If Rock hadn't recognized the chest tattoo of a busty blonde holding a frothy beer mug, he never would've known it was Sketcher, his face beaten that badly.

"Fuck. They did a number on him," Jax said, kicking the ice with his boot.

"And they cut off his balls." Rock bent down and tugged the dead man's pants up. "He didn't fuckin' deserve this."

"I hope he was dead when they did it. I put a call in to Hawk and Banger. We gotta find out who did this." Jax pounded his fist into the palm of his hand.

"I know he planned on making a buy to find out who was dealing the shit. I told him to call me. When I didn't hear from him, I figured he either chickened out or it got canceled." He stood up and stared down at the broken body. The chance that the dirtbags had made Sketcher as an informant had niggled in the back of his mind and was the reason he'd come out to that wooded area of Crenshaw Park; it was known for drug dealing.

"The fuckers left him like this as a warning to other. We gotta beat their asses." Jax spit on the ground.

"It's a damn act of aggression toward the club. Last thing Sketcher told me was that he heard some dudes had hooked up with Satan's Pistons and were vowing revenge on the Insurgents and Night Rebels.

We can't let this pass," Rock said.

"Sketcher had a mom in town. She should know he's gone." Jax stomped his feet on the snow-covered ground.

"Banger will take care of it. That's the kind of shit a president does." Rock took out two joints and offered one to Jax. He lit both of them, and the two men stood looking at Sketcher, their heads bent, the smoke billowing above them.

The crunch of tires made Rock look behind him, Hawk and Banger walking toward them.

"What the fuck happened? Weren't you monitoring his buy?" Banger asked Rock, his eyes fixed on the beaten man.

"I told him to set it up and call me so I could watch out for him, but I never heard back. That's why I came looking for him."

"Fuck!" Banger's voice echoed between the trees.

It was a gloomy afternoon, and Rock looked around the empty park. It was as quiet as a mausoleum, and the bare trees with just ice and a dusting of snow clinging to their branches looked grotesquely eerie against the backdrop of lethal violence.

"We gonna move him out?" Jax asked.

Hawk pursed his lips, shaking his head.

"The fuckin' badges will find him. Eventually. I heard his mom was staying with a sick friend," Rock said.

"More like she was in detox," Hawk retorted, turning away from Sketcher.

"Probably. I know she's had a rough time of it. Should be home now. I'll go by her place tomorrow and tell her about her boy," Banger replied.

"Unless the fuckin' badges beat you to it," Rock said, putting his gloves on.

"Then I'll offer her the sympathy of the club. We gotta find who the fuck did this, slice off his balls and cock, and feed them to him."

Rock went down on his haunches and rifled through Sketcher's pockets, making sure there was nothing in them that was incriminating against the Insurgents. All he found was some spare change and a crinkled photograph of Sketcher with his arm around a young woman. He shoved the picture back in and stood up.

"Nothing. We'll find out who did this, and I'm gonna enjoy killin' his ass." Rock clenched his jaw, rammed his hands into his pockets, and followed Hawk, Jax, and Banger to their cars. He glanced one last time at the lifeless body, then drove away.

When they entered the clubhouse, anger and sadness crackled in the air; the brothers had a soft spot for the likable twenty-six-year-old.

"Who the fuck snuffed the kid?" Bear asked as he shuffled behind Rock to the meeting room.

"Not sure yet, but I'm gonna find out," Rock answered.

Banger had called an emergency church regarding Sketcher and the encroaching threat of hard-core drugs in Pinewood Springs. The Insurgents knew meth was the drug of choice for some of the residents in town, but dealing coke, acid, and H in the county just didn't sit well with the brothers. There was no way in hell they were going to allow that shit to come through; they didn't want to blow their tacit agreement with law enforcement that they'd keep that shit out of Pinewood Springs in exchange for the badges looking the other way at some of the club's indiscretions.

As the brothers let their rage over what happened to their informant spill out, Skinless came in and went over to Banger. The president looked at the group. "The prospect says the fuckin' badges are in the great room."

"I'm surprised they found Sketcher so fast. They usually can't find their ass with both hands," Chas said, and several members chortled and grunted.

"Tell them we're in church and they need to wait," Banger told Skinless. The young man nodded and left the room.

"Hold up. I'll go out and stall the fucks," Rock said.

When he entered the great room, he saw two assholes in uniform and one in a suit. He went over to the bar and leaned against it, his foot propped up on a chair. The one in the suit came over.

"I'm Detective McCue, and I have a few questions about Tommy Horace."

Rock jutted his jaw out, smoothed down his cut, and snapped his fingers at Skinless, who promptly placed a shot of whiskey in front of him. Curling his fingers around the shot glass, he threw back the dark amber liquid, then crossed his arms. "I don't know who the fuck you're talkin' about." He motioned to Skinless for another.

"His street name is Sketcher. Know him now?" McCue shifted from one foot to the other.

Rock shrugged.

Putting his pad back inside his suit jacket, McCue stared at Rock. "The word is he was an informant for the Insurgents. He was found murdered in Crenshaw Park."

Rock stared deadpan at him and didn't say a word.

"We can do things the easy way or the hard way. The easy way is that you and your fellow club members cooperate and tell me what you all know about the killing. And the hard way is that I tear your clubhouse apart."

"I've never done easy in my whole fuckin' life. And good luck in getting a search warrant, 'cause that's the only damn way you're gonna get past where you're standing right now."

"Did Sketcher piss you guys off, betray you?"

Rock just stared at the detective until he heard Banger's and Hawk's voices behind him.

"Banger. Hawk," McCue acknowledged them. "Your informant Sketcher was found murdered in Crenshaw Park, and I need to clear up some things."

"Don't know him, McCue." Banger turned to Hawk. "Do you know someone named Sketcher?"

"Nope," Hawk said.

Soon all thirty-five members filled the room, each one asking the other if they knew the person the detective was yapping about.

"Fucking unbelievable! Are you that cold-hearted that you don't give a shit what happened to Sketcher?"

"Let me tell you something, McCue," Hawk said, leaning against the bar next to Rock, a shot of whiskey in his hand. "If we *did* know this Sketcher dude, we'd take care of things on our own." He threw back his shot.

"And we're not sayin' shit 'cause we don't know shit. You're wasting your time and ours," Banger said as he posted himself next to Hawk and Rock. Skinless set a shot of whiskey in front of him.

McCue shook his head. "There were tire tracks and a shitload of footprints at the scene of the crime. I'm going to guess they belong to some of your members." Dead silence descended on the room. Staring each of them in the eyes, McCue said, "I'll be back." He turned around and walked out, the two badges following him.

"If that one keeps getting in our business, we'll have to talk to the police chief," Hawk said.

"Agreed. I gotta get going home. I just wanted to let you know that next Saturday there's gonna be a big party." Cheers drowned Banger out.

Rock put two fingers in his mouth and whistled loudly. The din died down. "The president hasn't finished talkin'. Shut the fuck up!"

"As I was sayin', we have all the charter clubs coming, and many of the affiliate ones will be here. All the officers have to be here. No damn excuses." He glanced at Rock, who nodded, along with Hawk and Throttle.

As Banger talked about the party, Rock felt his phone vibrate. He slipped it out of his jeans and stared at the number flashing. Fire shot through his veins. *Why the fuck is Andrew's school calling me?* Ducking out to the back porch, he answered the call.

"Hello?"

"May I please speak to Mr. Aubois?"

"That's me. Is my boy in trouble?"

"This is Mrs. Crowe, the principal, and… well, yes, he is. He skipped school again. If he does it one more time, I'll have to report it.

That's the law."

Rock gritted his teeth as he tried to control the rage threatening to explode inside him. "He's not gonna do it again. Is that all?"

"It is. Perhaps we should make an appointment so we can talk."

"I don't have anything to say. I told you I'll handle it. I've gotta go."

Heat flushed through his body as he ground his teeth. When he returned to the great room, Axe came up to him. "Throttle's already got the balls stacked."

"I gotta pass on the pool game. There's a problem that needs fixin'. I'm outta here. Later."

The wisps of frosty air from his heavy breathing ribboned around him as he hoisted himself into his truck. With the fire of a pissed-off parent burning inside him, he made it home in record time. He waited several minutes in the garage, taking deep breaths to calm down before he confronted his son.

Opening the car door, he saw Clotille standing in the doorway of the kitchen. "I thought I heard the garage door open and close. Roche... what's the matter? You look like a bull ready to charge."

"I'm fuckin' pissed! Did the school call you?"

"Which school?"

James popped his head out from behind Clotille's legs. "Père!"

The boy's black eyes shone and his chubby hand waved at Rock, melting his heart. He laughed and came over, swinging James up and settling his son down on his shoulders. The boy's fingers pressed against his head tightly as Rock brushed Clotille's lips. "Andrew's school. He cut his classes again."

"Oh no," she said, fingers flying to her throat.

"Oh fuckin' yes." He walked into the family room and pulled James off his shoulders, setting him down on the thick carpet. "Andrew's out of control. I'm taking over the problem full time. All your coddling and wanting to talk things out hasn't done shit. I'm in charge now, and if he wants to keep this shit up, he's gonna be sorry he crossed me!" He slammed his fist on the coffee table and it splintered. James jumped and then began to cry.

"Calm down," Clotille said as she knelt down and put her arms around the young boy, pressing him close to her. "Anger fighting anger never solved anything."

Rock's heart lurched when he saw big tears rolling down his three-year-old's face. In a flash, he was back in his house in Lafayette, cowering in a corner as his dad ranted and smashed up the small living room. *Fuck! I don't want James to be scared of me. Shit.*

He went over to Clotille and gently took James from her, hugging him against his chest. "*Mon doux petit fils, ne pleure pas. Père* isn't mad at you. Don't cry." With his thumb, he gently wiped away his son's tears. After several minutes, James calmed down and squirmed to get back on the floor. Rock bent over and set him down, and the small boy grabbed a bright red firetruck under the table. As he played, Rock caught Clotille's gaze. "This is one of the reasons I don't want you working. The kids need you in the home."

"I'm not working and Andrew is still acting up. He needs to see a therapist to help him with any unsolved issues he has. The school has recommended it many times."

"Fuck, woman," he hissed, then stormed out the French doors, shutting them behind him. The chilly air made his eyes water. Taking out a joint, he cupped his hand around it and lit it. Inhaling deeply, he held in the smoke and then slowly exhaled, releasing some of the tension in his body. He had to calm down before Andrew got home so he wouldn't do something he'd regret.

Staring at the snow-covered grass, his mind floated back to his childhood and the beatings his father had given him and his siblings. *I don't want to raise my hand to Andrew. I promised myself I'd never do that to any of my kids. Why can't I control him? I'm the club's sergeant-at-arms, yet I can't do shit with Andrew.*

The door opened behind him, and he stubbed out his roach with the toe of his boot. Looking over his shoulder, he saw Clotille come outside, zipping her jacket up to her chin.

"You know, asking for help is neither a sign of weakness nor a sign you're throwing in the towel. It's simply another path to finding a solution," she said softly.

Clenching his teeth, he stared straight ahead without answering.

"We need to be honest with ourselves and with Andrew. He has to know that we're not perfect parents and we're scared we're losing him. We have to tell him we worry and feel inadequate as parents."

"There's no fuckin' way I'm saying that," he gritted.

"Anger is a part of him and a part of you, and we have to go beneath it. Your dad was always mad, never taking the time to listen to you, and you resented it like hell. My mother was the same. Your dad and my mom only knew how to communicate with their hands, and anger was the only emotion they ever showed us. I remember how I adored my dad and always responded so positively to him. I know you had the same experience with your mother. We can't fuck this up. We have to be better than your dad and my mom. And maybe we don't know how to be that way because our childhood was fraught with anger, beatings, and no communication. My mom never listened to me, and it made me feel shitty and unloved."

"There's no damn way Andrew doesn't know we love him." He didn't turn to look at her, but he heard her footsteps clack on the stone patio.

"He does, but he thinks you're unapproachable and I take your side all the time." She wrapped her arms around his waist. "And that's a horrible feeling for a teen. It's hard being a teenager. We have to put ourselves in his shoes. And we have to figure out why he's skipping school and acting out. We need to find the source of his behavior. Right now, all we're doing is treating the symptoms by punishing and lecturing him, and it's not working."

Rock leaned back against her and placed his hands on hers. "Fuck. I thought if I was the opposite of my old man, everything would be great with me and Andrew. It's hard to think I fucked this up when all I've been doing is trying to be the best dad I can."

"And you are an amazing dad. Don't think you're not. And you haven't fucked anything up. It's challenging to be a parent, especially of a teenager. Andrew has issues we probably should've addressed when I first brought him to Pinewood Springs to meet you. I was so wrapped up in loving you and our family unit that I thought everything was good with him. Obviously it's not."

He blew out the breath he was holding. Puffs of icy white vapor mingled with the cold air. "We need to make this right, *ma chérie*."

"We need help in doing that, and we have to be together on this. Andrew has to know we're a united front, and we're doing this because we love him and are scared of losing him."

Rock nodded. It was hard for him to ask for help. He knew Clotille was right, but a big part of him felt like he'd done something wrong. He went through so much shit in his life, but he'd survived, and he hadn't needed a damn shrink to get him through it. But Andrew wasn't him. And if he was being honest, he was still pissed as hell at his old man for treating his mother like shit and for beating him too many times. *Maybe getting Andrew therapy will help him deal with whatever's going on inside him.*

He turned around and pressed Clotille close to him. "*Que je t'aime, chouchou.*"

"I love you too, sweetie," she whispered as she gripped the back of his neck and pulled his face toward hers.

They kissed deeply, only breaking away when they heard the creak of the patio door. Rock locked gazes with Andrew, who stood in the doorway. Grasping Clotille's hand, Rock walked toward him.

Andrew lifted his chin, a defiant gleam in his dark eyes.

Rock knew he expected him to flip out, but he wouldn't get sucked into the old familiar pattern. He stopped in front of him. "Let's go inside. We gotta talk."

Andrew's eyes widened and he stepped back into the house.

Rock went into the study, Andrew close behind him. That night, no matter what, they'd have a long talk. He'd fight down the inclination to raise his voice, he'd listen to everything his son said, and then he'd tell him he loved him. The following day, Clotille would find someone to help them.

He had no intention of losing his son. No matter what happened in his life, he'd fight to the end to save Andrew, and he wanted him to know that. It was something he never had from his own father.

Rock sank down onto the couch and gestured for Andrew to do likewise. He looked fixedly at him. "We're gonna talk. I'm gonna listen to you, and you and I are gonna come up with a solution. Why don't you start first by telling me why you keep skipping school?"

Andrew hesitated, but Rock didn't say anything. Then the teen cleared his throat and looked downward. "I'm not sure."

It was going to be a long night, but Rock had time.

He had all the time in the world.

CHAPTER TEN

BANGER

I T WAS THE seedy part of town. Pawnshops, junkyards, strip joints, and dive bars filled the spaces between the run-down homes and trailer parks. It was where the forgotten people lived, too strung out on drugs or booze to give a damn. It was the hiding place for the ones who gave up on living for whatever reason.

Banger drove up and down the icy streets. It didn't look like a county snowplow had touched them. A rusty, crooked sign up ahead read "Buena Vista Mobile Village," and he slowed down to take the sharp turn. The sign lied. It wasn't a mobile village like the ones his cousins lived in, where the yards were pristine and the mobile homes were well-kept. Buena Vista Mobile Village was a first-class dump. Piled in front of several residents' trailers were junk cars and a slew of broken appliances.

Winding around the narrow, icy roads, Banger looked out for lot number 356. Some of the men who sat on cold porch steps smoking cigarettes and joints eyed him suspiciously as he drove around. He knew his presence didn't sit well with many of the residents; he was a newcomer, piercing their veil of anonymity.

Spotting the faded lot number on a blue trailer in disrepair, Banger parked in front of the curb, lit a joint, and took in Lynn Horace's mobile home. Rust patches dotted the blue metal walls, and it looked like the wooden porch was falling apart, the white paint on the two pillars peeled and chipped. A beat-up old Buick sat under the carport.

He inhaled deeply, the anger he'd been feeling ever since he learned of Sketcher's death bubbling under his skin, threatening to burst through. Whenever he thought of the young man, he got a burn deep in his stomach. The kid was only a few years older than Kylie. He knew Sketcher was trying to survive and help his mom out, and Banger respected him for that. Most of the punks he saw only gave a shit about themselves, leaving family behind, but Sketcher was there for his mom, supporting her the best way he could. Sure, he fucked up sometimes, but who the hell didn't? All Banger knew was the Insurgents let Sketcher down. *He* let the kid down. He should've seen what was coming.

"We're gonna get whoever did this to you, Sketcher. You got my fuckin' guarantee," he said under his breath, flipping his roach out the window. As he walked to the door, the neighbor next door, sitting on his porch steps, beer in hand, watched his every move. Banger rapped on the door and a woman's voice, amid wheezing coughs, yelled out, "Come in."

The stale, hot air hit him straight in the face when he walked inside. The house was messy and cluttered and in total chaos. Several cats scampered away, and the odor of grease, soiled kitty litter, and Bengay permeated the cramped quarters. Sucking in his breath, he took a few steps toward a woman sitting in a worn-out recliner and staring at him through weary and swollen eyes. She pushed back her lifeless gray mane that limply framed her aged face.

"Who are you?"

"Banger. I've come about Sketcher."

"The police were already here." She turned from him and stared at the dark TV screen.

"I just wanted to tell you I'm sorry about your boy. He didn't deserve that."

Tears filled the lines on her face, and she reached for a tissue from a box on a TV tray beside her. "He was a good boy."

Banger stared at the carpet, wondering why Sketcher never had it replaced; it had worn through in many spots. He'd been on the club's payroll, and they'd been generous. Glancing at the scratched kitchen cabinets and the broken wooden chairs piled in a small space he was sure was the dining room, he wondered what the hell the informant had done with all the money he'd earned over the last five years.

"Youse with that club he worked fer, aren't you? I can tell by your jacket." She blew her nose and threw the used tissue on the tray.

Sketcher was known to have a big mouth whenever he was drunk or high, but Banger didn't figure he told his mother about his covert operations with the club. Instead of answering her question, he folded his arms and stared at her.

"He told me he had something big going on with youse. Told me youse would pay him real good."

"What did you tell the badges?"

"Nothin'. I'm not stupid." She coughed and wheezed, grabbing a tissue and spitting into it. "You wanna know what he said?"

Banger shrugged. "I just came over to give you my sympathies. I tried to help your boy out with some jobs at some of the businesses I own."

She narrowed her eyes. "If youse wanna play it that way, okay. It's just that Tommy was a good son. He took care of his mama. He knew my disability and food stamps didn't go far in paying the bills. I don't know what I'm gonna do without him. I loved him. He was the only one of my kids who was worth anything." Wet streaks trickled down her cheeks.

Prior to going over to Lynn Horace's home, the brothers had agreed with Banger's proposition to give her a lump sum of money. He reached into the inside pocket of his jacket and took out a rolled wad of bills. Wiping her nose with the palm of her hand, she stared at the money. Banger handed it to her. "I hope this helps. I know it won't bring your son back, but it'll help you get by for a long while."

Lynn took the money and shoved it down her housecoat. "It's Chad Bridgewater and his no-good son who done this to my boy."

Chad Bridgewater? Banger didn't move a muscle or say a word. He simply stood there waiting for her to talk.

"Tommy told me he thought it was bikers bringing in the bad drugs to sell, but he found out it was Chad and the guys who stay with him. They bought the drugs from Texas, I think, and they're making a shitload of money selling them. They're already doing it in Silverton. Tommy smoked weed, but he didn't do the hard shit. He was good to his mama. Very good." The tears welled up in her eyes again.

"You take care of yourself. I'll come around again. You had a good boy." Banger turned around and walked to the door.

As he stepped out, Lynn yelled out, "Thank you. Youse a kind man."

He put his fist in the air and then walked out, closing the door behind him. The anger simmering beneath the surface rose to the top. Looking at the trailer next door, he was glad the guy who'd been staring at him earlier was gone because he wanted to hit someone real bad. Gunning the motor, he peeled out of the dilapidated trailer park and headed back to the clubhouse. Pressing the Bluetooth button in his car, his phone dialed Hawk.

"Dude. What's up?" Hawk said.

"I got some news on Sketcher. His ma told me he'd found out Chad Bridgewater's bringing in the shit. Already set up shop in Silverton."

"Chad? Is this reliable?"

"Fuck if I know. Remember we shut him down before with the meth and the gun smuggling when he was trying to fuck with our turf."

"Yeah. I thought he was done."

"According to what Sketcher told her, he's just getting started."

"You guys went to high school, right?"

"Yeah. He thought his shit didn't stink back then too. He was always competing with me when it came to girls."

Hawk chuckled. "Who won?"

"Do you have to ask?" Banger laughed. "And he was pissed as hell when he didn't patch into the Insurgents. I prospected a year before he decided to. He was a fuckup and never learned what loyalty and respect meant. Stinger threw his ass out after less than a year." Stinger had been the founding president of the Insurgents MC and reigned for twenty years before he handed over the gavel to Banger.

"Yeah, I remember you telling me that. It was before my time. I heard Stinger was tough."

"And I'm not?"

Hawk laughed. "You're tough and grouchy as all fuck."

"Anyway, get the brothers together for an emergency church. I'll be there in a half hour. We gotta move fast on this. Tell Blade to do some digging on this asshole and his goddamn son. What the fuck's his name?"

"Reggie. Getting forgetful, old man." There was a smile in Hawk's voice.

"Old man, my ass. Ask Belle about that." Both men laughed. "You better start rounding up the brothers. See ya."

An hour later, Banger watched as the brothers filed into the meeting room. Dressed in black leather cuts and jeans, many of them pulled out chairs, others preferring to stand. Banger wasted no time getting to the point, turning to Blade to see if he could find out anything about Chad and his pansy-ass son.

Blade stood up. "I did some quick searches and some surface digging because I didn't have much time, but there's something going on at that Chad's spread. I saw a lot of movement when I zeroed in on it from an aerial view. It looks like there're several metal buildings on the property that could be used to house shipments like guns or drugs. Some of them look like small warehouses."

"I thought we shut his fuckin' ass down with the gun smuggling a couple of years back," Throttle said.

"We did, but he may be at it again," Hawk said.

"Guess we're gonna have to kick his ass again," Chas said.

"How many people live at his place beside his puny-assed son?" Banger asked.

"Looks like the ones who are there for the most part are Beau Larker, Randy Lyon, and Calvin Schwind."

"I went to school with all those assholes. Fuck. It's like a damn high school reunion." Banger folded his arms over his chest.

"All reports indicate the Deadly Demons aren't involved with the drugs coming into Colorado. Looks like they're running drugs to northern Texas, Oklahoma, and Missouri."

"That's what Sketcher's ma said. He told her bikers weren't involved with this. I can't say I'm not happy knowing that."

"Our old ladies would kill us if we had a turf war right before Christmas," Axe said. The group laughed. "And can you imagine what they'd say with a lockdown?"

"I don't even want to think about it," Chas said.

"So what are we gonna do?" Rags asked.

"Pay them a visit." Banger looked around the room. "We're gonna have to be prepared for a fight, so we'll take machine guns and grenades in addition to our usual guns. I want Hawk, Rock, Jerry, Throttle, Wheelie, Chas, Axe, Bear, Cruiser, Billy, Ruben, Tiny, and Helm to come along on this one. I know they're cooking meth. The fuckin' badges know they're doing it. We're there to stop acid, crack, and H from hitting this area. Chad's too stupid to be doing this whole operation on his own. Who's supplying him?" He looked at Blade.

"From my preliminary investigation and the shit's that been tweaking over the grapevine, it's the Los Asesinos in Northern Texas."

"They probably need the cash flow since they're in a turf war with the Deadly Demons. I heard they were selling to small-time dealers. They need the dough to buy more guns to fuel their war," Jax said.

"Reaper's gonna be pleased we stopped one of their flows," Hawk added.

"We gotta stop this shit now. If we have to air condition their compound, we'll do it. We're gonna treat this as a hostile visit, and if any of them draws a gun first, they're fuckin' dead." For outlaws, "air conditioning" a standing structure meant riddling it with bullets, and Banger was prepared to do that and more to the men who threatened Insurgents' territory and killed a person who worked for them.

"When do we move in?" Rock asked.

"Soon. I'll let you know. We got the element of surprise, which is the best advantage." Banger brought the gavel down on the wood block, indicating church was over.

He went into the great room and picked up the bottle of beer Rusty had waiting for him on the bar. Across the room, Jerry, Jax, and Axe were talking. Remembering how Kylie had been upset after he questioned her about what was going on with her, he went over to the trio and put his hand on Jerry's shoulder.

"I need to talk to you," Banger said.

"Sure." Jerry followed him to the other side of the room where it was quieter and no brothers were around.

"Get the fuck off Kylie's case about grad school. She wants this. It's all she talked about when she was growing up. She wanted to be a teacher. She's got enough pressure with school. Back the fuck off."

Jerry's nostrils flared and he cracked his knuckles. "This is between me and Kylie. In here, you're my president, but outside, you're just my woman's father."

"I'm gonna forget you said that because I don't want to smash your fuckin' face and have to explain it to Kylie and Belle. Consider this a freebie. When my little girl's hurting, you can be damn sure I'm gonna fix it."

"We're working it out. It's just that she's always studying and she never has time to go out, or she's too tired."

Banger glared at him. "She's in school to better herself. She's the first one in my family to have a college degree, and now she's going for her master's. I'm damn proud, and you should be too."

Jerry lifted his chin, his face taut. "I am. It's just that we need some balance."

"That's what school breaks are for. And don't even think of looking at any of the club whores."

"What! Why would you say that? I love Kylie. She's the only woman for me."

"Then stop riding her ass."

"I'm not."

Banger ran his eyes over Jerry, who kept his chin held high. "You treat her right or you'll have me to contend with."

"You're going to have to let us deal with our problems on our own."

Banger laughed dryly. "Yeah… that's not gonna happen. You take care of her, and quit making her upset."

Banger marched away, lifted his fist up in the air to the brothers, who reciprocated, and walked out of the club. He went over to his SUV, started the engine, and headed home.

It'd been a long day, and the upcoming days would even be longer.

Switching on the windshield wipers, he drove into the darkness.

CHAPTER ELEVEN

WHEELIE

WHEELIE PUT TWO six-packs of Heineken and a bottle of blueberry-flavored vodka on the counter. The redheaded cashier gave him the type of smile that said she was available for more than ringing up his purchases. He grabbed several Jack Daniels shooters and pulled out his wallet.

"You look like you're having a party," she said, placing the bottles in a paper bag.

"How much is it?"

"I'll let you have the shooters, so for the beer and vodka, it's thirty-three bucks. Is it a private party?"

He counted out the bills and handed them to her. "Yeah." With a paper bag in each arm, he walked out of the store and over to his jeep. *Sofia's gonna love the blueberry vodka.* He'd remembered she'd told him that was her favorite flavored vodka on one of their many trips to Canon City. Tigger had been in prison, and it seemed like Sofia's car always had trouble, so Wheelie had offered to take her to see Tigger.

He'd enjoyed her company during the long ride there and back. Sometimes they'd talked the whole round trip, other times they just listened to music and spoke sporadically. It seemed like those trips had pulled them close together, or at least that was the way he felt.

Resting his arms on the steering wheel, he dipped his head down until his forehead touched his wrists. *What the fuck am I doing? Sofia's a brother's old lady.* A brother he didn't care for too much. Never had. When Wheelie had first met her at Steelers, Tigger's arm draped around her thin shoulders, he couldn't believe how dainty and pretty she was. With her porcelain skin, dark brown hair, and luminous green eyes, she'd looked like a china doll. She'd been wearing higher-than-hell heels that made her look taller than her five-foot-two inches, and when she laughed it'd sounded like wind chimes on a breezy spring day. He'd been blown away. And her eyes had sparkled when she'd get excited.

I'm fuckin' playing with fire. At that moment he should be at the clubhouse eating ribs and coleslaw, then fucking a couple of club girls instead of sitting in a liquor store parking lot remembering all kinds of dangerous shit.

Lifting his head up, he saw the redhead come out and light up a cigarette. That's who he should be spending the evening with, not a brother's wife. *Fuck!* But he didn't want to be at the clubhouse, or drinking and fucking the redhead. He wanted to be with Sofia, trying to make the sparkle in her eyes come back.

Over the years, he'd seen dullness replace the brightness her green orbs used to have, and he rarely heard her laugh. The longer she stayed with Tigger, the more weary and beaten down she became.

The redhead noticed him, waving her arm off as she bounced over. He switched on his engine and took off before she reached the vehicle.

Way before Sofia had come into the picture, Wheelie had a tense relationship with Tigger. The five-foot-ten, muscled brother loved to brag about himself to anyone who would listen. Most of the brothers ignored him, but it gripped Wheelie's ass and he'd usually call Tigger on it, which usually ended up with them throwing punches at each other.

In Wheelie's opinion, Tigger was a blowhard who cared more for himself than he did for the brotherhood. He'd always suspected Tigger just wanted to be part of the club because it was a chick magnet and it gave him an excuse to bash in heads. Tigger loved the way people stared at him and how intimidated they were when they saw the Insurgents patch.

Wheelie didn't deny it fuckin' rocked when men stepped away from him, or the way chicks cozied up to him, but he was loyal to the bone to the club. Something he didn't think Tigger was, and he wasn't the only one who felt that way. Axe, Throttle, Jerry, and Chas voiced the same opinion, and he suspected Hawk and Bear agreed with them even though they never said anything. The difference between him and Tigger was that he'd do anything for a brother, even butt out of Sofia and Tigger's life.

He pulled into the driveway in front of the garage. The door clanked open and he drove in. Before he'd left, she'd called and told him to park in the garage so no one would see his car. She hadn't wanted it to get back to Tigger that she'd had a lone brother in the house.

She stood in the doorway, dressed in a fuzzy purple pullover sweater and tight blue jeans, her hair gleaming under the fluorescent lights in the garage. A sliver of excitement lit up her eyes, and he thought she'd never looked prettier.

Easy. Tigger's an asshole, but he's a brother. Banger will have my ass if I step over the line.

She curled up her lips, and her smile excited him more than all the nakedness of the club girls. At that moment, all thoughts of Tigger, Banger, and loyalty vanished from his head. Pausing for a long moment, he got out of the jeep, reached over and grabbed the bags, and came up to her. A hint of nutmeg, orange, and violet circled around him, and he groaned inwardly.

"You smell wonderful. Is that a new perfume?"

"Sorta. It's super expensive, so I only wear it for special occasions."

He ran his thumb under her bottom lip and watched her cheeks turn all shades of red. "Glad you think our time together is special, 'cause it is." He started to dip his head down but reconsidered. If he kissed her, he'd never be able to stop. Pointing at the bag in his hand, he smiled. "I got blueberry vodka for you."

When she took the bag from him, their fingers brushed. She quickly walked into the kitchen. "I can't believe you remembered how much I love it. Thanks."

"Of course. You didn't think I tuned you out each time we drove to the pen, did you?" He winked at her and unpacked his bag, lining up the shooters on the counter.

"You want to try some?" Opening one of the cupboards, she stood on her tiptoes and reached for the glasses.

He came over and took two out, his body brushing against hers. "Here you go. And I'm good with my Jack and beer." He walked away quickly, not trusting himself. Tossing the decorative pillows on the couch aside, he sank into the cushion and grabbed a shooter, twisting off the cap. In one fluid movement, he downed it, welcoming the burn as it traveled down his throat.

"Good?" Sofia picked up her glass and took a long drink. "This tastes so good. I haven't had a drink like this in a long time."

No doubt Tigger's the reason why. He took another shot and threw it back. Tigger wouldn't be the topic of conversation. That night it would be all about Sofia and the two of them enjoying an evening together.

"I'm going to make another." She jumped up from the couch and walked into the kitchen, her hips swaying.

"Just bring the fuckin' bottle out here."

"I'm afraid if I do, I'll get smashed." Her laughter wrapped around him.

"It's good to hear you laugh. It's been a long time." Kicking off his boots, he settled back against the cushion.

With bottle in hand, she walked back into the room and plopped down on the couch. "I actually feel happy right now."

"Maybe it's the booze."

She locked her gaze on his. "I don't think it is." Without breaking eye contact, she brought the glass to her lips and drank deeply, then put it down on the end table.

He sucked in his breath and his cock stirred as she ran the tip of her tongue over the contours of her lips, lips that were made for sinning. *Easy.*

"What about that pizza you promised?"

"Yeah… sure. What do you like on it?"

"I love sausage, extra cheese, ham, and tomatoes, but I shouldn't have that. It'll go right to my hips."

Wheelie ran his gaze over her slender body and shook his head. "I don't think you have to worry."

"I do. I've gained a lot of weight."

Pursing his lips together, he took his phone out of his pocket. "That's bullshit. Is that what Tigger's been telling you?"

The mention of his name made her smile fade and her eyes dull.

"Don't believe it for a minute. You're a beautiful, sexy woman. You need a man who'll tell you that often, no matter what you weigh." He tapped in the numbers to the pizza place and ordered a large with everything she wanted. "Should we get a salad?" She nodded and he ordered it with creamy ranch dressing.

Reaching over for the remote, he brushed his hand against Sofia's and heard her gasp softly. From his peripheral vision, he saw her throwing peeks at him as he flipped through the channels on the TV. Settling on a show where there were a lot of explosions, he muted the television and turned toward her.

"What's going on in your pretty head?" he asked.

"I was just wondering if you had a girlfriend. I mean, it's Saturday night and you're stuck babysitting me. If I was your girlfriend, I'd be pissed about it."

"Oh yeah? Why?"

All of a sudden, her cheeks burned brightly and she shifted in place. "I guess I wouldn't want you spending the evening with another woman."

"Even if it was with a friend?"

"I'd be afraid something may go farther than that. I don't think men and women can just be friends. I mean, there's always a strain of sexual tension between them."

Wheelie swept his fingers over her hand. "Are you feeling sexual tension between us?"

Moving her hand away, she locked onto his gaze and they sat still, barely daring to breathe. Heat brewed between them.

"Well, are you?" he whispered, scooting closer to her.

"Yes. What about you?"

Grasping her upper arm, he pulled her toward him. "Fuck yeah, baby."

She tilted her head back and he brought his face close to hers. He could feel her warm breath fanning over his face.

Ding dong. Ding dong. Sofia jumped up like a bee had stung her and rushed around the room, panic plastered on her face.

"Relax. It's the doorbell. Probably the pizza guy." Wheelie rose to his feet and looked out the window. An older man carrying a pizza stood on the porch. "That's who it is." As he opened the door, he saw Sofia lean against the wall, holding a hand over her heart and breathing heavily.

After paying the guy, Wheelie brought the food over to the coffee table and then went over to her. She was still leaning against the wall. Grasping her wrists, he tugged her to him; she didn't resist. He looped his arms around her and held her tightly.

"You're shivering like a leaf," he said. "It's okay. I'm here. I won't let anything hurt you."

Resting her head on his chest, he felt her relax and snake her arms around him. A shock of physical awareness jolted through him at the feel of her soft body molded to him. He felt a tug in his jeans and he pulled away slightly in an attempt to cover his desire.

"You never answered my question," she said into his shirt.

"What was it?"

"Do you have a girlfriend?"

"No."

"I'm surprised a nice, good-looking guy like you doesn't have one. Why not?"

Because the one I want is already taken. "Not looking for one, I guess." He pulled away. "Pizza's gonna get cold." He turned and went back to the couch.

For the next few hours, they laughed, watched a movie, and played

Resident Evil 7. It was one of the best nights Wheelie'd had in a very long time.

When he glanced at his phone, he saw it was almost two in the morning. The time had just flown; it seemed like he'd only been there for a couple of hours. Sofia came back from the kitchen with a plastic bag and put the pizza box and paper plates in it. He helped her tidy the room, and then he picked up his jacket.

"Are you leaving?" Her voice had a tinge of sadness to it.

"It's getting late."

"Are you going back to the clubhouse?"

"Nah. I'm just going home." Wheelie had moved out of the clubhouse in the early part of the year. Most of the single brothers lived at the club, but after years of not having much privacy, he decided he needed his own space, so he bought a three-bedroom home overlooking the Colorado River. It was in the Pinehurst community, and each morning when he woke up to peace and quiet, he wondered why it'd taken him so long to get his own place.

"Do you mind taking the vodka with you? You can keep it for the next time we get together," she said softly.

"Next time you can come to my place. You'd really like it."

She nodded, her eyes fixed on him. He went to the door and smiled. "It was nice tonight. One of the best times I've had in a long while."

"Me too." She padded over to him. "Thanks for the vodka, the pizza, the laughter, and telling me I'm pretty." Her voice quivered and she dipped her head down.

He cupped her chin and tipped her head back. Latching his gaze on hers, he pressed his mouth on the soft cushion of her lips. A startled yelp escaped from her and she pulled away.

He straightened up. "I'm sorry. I crossed the fuckin' line." He spun around and had his hand on the doorknob when soft hands touched his forearms. She slid in front of him, stood up on her toes, and hooked her arms around his neck, pulling his face closer to hers. Desire shone in her eyes, and he yanked her to him and crushed his lips on hers, kissing her deeply. He wanted to devour her whole.

Clinging to him, her lips parted, allowing her moans of pleasure out and over his cheek. Raw intensity sizzled between them as they kissed frantically—breathing fast, heart rates faster.

Wheelie could feel her tits pressed against his chest, his jeans tightening painfully. Then the faces of his brothers flooded his mind. He willed them to go away but they were stubborn sonsofbitches. He owed loyalty to the brotherhood and to each brother, even Tigger.

Fuck! What a cock blocker. He pushed away gently and put his hands on Sofia's drooping shoulders.

"I better get going."

"Okay." Her chin trembled, and he wanted to take her back in his arms and cover her in long, deep kisses.

"I shouldn't have done that. I'm not sorry I did, but it's just not cool with Tigger being a brother, you know?"

Lowering her head, she nodded. "I shouldn't have done it either. I mean, I'm married."

"I know." He ran his fingers through her soft hair. "If you weren't, I'd be all over you. Don't ever think for a second I wouldn't. If you need anything, call me. It's too snowy for that bike ride. Maybe when the weather gets better."

"Oh sure. That's fine. I've got a ton of stuff to do around here, anyway. No worries." Her voice quivered on the last two words.

"Okay. I'm off."

"I'll open the garage door for you. Goodbye, Wheelie."

He walked out the back door, his boots crunching on bits of gravel on the concrete floor. The door opened and he slid into his Jeep. Waving at Sofia, he backed out and turned out of the driveway. Waiting for the door to close, he cursed his lack of self-control. He watched the house for a long time, and when all the lights turned off, he drove away and made his way home.

Inside his house, he kicked off his boots, grabbed a bottle of Jack, and stretched out on the couch. Taking a few gulps of whiskey, he stared out the window into the inky darkness.

The scent of Sofia still lingered on him. Her lips were so soft and her body felt damn good pressed into his.

I can't go there.

But the problem was he already had.

CHAPTER TWELVE

CHERRI

"I CAN'T BELIEVE I agreed to a fake tree," Jax said as he spread out the folded branches on the seven-foot tree. "I like the scent of pine."

"Stick your head outside and breathe in deeply. We have a ton of pine and evergreen trees in our front and backyard," Cherri answered.

"I like the smell of real pine in the house, smartass." Jax made a face at her and she laughed.

"But we can have the tree up longer because it won't dry out, and vacuuming up the needles is a pain in the butt."

"Speaking of butts, I oughta spank yours for talking me into this."

"Later, baby." Cherri winked while staring at his tight ass. Thoughts of being with him after Paisley was tucked in bed made her skin tingle. She still couldn't get enough of him, and the way he kissed and hugged her every chance he got meant he felt the same. And that made her very happy. After so much crap in her life, she finally got it right with Jax.

"These are pretty, Mommy," Paisley said, showing her mother two shiny ornaments. "Can I put them on the tree?"

"After your dad puts the lights on."

"When's that gonna be?" Paisley carefully put the two ornaments down.

"Shouldn't be too long, honey," Jax said as he wound a string of multicolored lights around the branches.

An hour later, Cherri, Paisley, and Jax stood back and admired the tree.

Paisley clapped and jumped in place. "The ormaments look real pretty with the lights on."

"Or*n*aments, sweetie." Cherri ruffled the little girl's blonde hair. "And they do look pretty."

"Best tree ever," Jax said, leaning over and kissing Cherri on the lips. He drew Paisley to him and gave her a tight hug. "You did a great job decorating." Paisley giggled, then looked back at the tree.

"What about hot chocolate and sugar cookies?" Cherri asked as Paisley skipped around the room.

"Yay! I'll put on one of my cartoons. The one about the anominal snowman."

Cherri laughed. "*Abominable*, and I love that one." She went into the kitchen to make the cocoa. As she placed a few cookies on a plate, Jax came up behind her and curled his arms around her, nuzzling her neck. "You smell like chocolate and sugar. I want to taste you."

She giggled and turned around in his arms, and he captured her mouth, delving his tongue deep inside as he pressed her closer. Heat burned between her legs as he rubbed his hard dick against her. "Let's go in the pantry and have some fun," he said against her lips.

"Paisey's—"

"She's watching the mean snowman. I need my cock inside your pussy, woman."

Cherri glanced at Paisley, who was sitting on the couch, engrossed in the cartoon. "She'll want her cookies and hot chocolate."

"We can have a quickie."

"Paisey?" Cherri said, smiling when her daughter turned to her. "It's going to be a few more minutes for your cocoa and cookies, okay?"

Her head bobbed up and down, and she turned back to the television screen. Before Cherri could say anything, Jax had her inside the walk-in pantry, her hands on the wire shelf and her knit top pushed up around her shoulders.

"I love it when you don't wear a bra," he rasped in her ear, cupping her tits.

She moaned and pushed her ass back, rubbing against his tight bulge.

"Fuck, sweetie. I love you so much."

Hearing him unzip his jeans had shivers gripping her spine. He nudged her feet farther apart and cupped her sex. A low grunt rumbled from his throat. "You soaked right through your panties." His voice was raw. She ground into his hand, her pussy twinging with an aching throb only his cock could relieve. "I love you too, and I want you so badly right now."

Fingers pushing her panties down her pebbled skin made her arousal shoot through the roof. Bracing herself, she groaned when his iron-hard dick hammered into her. She craved it hard, fast, and rough. When Jax yanked her head back by her hair and shoved his tongue into her mouth, she slipped her hand down and played with her clit. With him pounding away, tweaking her nipples, and her finger moving rapidly over her nub, she bit down hard on her bottom lip as a rush of molten liquid rushed through her.

"Oh fuck," she gasped, trying to keep her cries at bay.

"Fuck!" Jax dug his fingers into her hips, and, in the midst of her feral fireworks, the heat from him exploded inside her.

Their jagged breaths filled the space around them, and Jax ran his hands over her back as he gently kissed her neck. She straightened up and leaned back into him, reaching over and looping a hand around his neck.

"I better see how Paisey's doing. I'm surprised she hasn't called out for her cookies." She pushed away and he swatted her butt gently. She giggled as she pulled up her leggings and pulled down her top. When she turned around, Jax was zipping up. "Do you want a shot of whiskey in your hot chocolate?"

He drew her to him and brushed his lips across hers. "I'm going to the clubhouse to shoot some pool with Axe. I should be home in a few hours. Cool?"

Nuzzling her face into his chest, she nodded. "Cool. I have to go to the grocery store anyway."

When they came out of the pantry, Cherri saw Paisley lying on her stomach on the floor, her chin resting in her hands, her eyes fixed on the raving white monster with yellowed, crooked teeth.

"Do you want your cocoa and cookies now?" Cherri asked her.

"Yes, please," she answered without taking her eyes off the cartoon.

Jax pinched Cherri's ass, then kissed her quickly. "I won't be back late."

"We're having steak and mac and cheese for dinner. About what time do you think you'll be back?"

"Five thirty or six. Bye, honey," he said to Paisley, who yelled "Bye" with her eyes fixed on the TV.

Cherri placed two cups of cocoa on the coffee table and a plate with two cookies. "You have to sit up to have your snack," she said.

Paisley sat up, took a cookie, and slowly chewed as she watched the rest of the cartoon.

★ ★ ★

WITH SEVERAL PLASTIC bags hanging on her wrist, Cherri opened the back door and went into the kitchen.

"Why isn't the door making noise?" Paisley asked, setting down a small bag.

"I guess I forgot to turn on the alarm, sweetie. Here, give me your bag."

Paisley handed her the bag and she took out a box of vanilla wafers.

"Can I have some, Mommy?"

"Just one. I don't want you to spoil your appetite. I'm making your favorite, mac 'n cheese."

Lifting her arms in the air, she giggled. "Yay!"

Cherri laughed and ran her fingers through her soft hair. "You goofball." She leaned down and kissed her. "You're the cutest." She opened the box and placed one cookie in a small plastic bowl. "Here you go."

"Thanks, Mommy."

Paisley scrambled out of the room and Cherri continued putting away the groceries. Then a high-pitched cry cracked the air and Cherri rushed into the living room to find a crying Paisley kneeling beside their Christmas tree that was toppled over and lying on its side. Slivers of broken ornaments picked up the afternoon sunlight. Paisley reached toward a shiny blue shard.

Cherri leapt forward. "Don't touch it. You'll cut yourself." She pulled Paisley's hand away and enveloped the sobbing six-year-old in her arms. "It's okay, sweetie. Daddy will put it back up when he gets home. I guess it was too heavy. You and I were pretty heavy-handed with the decorations." She wiped her daughter's wet cheeks.

"Where are all the presents?" Paisley asked between sobs.

"They're probably under the tree. It's all good. Mommy will clean it up and Daddy will fix it."

"But everything's broken."

"I know. We'll get new decorations. That'll be a ton of fun. Would you like to do it after I clean up the glass?" Paisley nodded while wiping her nose. "This is going to be great. We'll get everything new and you can pick out the ornaments." She hugged her daughter and kissed her.

Paisley smiled. "Can I get any colors I want?"

"Sure. Your job will be ornaments and mine will be garland. Let me just get the vacuum. If you stay here, you have to promise me you won't go near the tree or touch anything on it or the floor. The glass is really sharp."

"I'll just sit and wait for you, Mommy." Paisley climbed up on the sofa and folded her hands in her lap as she stared at the tree.

"I'll be back in a sec." As she rushed to the kitchen, she glanced behind her to make sure Paisley hadn't moved, smiling when she saw her still seated. *She's such a good girl. I can't believe the fucking tree fell over. I've never had that happen before. Shit. Like I don't have enough to do.*

When she walked into the kitchen, she stopped dead. *Something's off in here.* A chill skated down her spine. Glancing at the counter, she realized the bag of chips was gone. Her mind whirred as she tried to remember if she'd put them away before she heard Paisley cry out. *I must have, or they'd still be on the counter. I'm being silly.*

Instead of going to the broom closet, she just stood there glancing around the large kitchen. An ominous silence crept into the room and her pulse banged in her ears. *What the fuck's wrong with me?* She tried to dispel the dread weaving around her nerves, but she couldn't.

"Are you coming back, Mommy?" Paisley's small voice broke through the dead quiet.

"Uh… yeah. Stay seated. I'm getting the vacuum now." *I can't believe how silly I'm being.* She forced herself to take a step, then another and another until she was in front of the broom closet. With clammy fingers, she opened the door wide. She didn't know what she'd expected, maybe a fanged demon or a demented doll. She giggled nervously. *That's the last time I let Jax talk me into watching a horror movie.* The night before, after Paisley had fallen asleep, Jax had put on *Black Christmas*, drew her close to him under the covers, and held her tight as a madman attacked sorority sisters. *And now I'm imaging all kinds of crazy shit.*

Sighing, she saw the vacuum buried in the back of the closet. *Great.* Pushing the mop out of the way, she moved things around.

Creak. The hairs on the back of her neck rose and she stood frozen in motion, her hand clutching the top of the vacuum. *Creak.* A door groaned on its hinges. Paralyzed in place, she couldn't move, breathe, or speak.

Then in one heart-stopping moment, she felt watched, as if the Devil himself was scraping a fingernail along her spine. *Fuck. Someone's in the kitchen with me. I know it.*

A choking stench of body odor assaulted her nostrils, making her eyes water. Droplets of sweat formed on her forehead as goose bumps laminated her cold skin.

"Mommy, can I get up? I wanna come in the kitchen."

Terror sliced through her. "No! Stay where you are." Her voice trembled.

"Are you okay, Mommy?"

Forcing the bile down her throat, a tight pull of fear threatened to erupt from her. "I'm more than okay, sweetie. I just had to find the vacuum. I'm coming. Be a good girl and stay where you are."

"Hurry."

"I will."

She dragged the vacuum out of the closet and shut the door. From her peripheral vision, she saw someone standing next to her. Jumping from fright, she gasped and clutched her hands to her throat. Turning around quickly, she screamed when a man in a black ski mask faced her, his brown eyes fixed intently on her.

"What's wrong, Mommy?"

She dropped the vacuum and stepped away, but the masked man reached out and grabbed her arm, jerking her to him.

"Who's that, Mommy?" Paisley's voice quivered.

Cherri darted her eyes away from him and saw Paisley standing near the kitchen island. Like a lioness protecting her young, Cherri kicked the guy hard in the balls and he groaned, releasing her. Using the few seconds he'd be incapacitated to her advantage, she grabbed Paisley's hand and dashed down the stairs. Behind her, she heard him grunt.

Thud. Thud. Thud. His heavy footfalls on the stairs pounded in her ears.

With her heart slamming against her rib cage, she dragged Paisley through rooms, ignoring her questions. The only goal she had was to reach the safe room.

In her panicked state, she thought she could feel his breath on her neck, but she didn't dare turn around. Every second counted.

With trembling fingers she punched in the code, and the steel door swung open. Cherri shoved Paisley in, and just as she turned to close the door, the intruder stuck his foot inside. Anger flashed in his eyes.

"No!" she cried.

With all of her strength, she lifted her leg and slammed her foot on his. He laughed. The voice of her self-defense instructor echoed in her head: "Jab your fingers into his eyes." The intruder started to push himself into the room, and she poked him hard in the eyes. He yelled out and stumbled backward. Then she quickly put a knee between his legs and pushed hard, forcing him to the floor. Without any hesitation, she kicked him viciously in the groin. Immobilizing him, she spun around and dashed into the safe room, slamming the steel door shut.

With her back against the door, she slid down to the concrete floor, sobbing. Paisley came over and sat in her lap, pressing her head against Cherri's chest.

"It's okay, Mommy," she said over and over as all the fear and terror spilled out of Cherri.

Loud pounding on the steel door startled her, and horror seized her again. *I'm in the safe room. He can't hurt us.* The thought ran through her mind each time he slammed his hand on the door. Paisley covered her ears with her hands.

When Jax had first built the room, she thought he was being paranoid, but he told her all of his brothers had them in their homes, and now she was grateful for the protection. She glanced at the screens and breathed a huge sigh of relief when she saw the intruder climbing the stairs. Her stomach flipped over when she saw him take a butcher knife from the kitchen and go into the living room. Raising his arm, he swung it down, slashing strings of lights and synthetic needles on the tree. Lifting his foot, he stamped over the downed tree, breaking what little ornaments remained intact.

As she watched his angry attack, her blood ran cold. *That's the fucking nut who's been in the news. I can't believe it.*

"Why's he hurting our tree?" Paisley asked softly, her eyes brimming with tears.

"He's crazy. Don't look anymore, sweetie. I'm going to call Daddy. He'll know what to do."

She held Paisley tight, then slowly rose up from the floor, grabbed the landline, and dialed Jax. As she waited for him to pick up, she saw the psycho jump up and down on their tree and presents, then walk out of the house.

"Hi, sugar. What's up?"

"You need to come home. That nut who's been breaking into people's homes and destroying their Christmas decorations was here. He was here when Paisey and—"

"I'm on my way. Where are you?"

"In the safe room. I saw him leave, but I don't know if he's coming back."

"Stay there and don't move. Did he hurt you?"

"No. I got away before he could." The man's penetrating brown eyes flashed into her mind and she shivered. "But he wanted to hurt me."

"The fuckin' bastard."

"I don't know why he picked our house. We only have a simple tree. And it's light out. I'm surprised he even saw it. I can't believe he waited for me to come home."

"Did you put the alarm on when you left?"

"No. I know… I know."

"It's okay, sweetness. The important thing is you and Paisley are safe. I'll be there real soon."

When Paisley saw Jax and Axe rush into the house, she jumped up and down while pointing at the screens. "There's Daddy and Uncle Axe."

Relief washed over Cherri, and for the first time in the past two hours, she relaxed. When the door swung open, she fell into Jax's arms. "You're here," she murmured as she peppered his face with kisses.

"I'm always here for you. I'm just relieved you and Paisley are safe."

With one of his arms wrapped around her shoulder and the other one carrying Paisley, she rested her head against his shoulder as they left the room.

We're safe now.

And she knew they always would be with Jax in their lives. He'd come into her life like a candle in the night. He was her beacon then and now, her yesterday, her today, and her tomorrow.

She put her finger under his chin and turned his face toward her, then kissed him hard and messy and passionately.

Then they went upstairs.

CHAPTER THIRTEEN

AXE

WHEN AXE PULLED into the parking space, he wrinkled his brow when he saw Baylee's car in one of the two spots. She'd told him she was going to Aspen after her doctor's appointment and she'd be home after dark, but she was already home and it was only three o'clock in the afternoon which meant that she wasn't feeling well. *Again.* The knot that had been forming in the pit of his stomach for the past few weeks tightened. *I hope everything's all right with her.*

The smell of gas and hot motors washed over him as he walked over to the elevators. He leaned back against the cold metal wall as the elevator ascended to the fourth floor. He'd stopped by the grocery store and picked up a quart of vegetable soup for Baylee and a meatloaf dinner for him. It seemed that soup was the only thing she could keep down most days.

Unlocking the door, the aroma of onions, garlic, and roasted chicken greeted him, and he threw his keys on the entry table and walked to the kitchen. Baylee stood by the stove stirring something, and the sight of her attempt at being domestic touched him and made the corners of his mouth turn upward. Baylee and cooking didn't see eye-to-eye, and take-out and delivery dinners had been the norm since he'd asked her to be his old lady a few years back.

"Never thought I'd see you in that position," he said walking over to her.

Baylee spun around, a wooden spoon in her hand and a thin cloud of steam rising steadily from a pot on the stove. "You're home. I expected you much later." She pointed at the bags in his hand. "Did you stop off at the grocery store?"

"Yeah. Vegetable soup for you and meatloaf for me, but what you're making smells fuckin' good."

She took the two bags from his hand and unpacked them, putting the perishables in the refrigerator. "I'm making roast chicken, mashed potatoes, a tomato salad, and peas. Belle gave me the recipe for the chicken and potatoes, and Cara told me what to do with the tomatoes. The frozen peas had directions on the bag. It's not so bad. It's kind of relaxing." She looped her arm around his neck and kissed him.

"Why'd you decide to cook? I mean it's been over a year since you tried your hand at it." His hand glided down her back, resting on her butt.

"And that was a disaster. I was really craving roast chicken and mashed potatoes. When Belle told me how easy it was, especially with these roasting bags, I decided to give it a try. I hope it tastes as good as it smells."

"I know you do." Axe rubbed his hands over her ass while kissing her deeply.

Giggling, she pushed him away. "I have to turn the heat down."

"I like where the heat is taking us." He turned her around and kissed her again. The hiss of water boiling over made Baylee jump and wiggle out of his arms.

Grabbing a rag, she pulled the boiling potatoes off the burner and wiped away the water. "I hope I didn't burn them," she said as she looked into the pot.

"I think you're good, babe. Just lower the temp and put them back on." Picking up the lid from the counter, he smiled at her. "Use this."

"Maybe I should have you making dinner," She took the lid from him. "Thanks, sweetie."

"Did you go to the doctor today?" He took one of the mini carrots she had in a bowl and chomped down on it.

"Yeah. We can talk about it later. I have to concentrate right now.

Why don't you relax and watch TV? Dinner will be ready soon."

Axe hesitated for a moment then went into the family room. He glanced over at her while she rushed around the kitchen, streaks of red painting her face from the heat of the stove and oven. He'd thought it was a little odd she didn't tell him what the doctor said, but then, it was her first big dinner from scratch in over a year. He'd decided that even if the chicken was dry as a bone and the potatoes watery, he'd tell her it was decent. The fact that she was trying so hard hit him and pleasure and warmth spread through him.

A few hours later, he had Baylee snuggled in his arms, a fire snapping in the fireplace, and a comedy in the DVD player. Dinner had been surprisingly good and Baylee had kept beaming with each additional helping he'd taken.

He dipped his head down and kissed her hair. "You seem like you're feeling better."

"I am. I love this movie, don't you?"

"Yeah. What did the doctor say? Was it the flu like you suspected?"

"No. This part here is real funny. I've seen *When Harry Met Sally* a zillion times, but it still cracks me up."

Staring at her, he noticed she purposely avoided him, her eyes glued to the screen. *She's not telling me something.* "What did the doctor say?"

"Axe, I'm trying to watch the movie. Don't you want to see it? We can talk later."

With the remote in hand, he hit Pause and set it down on the couch next to them. "What's going on?"

Without looking at him, she answered, "I don't know what you're talking about."

"Did the doctor tell you something bad?"

"No. Just something unexpected."

"What do you mean?"

Still staring at the frozen actors on the screen, she said softly, "I'm pregnant."

Did she say pregnant? *What the fuck?* He tried to grasp what he thought he'd heard. Silence snapped between them. "What did you say?"

She pulled away from him and tucked her legs underneath her. "I'm pregnant."

Fuck. That is what she said. "How?" Axe shook his head when she rolled her eyes. "I mean, aren't you on the pill?"

"Yeah, but I still got pregnant."

"Did you forget to take it?"

"No. It's not foolproof, you know. Addie said the same thing happened to her and Chas with Hope."

"But we talked about kids and decided we didn't want them. Fuck."

"I know. I didn't plan this, Axe. It just happened."

"How did you let it happen?"

Baylee narrowed her eyes. "*Me?* You're responsible for this too. And if you wanted to make extra sure, you should've worn a condom."

"Are you nuts? I'd never wear a rubber with my old lady."

"Well, there you have it. Don't you dare blame me for this."

"It's just that we didn't want kids. Fuck. I don't know what to say."

Baylee's chin trembled. "You could say you're happy and give me a fucking hug."

Axe knew that's exactly what he should do, but he wasn't happy about it. The shock of her pregnancy shook him to his core. Thoughts looped around in his mind until there was no room for anything else. Thoughts of the unknown: how will it be with three instead of two, would he be a good dad, how would it affect their sex life.

Baylee jumped up from the couch. "I didn't expect this either, but that's the way life turns out sometimes. I have our baby growing inside me, and when I think of it that way, I'm happy. You're acting like a first-class asshole!" She rushed down the hall toward their bedroom. The slamming door echoed around him as he sat there unable to move.

I don't know jack shit about being a dad. I had a shitty one. His dad was never the father he needed him to be. Axe had always known him to be a cold and heartless person. Ever since he could remember, his mother and father communicated through fighting. To him, it seemed like they brought out the very worst in each other, each of them backing up the other's vices like they were virtues. Boozing, gambling, and cheating consumed the household, and at a young age, he was left to fend for himself emotionally. The only thing he could count on when he was growing up was that neither of his parents would be there for him. They were too busy worrying about themselves. Thinking back on it, the only thing they'd had in common was their selfish streaks.

What if I'm like my parents? My dad split when I was nine, and he never contacted me again. How the fuck does a father do that? What if I do the same shit? How the hell could Baylee be pregnant? Damn! I never thought this would happen. Instead of happiness, anxiety, apprehension, and dread twisted his insides. He knew he should go to Baylee, hold her close, rub his hands down her back, and tell her it would be all right, but he couldn't. A large part of him wanted the status quo. He didn't want a baby coming between him and Baylee. They'd fallen into a rhythm and he loved it. With a kid around, they couldn't be as free to love and fuck whenever and wherever they wanted, and he wasn't sure he liked changing those dynamics.

All of a sudden the room grew hot and suffocating like the walls were closing in on him and he couldn't breathe. He couldn't sit there anymore. He had to move around, breathe in some cold air, and get the hell away. Grabbing the car keys, he opened the front door and took the elevator to the parking garage. He backed the car out and headed to the clubhouse. He needed to have some shots, talk shit with the brothers, shoot some pool, and not think about anything. He needed a sliver of his old life back.

When he walked inside, the brothers yelled out his name, surprise registered on many of their faces to see him mid-week at that hour in the club. A few of the club girls waved at him, their faces lit up with huge grins.

"How's it going?" Cruiser asked as Axe came over to the bar.

"Good. I thought you were working at Dream House during the week." Axe picked up the shot Skinless placed in front of him.

"I am, but I traded nights with Helm. He's got some shit going with his girlfriend on Sunday, so I'll work for him. Is your ol' lady tied up tonight?"

Axe shook his head. "No. Just needed some fresh air and my brothers. Wanna shoot some pool?"

"You got the money to pay when you lose your ass?" Helm chuckled, picked up his drink, and ambled to the back of the room. "I'll rack them up. Solid or stripes?"

"Solid." Axe lit up a joint and inhaled. *This is what I fuckin' need. A joint, a shot, and playing pool with a brother.* Diapers, sleepless nights, and an exhausted old lady weren't on his agenda. *We talked about this. We agreed we didn't want kids.*

"You take the first shot, dude." Helm took the joint Axe offered him.

Axe hit the ball so hard that some of the brothers across the room raised their heads from between the club women's legs and stared at him. After he hit the first ball, nothing was on his mind but winning the game.

It was well after midnight when he entered the bedroom, his eyes fixed on Baylee's sleeping form. He ducked into the bathroom as quietly as he could, washed up then went over to the bed and slid between the sheets. The room spun around even with his eyes closed, and he knew he should've stayed at the club instead of driving home, but he didn't want to leave Baylee alone.

Emotions still whirled inside him like a cyclone spinning round and round, bringing him down. He turned on his side and punched the pillow underneath his head as he tried to get comfortable. Closing his eyes again, visions of rocking horses, his parents fighting, holidays without his father cluttered his mind driving him crazy.

Soon the booze took hold and blackness slowly erased the images until there was nothing but darkness.

CHAPTER FOURTEEN

HAWK

CARA PLACED A breakfast burrito with green chiles in front of Hawk and sat down on the chair across from him.

"How crazy weird is it that the Crazed Grinch picked Cherri and Jax's house? Is it possible that it's just a copycat because it didn't fit the psycho's MO."

"It's the fucker." Hawk cut into the burrito and took a huge bite. "This is damn good, babe."

Cara tapped her fingers on the table. "Thanks. How do you know it was him? I have to agree with you, but I want to know your reasoning."

"Babe, I just wanna eat and not be cross-examined. We know it's him, but he targeted Cherri. My thinking is that the tree was an afterthought."

"Mine too. So that means he saw Cherri somewhere in town. Could be anywhere. He had to have watched the house because he knew to go in when Jax wasn't there."

"The club's looking into it. Aren't you eating?"

"I have another meeting at Brighter Lives. I can't wait for next Saturday when the whole thing will be done. The good news is I just snagged another sponsor, so the club will have little to no expenses."

"You're a powerhouse fundraiser, babe."

"I learned it from my mom. She makes a ton of money for charities. I also have a hardworking and killer committee. I never could've done it without them. I love seeing the smiles on the kids' faces whenever we help make their lives a bit better. There's so much poverty and heartache in the world."

"The club's favorite charity events deal with kids. When you're young, you can't do shit, so it's good to have people looking out to help you." For a brief second, a memory of him at thirteen scavenging through trash cans in alleys in LA flashed in his mind. "Are the kids still sleeping?"

"Braxton's playing in his room and Isa's still snoozing. I can't believe how she loves to sleep. Remember how Braxton kept us up most of the night until he was almost three? Isa's the opposite. She doesn't take long naps but she sleeps through the night."

"Enjoy it." He smiled and pushed his chair back. Rinsing the dishes in the sink, he looked out at the deer walking across the back lawn.

"Are you wearing your dress shirt tonight? I'll press it if you are."

"Dress shirt?" He put the dishes in the dishwasher. "Why would I wear one tonight?"

"You look even more handsome when you're all dressed up. My mom's freaking out about the dinner tonight, so I'm going to leave a couple of hours before it starts. You can bring the kids, okay?"

Closing the dishwasher door, he leaned against the counter and ran his hand through his long hair. Inhaling deeply, he slowly blew it out. "I thought the dinner was tomorrow night."

"No, it's tonight. I really do think you should wear your dark green pinstriped shirt. It looks really good on you. It'll only take a minute to iron."

"Fuck, babe. I thought it was tomorrow. I can't go. I have to be at the club's party tonight."

Cara's face tightened and her lips curled down—the telltale signs she was pissed. "What? You have to go. I need you to bring the kids and help me pack the car because I have to help my mom. I've been telling you about it all week. You never mentioned you had to go to a club party."

"I can still help you pack the car. I can drop the kids off too, but I just can't stay. If I thought your dinner thing was tonight, I would've told you I couldn't go."

"You have to come. I'm going to be the only one without her husband. How stupid is that? And because you have to go to a club party where everyone's getting drunk and fucking? That's what you're canceling a family outing for?"

Licks of anger singed his nerves as he watched her grow madder. "You don't understand. This isn't just a club party. They have those every fuckin' weekend and I haven't been to one in months. This is a big deal. All the charters and affiliates are gonna be there. I'm the goddamn vice president. I have to be there. All officers do."

"Oh… well, that explains everything. You're choosing to spend time tonight with a bunch of sweaty men instead of your wife and children during the holiday season. When the hell are you going to understand that you're married? You're not a bachelor who can just do what the hell he wants without thinking about anyone else."

"You're totally overreacting. I'm always with you and the kids. If this were a regular party, I'd be going with you to *your* family's dinner. But it isn't, and I need to be there. All the officers will be there. There's nothing more to say about it." He walked out of the kitchen.

Cara came rushing up to him, grabbing his arm to spin him back around. "It's either your family or the club."

A jolt of white-hot anger shot through him. He whirled around and put his face close to hers. "Don't you ever fuckin' ask me to choose," he hissed.

Moving back, Cara glared at him. "You can't go. We have to be at my parents' tonight."

He glowered at her, burning rage seeping through all his pores. "What the fuck did you say?"

Cara crossed her arms and lifted her chin. Her defiant gaze met his. "I said you can't go."

Gritting his teeth, he grabbed his money clip and keys from the side table. From the corner of his eye, he saw her watching him. He went over to the door and turned the knob. Turning slightly, he swept his gaze over her frowning face.

"Don't you ever tell me what to do, woman." Cara started to say something, but he cut her off. "You need to fuckin' respect me. I don't tolerate that shit from anyone, even you."

"And running off to the club and abandoning your family is treating me with respect?"

The vein in his temple pulsed. "I'm not abandoning anyone. You know I have to go tonight."

"I don't know that." She continued to glare at him and it just made him madder.

Afraid he'd put his fist through one of the walls, he shoved his hand in his pocket. "Then you should. We've been together long enough for you to know I'm VP and there's shit I have to do." He held his hand up, silencing her. "Don't say another fuckin' word. I'm not one of your goddamn clients you can tell what to do. I'm outta here."

He stepped out and slammed the door behind him. When he jumped onto his Harley, his whole body trembled with fury. He'd planned on taking the SUV, but he was so pissed he needed the frosty air to cool him off. *Cara went too damn far. Abandoning my family. Fuck her!*

The frigid wind roared around, chilling his skin beneath his jacket. In his haste to get away, he'd forgotten to tie back his hair, and the wind whipped the strands against his face and blew them above his head. Instead of cursing the cold, he embraced it as it revitalized him. His breath rose before him in puffs of moisture, and he squinted against the blinding glare of sunlight bouncing off the pristine snow.

By the time he arrived at the clubhouse, his nose was numb, his hair wet, and his fingers were almost white from gripping the handlebars. The warmth of the great room seemed suffocating after coming in from the bitter, energizing cold.

"Hey, brother," Throttle greeted him as Hawk went over to the bar and grabbed several napkins, running them over his hair. "Did you ride your Harley over here?"

"Yeah. It was fuckin' awesome." Hawk drained the shot Rusty put in front of him, then held up three fingers to the prospect, indicating he wanted a triple. Rusty nodded and in less than ten seconds, Hawk grasped a larger glass of Jack.

The great room was beginning to fill up as brothers from all over Insurgents' territory filed in. Steel strode in with Goldie and Diablo, and the trio came over to Hawk and Throttle.

"How was the ride?" Hawk asked.

"The drive was good. We couldn't take the bikes because the snow was fucking insane in the San Juan Mountains," Steel said as he sat next to Hawk.

"Heard the Deadly Demons and the Satan's Pistons aren't involved in the drug shit threatening the territory," Diablo said, grabbing a handful of pretzels from a bowl on the bar.

"Damn straight," Rock said as he joined the group.

Hawk nodded and looked at his phone as it vibrated. It was Cara. He slipped it back in his pocket. There was no fucking way he was ready to talk to her. *Asking me to choose was not the way to go, babe.*

A portly man with long blond hair came over to Hawk and high-fived him. "Long time, brother," he said.

"Rollo. How the fuck have you been?" Hawk handed the brother a bottle of Coors.

"Can't complain. I hear the pussy's real good around here." He brought the bottle to his lips.

Hawk, Throttle, and Rock laughed. "That's what we hear too, but you're gonna have to ask one of the brothers who isn't hitched," Throttle said.

"That's right. You all went and did some stupid shit and got old ladies." Turning to Steel, he pointed to Goldie and Diablo. "What about you guys? Are you pussy-whipped?"

Goldie shook his head. "Hitched, but not pussy-whipped."

As the men talked, Hawk saw Banger heading his way. They bumped fists, and Banger said his greetings to the Night Rebels brothers. Several of the club girls came in and out of the kitchen, bringing in trays of food that they set down on a long table.

"Your club women fix the grub?" Goldie asked.

"The old ladies," Banger said. "Belle's in charge, and she got a few of them together to help." He looked at Hawk. "She said Cara couldn't make her delicious sausage and peppers because she was cooking for a family dinner. If you gotta leave to join her, that's cool. Just make sure to stick around until all the officers from all the chapters get here. It may be kinda late. Not sure how long the dinner's gonna go on."

"I'm here for the night." Hawk turned away and watched Kristy and Lola as they carried in platters of ribs and fried chicken. Kristy smiled and waved at him, and he lifted his chin to her.

"Who makes your food?" Jax asked Steel.

"We have a cook, Lena."

"Fuck, aren't you all sophisticated and shit? You have a cook," Jerry said, and they laughed.

"Hey, Hawk," Wheelie said, squeezing between him and Axe to get a drink.

"What're you up to?" Hawk felt his phone vibrate.

"Not much. This should be a good party. I've seen some brothers I haven't talked to since August in Sturgis." He grabbed a drink and stood in front of Hawk.

"You doing good?" Hawk watched Wheelie's face to see if he could pick anything up. Ever since Wheelie had offered to watch Sofia that weekend Tigger had gone on a poker run, Hawk had been anxious. He really liked the brother and didn't want to have to beat his ass. The brother he couldn't stand was Tigger, but he was a patched member and deserved the respect and loyalty afforded to all in the brotherhood.

"Yeah. Why?"

"Just asking."

"I'll see you." Wheelie ambled away and vanished into the crowd.

Hawk looked at his phone. Another call from Cara. And a text. He put the phone in his pocket. She had to respect him and not question his decisions when it came to the club. He loved her so much and had shown her in so many ways that she was number one in his life, and her questioning that left a real bitter taste in his mouth. *I bet Belle wouldn't have said shit to Banger. She understands he's got a responsibility to the club. She knows her role. Cara could take some fuckin' lessons from her.*

"Hey, cutie. You look super pissed. Aren't you having fun?" A soft hand curled around his bicep.

Glancing sideways, he saw the new club girl who kept trying to get his cock in her pussy. For the life of him, Hawk couldn't remember her name.

"Don't feel like talking? That's okay. Do you want me to get you some food?" She came in closer, and he could see her tits through her skimpy top.

"I don't want anything. Circulate. They're a shitload of out-of-state brothers who need taking care of."

"Just call me if you get lonely." She sashayed away.

His phone kept vibrating, and he almost answered it when the presidents of three of the chapters came up to him, pulling him into a bear hug.

As the night wore on, Hawk talked too much, smoked too much, and drank too much. By the time two thirty rolled around, he was plastered, sitting on a bar stool breathing in smoky air. His head spun and the whole room whirled around as if it were on a carousel, slow at first and then faster and faster. Swaying on the stool, he gripped the edge of the bar and stood up. Blood rushed to his head, and he pressed his hands to his temples as if the simple gesture would stop the constant throbbing.

"Need some help, cutie?" A woman in a low top with big tits pressed her soft body against his.

"Cara? What the fuck are you doing at the club, baby?"

"My name's Heather," the woman said stiffly.

"Heather? Who the fuck are you?" He swayed on his feet.

"I'm just here to help you make it to your room safely. That's all."

"I don't want you. Get Cara. Tell her to get her ass to my room. I need my woman." He pushed Heather away and staggered, his hands gripping anything he could to steady himself. Officers maintained rooms even if they didn't live at the clubhouse, and he slowly clumped up the stairs to his on the third floor.

It took several minutes for him to put the key in the lock, but finally the door opened. Pushing it closed, he leaned back against it, waiting for the room to stop swirling. With much effort, he made it to the bed, pulled off his boots, and flopped on his back. Closing his eyes, darkness came.

HAWK RAISED HIS heavy eyelids, quickly closing them halfway when shards of sunlight pierced them. Draping his arm over his eyes, he groaned. His head felt like an axe was planted in it, and his throat was like sandpaper. *Fuck.* Taking his arm away from his pounding head, he forced his eyes open again and cursed the brightness of the morning as he struggled to cope with it. On the nightstand, he saw his phone and fumbled for it. When he saw a ton of texts and several missed calls from Cara, his stomach turned sour. *I really fucked up.* Deciding he better get his ass home and smooth things over, he tried to move but it felt like he was in quicksand.

Then he heard a soft sigh and something bump against his left leg. Glancing over, he saw a woman sleeping next to him. He bolted up. "Fuck!" he yelled, then held his head. Nausea grabbed him as realization hit him: a woman other than Cara was in his bed. Squeezing his eyes shut, he tried to remember what the hell had happened the night before. *Did I fuck her? I couldn't have. I never would've done that to Cara.* He was pissed at her, but he'd never take another woman in his bed. But there *was* another woman lying next to him.

What the hell did I do?

Nudging her with his leg, Heather turned around, smiling. She stretched like a cat, then wrapped her arm around his waist. He moved it away.

"Why the hell are you in my bed?"

"I was so tired, I fell asleep after you did." Smiling shyly, she ran her finger up his arm. "You're way better than your reputation, and that's pretty awesome."

"What the hell are you talking about?"

Her gaze widened. "I've never been fucked like that before. It was pretty incredible."

Forcing himself up, he grabbed his T-shirt on the floor. "You're bullshitting."

Jutting out her lower lip, she pushed herself up and leaned against the headboard, the falling sheet revealing her naked breasts. "I'm insulted you don't remember our night of passion."

"Cover your damn tits." He went over to the window and looked at the mountains, squinting. *Did I really fuck her? How could I do that? Yeah, I was drunk as shit, but there's no way I'd betray Cara.* Since he'd first seen her, she was the only woman he'd ever wanted. Women came on to him all the time, but he never considered going behind Cara's back. He didn't want to; she was the love of his life and was enough for him for a zillion lifetimes. He glanced down. *I still have my jeans on. Something's not right.*

"Do you wanna take a shower together? I can rub you down real good."

He looked over his shoulder. "I want you to get the fuck outta my room. You shouldn't have been here in the first place. Club whores aren't allowed in an officer's room."

"Unless he invites her, and that's what you did." Naked, she bent over and scooped up her clothes. She blew a kiss at him, winked, and closed the door behind her.

Staring at the closed door, he rubbed his temples, trying to remember if he did something so despicable and disloyal to the only woman he'd ever loved. In his past, he'd been wasted to where he blacked out, but he'd never fucked a woman and didn't remember it. *This is bullshit. There's no way I would've touched another woman, drunk or not.*

He trudged to the bathroom and stepped into the shower. The cool water calmed his aching head and gave him renewed vitality. After drying and dressing, he gulped down three aspirins and headed downstairs.

The great room looked like a tornado had hit it: bottles strewn everywhere, furniture topsy-turvy, blinds torn from the windows. When he went into the kitchen, Kristy hovered over the counter, pouring orange juice into a glass.

"You don't look so good. Want some?" She lifted the carton and reached for a glass when he nodded. "You tied on a good one last night." She smiled as she handed him the glass.

In one long gulp, he drank the juice. "What the fuck happened last night?"

"You were in a real sour mood and you got real drunk. I haven't seen you that drunk in a really long time. Remember how we used to party?"

He slowly nodded. "When we did, I always remembered it the next morning."

"Of course you did. I was unforgettable." She laughed.

"Yeah, but I always remembered when I fucked a chick. Something's not gelling here."

Kristy pressed her lips together and turned away.

"What's wrong?"

She shook her head, shrugging.

"Don't bullshit me. We go back a long time. I know when you're hiding something."

She walked over to the kitchen door, looked out, and then closed it. Taking the seat next to his at the breakfast counter, she placed her hand on his forearm. "That shit last night was staged."

"What do you mean?"

"Heather concocted it. She's pissed as hell that you're ignoring her, and she hates Cara. Lola egged her on, but it was all Heather's doing. I told her not to do it, and Brandi and Wendy said she was fuckin' nuts. We thought she was all talk until Lola came to our rooms telling us

Heather snuck into yours."

His temples pounded. "So I didn't fuck Heather?"

"No way. Do you think I would've let that happen?" She laughed dryly. "If you're gonna stray for one night, it's gonna be with me. I was your go-to girl back before Cara came into the picture."

"That fuckin' bitch." Muscles strained against his skin.

"You were so wasted you forgot to lock your door. The slut snuck in there early this morning."

"She's fuckin' history."

Kristy stretched her arms over her head. "I never liked her. She doesn't know her place. I'm the head club girl, but she acts like she's all that just 'cause she's twenty-two and all the brothers are into her 'cause she's new meat. She's nothing but a skank."

Hawk put his hand on her shoulder and squeezed it. "Thanks for telling me." He stood up. "I gotta take care of something before I go." He walked to the door and stopped when Kristy called his name. He turned around and looked at her.

"I just wanted to give you a heads-up that Doris was in here earlier this morning and Lola was making sure she was talking real loud in the hallway about you fucking Heather. I know Doris is an old lady and I gotta show her respect, but that woman lives for gossip and the nastier it is, the more she loves it. I wouldn't be surprised if she's already called Cara."

Knots formed in his stomach; he had no doubt Doris raced to call Cara. The woman never cared when something good happened to another old lady or to a brother, she only lived for the stuff that caused the biggest drama. And this would be the fucking atomic bomb in his household. He had to get home and explain it to Cara.

Fuck, I screwed this up. I should've gone home after the party, or at least told her I was too drunk to ride and was crashing at the clubhouse. He grabbed a few plastic bags, nodded to Kristy, and then left.

Climbing the stairs, he went to the attic where the club girls had their rooms. He kicked open Heather's door and saw her and Lola sitting on the bed chatting. They both avoided eye contact with him, and Heather clutched her arms to her chest. Without a word, he opened her drawers and threw all her stuff on the floor.

"What're you doing?" she asked in a quiet voice.

"Clearing your shit out so the room's available for the next girl on the list. Your ass is outta here."

Heather's mouth dropped open and her eyes shimmered. "I'm sorry, I didn't—"

"Sorry doesn't even begin to cut it." He threw dusting powder, lipsticks, and a mini hair dryer on top of the pile of clothes on the floor.

"Hawk, she didn't mean—"

He stood cracking his neck from side to side, his feet planted wide. Adrenaline surged through his body and he knew if either of the bitches said another word, he'd lose it.

"Don't say another damn word or your ass is outta here too," he gritted to Lola. She hung her head and folded her hands in her lap. He threw the plastic bags at Heather. "You've got fifteen minutes to bag this shit and get your ass out. If you're still here after fifteen minutes, I'll throw your ass out and I won't be gentle. Leave your cut on the bed."

Lola glanced up at him and offered him a small smile that seemed to say she was sorry and grateful he was letting her stay. He clenched his fists. "And this is the last time you fuck with me and my wife. If you even think about doing shit to me or any other brother in the club, I'll kick your ass out next."

He stormed out and went into the great room, checking the time. He meant every word he said: if the club whore wasn't gone in fifteen, he'd drag her out.

"You still here?" Wheelie asked as he sidled up to the bar.

"Yeah. I threw one of the club whores out."

"Which one?"

"The new one."

"She disrespect you?"

"Yeah."

"Then her ass has gotta go. We got someone already waiting to fill her spot. I'll let the brothers know."

Hawk saw Heather dragging two large black bags behind her as she walked toward the front door. She didn't look at Hawk, just kept walking with her head down until she was outside. Satisfied, Hawk slid off the stool and put on his leather gloves.

"I gotta get home. See ya." He fist bumped with Wheelie, put on his sunglasses, and went out into the bright sunshine.

After switching off the motor, he quietly turned the doorknob and slipped into the mudroom. The aroma of warm butter and maple syrup greeted him as he heard the small voices of Braxton and Isa in the kitchen. Pulling his hair back in a ponytail, he walked in. Cara was by the griddle flipping pancakes, and Braxton and Isa were at the table.

"Daddy!" Braxton cried as he scrambled out of his seat. Isa laughed and extended her hands, her green eyes sparkling.

Hawk scooped Braxton up and kissed his cheek, then went over to Isa and grabbed her chubby hands. "Are you guys waiting for the killer pancakes your mom makes?" He glanced sideways at Cara but she ignored him, her eyes on the griddle, her lips pursed together. He sat Braxton back on his chair and went over to Cara. Wrapping his arms around her waist, he felt her stiffen like a board.

"Don't touch me," she said, pushing him back with her behind.

"Babe, we need to talk."

"I'm not going to fight in front of the kids."

"We don't need to fight, but we need to talk. I got fuckin' wasted last night and passed out. I shoulda called you but I was too bombed."

"And were you bombed the minute you stepped into the club? You ignored my texts and calls." She placed three more pancakes on top of an already growing stack.

"I was pissed."

"How mature."

"We just need to talk."

"I'm making breakfast for our kids. Unlike you, I'm concerned about them and making sure they have a responsible parent in the house."

In a low harsh voice, he said in her ear, "Don't ever fuckin' accuse me of not caring for our kids. That's a goddamn low blow. I got drunk and spent the night at the club. Fuckin' deal with it."

"Get away from me. I have nothing I want to say to you." She pushed past him, brought the stack of pancakes to the table, and placed some on Braxton's plate.

Hawk watched as she fussed over their kids. *I lost my cool. Fuck.* He poured coffee into a large mug, then came over to the table.

"Aren't you gonna give Daddy any pancakes?" Braxton asked as he brought the fork to his mouth.

"I don't have enough," she said, glancing at the stack on the serving plate.

"Isa and me can't eat all those." Braxton giggled.

"Don't talk with your mouth full, honey." Cara whipped the serving plate away and placed it in the warming oven.

"No worries, little buddy," Hawk said as he ruffled his son's hair. "I'm good with just coffee."

Cara came over and wiped Isa's mouth with a napkin. "We're going to see Nana and Noni."

"Am I going too?" Braxton said.

"No. You can stay with your father today. Isa, Nana, and I are going shopping. I don't think you'll like that."

"Uh-uh!"

"I'm just going to change. I'll be right back." She ran her hand through his hair and stroked Isa's cheek with her finger, then left the kitchen.

Hawk's jaw tightened as he watched her bounce up the stairs.

"Did Mommy put you in timeout?" Braxton asked, his blue eyes wide.

"It looks that way."

"When I do something I'm not supposed to, Mommy puts me in

timeout too. It's not so bad, 'cause I say I'm sorry and that makes Mommy happy. You should tell Mommy you're sorry. Then she won't be so mad at you."

Hawk smiled dryly as he brought the mug to his lips and took a sip. The bitter taste burned down his throat. "I'll have to try that. Thanks for the tip, little buddy."

"What did you do?" Braxton stuffed another bite into his mouth.

"It's complicated."

"Do you want some of my pancakes? They're good."

"Nah. I was gonna make some eggs and bacon. You want some bacon?" He pushed away from the table and laughed as Braxton bobbed his head up and down.

Bent over looking for the frying pan, he knew Cara had come back into the room. The scent of spiced vanilla wisped around him, and his dick twitched. He stood up and saw her in black skinny jeans, a sweater that clung temptingly to her tits, and knee-high black leather boots. Her wavy chestnut hair spilled down around her.

"You look real good," he said, his muscles tensing when she threw him a dirty look.

She took Isa out of the high chair, wiped her face, and slipped her arms into a plaid fleece jacket with a panda bear on the front. "All set?" Isa giggled and clung to Cara. "Have a good day with your father." She bent over and kissed Braxton on top of his head.

When she walked past him to go to the garage, Hawk pulled her back and nuzzled his face into her neck. "I know you're pissed at me, babe. I fucked up, but don't be this way."

With cold eyes, she stared at him. "Doris called me this morning." Ice dripped from her words.

"You can't believe the shit she told you. I was set up, and I threw the whore's ass out of the club."

"Watch your language around Isa. I'm not in the mood for excuses." She jerked away from him and walked away.

A few minutes later, the rumble of the garage door opening and closing told him she was gone. *She can't stay pissed off at me forever. Or can she?* Cara could be very stubborn, and he'd have to bide his time. But if she took too long, he'd have to remind her why she fell in love with him.

She was his woman to the end, and nothing was ever going to change that.

CHAPTER FIFTEEN

CHAS

JACK SAT ON the couch, his head down, and Addie stood in front of him, her face taut, hands on hips.

"What's going on?" Chas asked, entering the living room.

"Mrs. D'Angelo called about Jack."

Tossing his jacket on the chair, Chas darted his gaze to Jack and then back to Addie. "Who's she?"

"His principal. She said Jack got in a fight with a boy at school."

Thrusting his chest out, Chas grinned and put his hand on Jack's shoulder, squeezing it. "Way to go, Champ."

Jack looked up and Chas high-fived him.

"You're not mad?" his son asked.

"Fuck no." Addie clearing her throat reminded Chas she was still in the room. He glanced at her furrowed brow. "What?"

"You're applauding him for hurting another boy? Are you thinking this through?"

"I'm telling him he did a good job standing up to a fuckin' bully."

"Are you being bullied? You never told me."

"That's not the kind of shit a boy tells his mom. Anyway, I took care of it." Chas sat on the arm of the couch.

"And how did you do that?" Redness mottled her face.

"By teaching him some moves to protect himself. I can't believe you're so bent outta shape over this. A man needs to know how to stand up for himself."

"But he's not a man, Chas. He's a boy, or can't you see that?"

"Every man was a boy. It's never too early to show that you're tough. You get respect that way and people don't mess with you." Chas looked at Jack, who had his head down again. He went over and ruffled his hair. "You did good. Did the fucker go down and stay down?"

A gleam shone in his eyes and he laughed. "Better than that, Dad. He ran away and everybody cheered and came up to me. It was awesome." He glanced at his mother. "Sorry, Mom," he mumbled.

"This is unbelievable. I was wrong in blaming you. This is your father's fault." Narrowing her eyes, she pointed at Chas. "You can meet with the principal at ten o'clock tomorrow morning." She stormed out of the room.

Inhaling deeply, Chas watched as Addie put on her coat, grabbed her purse, and slammed the back door. A few seconds later, the Land Rover's engine revved to life and the familiar clang of the garage door closing seeped through the walls.

"Mom's pissed." Jack leaned back and put his feet up on the table.

"She'll get over it. Women are like that. They're all into talking and shit because that's the way they resolve stuff with their girlfriends. Us guys just throw a few punches and we're good. Women don't get it. So, you must've been practicing what I taught you."

"I did, and when Owen came for me, I didn't cower or run like I always did. I just stood there. He seemed surprised. Some of the kids came over to see what was going on. Owen came toward me and I knew he was going to punch me, so I did like you told me to do—anticipate his move and do the opposite of what he expected me to do. He missed me and I punched him in the gut real hard. Then the fight was on."

Chas loved seeing the confidence in his son's face, the way he became animated in talking about the fight, and his booming laugh made Chas's heart swell. No matter how many arguments Addie threw at him about peace versus violence, he'd never regret teaching Jack how to defend himself. The glow over Jack's face was priceless, and as he watched him hold his chin high and push his shoulders back, Chas knew Jack would never cower in another corner again. When six o'clock rolled around, Chas took out a package of hot dogs and put them in a pot of water on the stove. He opened a couple cans of chili beans and put them in another pot.

"You're cooking?" Jack said, coming into the kitchen.

"I'm hungry, Daddy," Hope said.

"I'm making dinner, sweet bear." He looked at Jack. "And I used to cook all the time for us before your mom."

"It was hot dogs and beans, pretty much," Jack said as he pulled the kitchen chair out for Hope.

"Then it'll be like old times because that's what we're having. You like hot dogs, don't you, sweet bear?"

"I love them. Mama doesn't make them too much."

"I'm an expert with them."

Addie didn't come home until well after Hope had gone to sleep. Chas was watching television on the couch when his ears pricked at the sound of the garage door. As she entered the house, a rush of cold air coiled around him, making the flames in the fireplace leap and dance.

"You have a good evening?" he asked, his gaze still on the television.

"I did. I went to the mall, then went over to Clotille and Rock's house. She made the best rice and beans I've ever had. Did you order a pizza for the kids?"

"I cooked. It would've been nice for you to have sent a fuckin' text or something. I get that you needed some space to cool off, but not sending a text to me or Jack is shitty. The kids kept asking where you were."

"I sent you one."

Chas looked at his phone and saw a text had come in fifteen minutes before. When he looked at the time it was sent, it was two hours before. "These damn phones."

"Did you get it?"

"Just recently."

Sitting at the other end of the couch, she lifted his feet and put them on her lap. "I know we're never going to agree with the fighting thing with Jack. I was so mad at you."

"I know you were. And you're right, we're not going to agree. Women just see things differently. You're pissed at Jack because he stood up for himself by punching the brat, and I'm proud. It'll be like that forever. My mom is still appalled to know that I'll beat the shit out of anyone who messes with me. My dad gets it. There you have it."

"I suppose. I hope you told Jack that it's not good to start fights, just fight to defend himself."

"Yeah, I told him that." Chas thought about how many barroom brawls he'd had when he was younger. Some of them were because he was provoked, while others were just because he didn't like the way some fucker looked at him. He pushed up and swung his legs off the couch. "You still pissed at me?" Scooting toward her, he reached out and grabbed her hand.

"Maybe."

"Don't be." He swept her hair aside and slowly licked her neck.

"I don't forgive that easily," she said as she moved closer to him.

"That's too bad," he breathed in her ear, then slipped her earlobe between his teeth and sucked gently. A small moan slipped from her lips. As he sucked her ear and neck, he unbuttoned her blouse, then slipped his hand inside her bra, squeezing her breast. "I fuckin' love your tits, precious."

She unsnapped the front of her bra and her big tits spilled out. "What about Jack?"

"He's in the middle of a video game. We got time."

Grasping her waist, he scooted her down until she lay beneath him on the couch. As he unzipped her pants, he drew one of her nipples into his mouth, sucking and nipping it as he felt her shiver.

"Are you closer to forgiving me?" His words were smothered against her skin.

"Yeah," she breathed.

He ran his tongue from the base of her throat down to her belly button, swirling in and around it, his hands pressing down on her squirming body beneath him. Locking his gaze on her, he slowly slipped his hand inside her panties, his lips twitching as he watched her face contort while he sank his finger deeply inside her. "You're wet as hell. I love that." Using the tip of his tongue, he teased her nipple, making it grow rock hard as he thrust his digits in and out of her heat. Low moans came from her throat and she stuffed her fist in her mouth as if trying to contain them.

"When I'm done loving you, you're not going to even remember why you were pissed at me."

The light from the crackling fire bathed her creamy skin in an amber glow and made her red hair shimmer like it was gold.

"You're stunning," he said.

Slipping her hands under his shirt, her fingers outlined his defined muscles. "So are you," she said softly.

Electric heat moved through him as his need for her intensified. As she stared up at him, desire brimming in her gaze, he slowly started taking her clothes off, piece by piece, kissing and caressing her skin as he revealed it. He'd be gentle, making sure each lick, kiss, bite, and touch reminded her why she fell in love with him. And then he'd go rough, claiming her all over again as only an outlaw knew how.

LEG CROSSED OVER his thigh, Chas sat in the principal's office, glancing at the clock and growing madder by the second. The door opened and a man in his late thirties dressed in a suit walked in, a tall, stocky boy beside him.

"Mr. Price. Thank you for coming."

"You're late," Chas said, and Jack giggled.

Mrs. D'Angelo glowered at both of them, then smiled sweetly at the man and the boy.

The man leaned forward and held out his hand to Chas. "Deke Price. This is my boy, Owen."

"Chas." Ignoring Deke's gesture, he jerked his head at his son.

"Jack."

Deke frowned and let his hand fall to his lap.

"What do you want to talk about? I got stuff to do." Chas stared at the gray-haired principal, who shuffled some papers on her desk.

"Jack was in a fight yesterday. He punched Owen several times, causing the boy to have to seek the assistance of the nurse."

Chas turned to Owen. "Did he break your nose?" Owen shook his head, his gaze downcast. "Any bones broken?" Another shake of the head. "Any internal injuries?" Another shake. Chas cracked his knuckles. "So why am I here? Two boys fought out their differences."

"Mr. Vickers, that is hardly the attitude I'd like to see from a parent," the principal said.

"That's the attitude you're gonna get. Are we done here?"

"We're most certainly not. Your son attacked Owen."

"The way I heard it, Jack was just defending himself."

"Is that true, Owen?" Deke asked.

"No. He started it." Owen threw Jack a dirty look.

"Did not! You're always starting something with me, but this time I showed you." Jack moved forward until he was on the edge of the chair.

"Enough, both of you. Jack, if there was a problem, you should've looked for a teacher to help. Fighting is never the answer."

"Sometimes it's the only one. I don't tell Jack to pick fights, but if someone messes with him, he's got a right to give it back. This kid here threw the first punch. It was a fair fight," Chas said.

Deke scoffed. "Of course you'd think that way. Aren't you in that outlaw gang?"

Bristling, Chas clenched his hands. "It doesn't matter who and what I am. Your son's nothing but a damn bully. He's been picking on my kid, and now he's fuckin' eating crow because his ass got beat."

"Mr. Vickers! We don't allow language like that at the school." Blotches of red had crept onto the principal's face, especially around her chin and cheeks, and her brown eyes flashed.

"They're just words, lady." He stood up. "I gotta get going."

"We're not finished," Mrs. D'Angelo said.

"I am, and so is Jack."

Deke shook his head at the principal and threw her a knowing smile.

Chas glared at the prick. "Instead of thinking you're better than everyone because you wear a suit, I'd deal with your kid and figure out why he's picking on younger kids."

"There's nothing wrong with Owen."

Chas looked at the principal. "Jack's been going to school here for the last seven years. Have you ever had a problem with him?"

She splayed her hands out on the desk. "No, I haven't. That's why I was so surprised by all this."

"Then you should've figured something was up. Jack told you what the deal was."

"You're right, but fighting still isn't allowed at school. I'm going to have to suspend both boys for it."

Deke jumped to his feet. "This is outrageous! Owen didn't do anything. This boy attacked him."

"Mr. Price, I'm not sure who did what. The fact is both boys were fighting, so they'll be suspended for two days."

"Works for me," Chas said as he motioned Jack to get up.

"The suspension will start now. Hopefully both Owen and Jack will learn from this and think twice before fighting."

Chas nodded, put his hand on Jack's shoulder, and walked out of the school. When they got to the car, Chas turned to Jack and winked. "You got a couple days free. Wanna grab some food at Ruthie's?"

"Mom's gonna be real mad at me."

"I don't think so. I kind of softened her up last night." Memories of Addie's legs spread wide and his tongue buried inside her pussy reeled through his mind. "Let's get some breakfast."

The snow covered both of them as they walked through the parking lot. A bell chimed when Chas opened the diner's door and heat surrounded them, warming their cold bodies.

As they ate steak, eggs, and hash browns, Chas saw his ex-wife near the cash register, staring at him. *What the fuck's she doing back in Pinewood Springs?* She waved at him, then started walking over to their booth. *Shit.*

"Hi, Chas. And Jack. How are you guys doing? You don't mind if I sit for a few," she said as she scooted in next to Jack.

The cheerful look on Jack's face switched to a stoic one and he moved stiffly as he made room for her to sit down.

"Why're you here, Brianna?" Chas asked.

"That's the first thing you ask me after all these years? Don't you want to know how I've been doing?" She put her arm around Jack. "What about you, baby? Do you want to know how your mama's been?"

Jack shrugged off her arm and stared down at his plate.

"Fuckin' cool it. I know you too well. Why the hell are you here?" Chas glared at her.

"My mom's real sick. They don't think she's going to make it." She brushed her finger over her cheek.

He liked his ex-mother-in-law; she was a genuinely nice person. In all the years that he and Brianna had been married, he'd tried to figure out how such a good person could have had such a mean and conniving bitch for a daughter. He'd thought it must've come from Brianna's dad. He'd heard the man was one cruel sonofabitch, but he'd run off years before Chas and Brianna had met.

"Mom said she hasn't seen Jack in a long time. I think she'd like to see him before she dies." Her voice hitched on the last word.

He placed his hand on hers. "This must be tough on you. Your mom's a good woman. The last couple of times I was gonna bring Jack over, she said she was busy. She didn't tell me she wasn't feeling well."

"That's the way she is. Doesn't want to stress anyone out. I had no idea she had cancer. None of us did. It sucks."

"I'll bring Jack to see her. I'd like to see her too. Is she at Pinewood Hospital?"

Brianna nodded and grasped his fingers. "I'm so scared I'm gonna lose it when she dies. I've been working so hard to straighten out my life."

"That's good. Are you still in Durango?"

"No. Me and Johnny split up. It was the best thing for me. I got clean and sober."

"Where're you living now?" Chas smiled at the waitress as she re-filled his coffee cup.

"You want something?" Stella asked Brianna. She shook her head and the waitress ambled away.

"I'm living here at my mother's house. I got a job and everything."

All of a sudden, he had a sour taste in his mouth. Glancing over at Jack, his heart squeezed as he watched the color drain from his face. *He's remembering how she treated him. There's no fuckin' way she's getting close to him. Or me.* He pulled his hand away from hers.

"Where're you working?" he asked.

"I'm a receptionist for this charity. It's called Brighter Lives."

"Mom does stuff with them," Jack blurted out, then clammed up when Brianna gave him a death stare.

"That's right. Addie and several of the old ladies are involved in a fundraiser we're doing next Saturday."

"Are you still with *her*?"

"Yeah. Of course. We're married and have a daughter."

The lines around her mouth deepened. "Mom told me. She was surprised we didn't get back together."

"She never said anything to me like that." What he wanted to tell Brianna was that her mother told him she was finally happy he'd found a good woman who would love him and be loyal to him. He waved Stella over. *Visiting time is over.* "Check, please."

"How're you doing, Jack?" Brianna asked sweetly.

Jack shrugged. "Okay. Are we going now, Dad?"

"Yeah." Chas slid out of the booth.

"We should get together for dinner sometime." She brushed against Chas.

"I don't think so. I'll take Jack to see his grandma."

"When? I mean, I'd like to be there when you do."

"Just when I get some free time. We gotta go."

"It was great seeing you again. You look real good still. How do you think I look?" She ran her hands over her body.

"You look fine." He walked to the cash register and Jack rushed in front of him. After paying, he headed for the door, and Brianna came up to him.

"Don't I get a hug?"

"No."

"Jack?"

Jack's eyes darted to Chas. He pulled Jack to him. "He's not into that."

Bracing himself, he stepped out in the cold, and with his hand on Jack's shoulder, they went to their car.

As they drove to Pinewood Hospital, Jack blew his breath on the window and made patterns on the steam with his finger. "Do I have to start going over to Mom's again?"

"No way."

"For real?"

"Yeah. I mean, if you want to, I'm not gonna st—"

"I don't want to. I love Addie. She's my mom. Is that bad?"

Chas shook his head. "Not at all. Addie loves you too. Your blood mom wasn't so good to you. It's okay not to love her the way you do Addie."

A satisfied smile spread over Jack's face as he settled back in his seat. Chas reached over and ruffled his hair, then turned on the radio.

There's no damn way I'm letting Brianna start trouble. Clean or not, Brianna only had one agenda in life—getting whatever she could for her. It was her world and she didn't give a shit about anyone. She gave up her parental rights to Jack years before, and there was no way she was going to start anything up.

Snowflakes swirled around and landed on the windshield.

"It's snowing again. Maybe Ethan can come over and we can build a snowman. Can I ask him?"

"Sure."

Jack took out his phone, and as he tapped his text, warmth spread through Chas. Seeing Brianna reminded him how lucky he was to have Addie in his life. His family was everything to him.

The SUV rambled down the slick, snow-packed street.

CHAPTER SIXTEEN

THE CRAZED GRINCH

LAUGHING AS HE checked off the names of three more families, he leaned back against the car's leather seat and turned the heater up. An eerie stillness sheathed the world outside as the falling snow choked the land, covering trees, lawns, roofs, and cars. It was like he was in a cocoon, safe and protected, all the windows covered by white making his world inside the vehicle charcoal gray.

As he stared ahead, a small boy appeared in the theater of his mind. The image was in full color and the boy sat on the soft cushion of a brocade chair, the fire's glow highlighting wet tracks on his face. His father, bent over, stuffed brightly wrapped presents into a large black bag. Standing in the corner of the room was his mother, her hands covering her mouth as she looked at the scene unfolding before her.

Gripping the steering wheel, memories from his younger days flooded his mind. He'd come from a wealthy family, lived in a mansion, took equestrian lessons, and had a lifestyle a lot of children would've killed for, but they didn't know what was hidden behind the columned porch and hand-carved front door. Inside, a monster ruled them—all of them. The mother he'd clung to before he went to school had betrayed him and his sister. She'd stood by and watched as the puppet master yanked their silvery strings, manipulating, humiliating, and punishing them without mercy. And all she'd done afterward was offer them cookies and lemonade.

Scrubbing his face with his fist, he glanced at the illuminated blue numbers in the car—midnight. *Darkness without a glow.* Closing his eyes, he tried to remember when there was a life without misery, but he couldn't. Blackness crept in when he hadn't been looking, and it never left.

His father had been a cruel and controlling man. There'd never been any physical signs of abuse on his wife and children—his dad was too clever for that. All the scars he'd given them were internal, and they never healed.

"You're a loser. You'll never amount to anything, you stupid, worthless brat. The day you were born was the worst day of my life." His father's words resonated through him, making him wince and shudder even all these years later.

All the commercialism in the world couldn't ruin Christmas the way his father had—he'd been an expert at it. From the age of four, he remembered the puppet master taking away their gifts to give to needy children. In the beginning, his mother had sneaked a gift to them, but somehow their father had always found out; the gift was taken away from them, and then he'd berate their mother for days. Then one year, she stopped trying: no secret gifts, no Christmas tree, no lights in the window, no cheer of any kind. The fight had seeped out of her, and she let the puppet master reinvent the holiday for their household.

After that, he'd outdone himself: forcing them to go to parties and give their toys away, taking them shopping for ornaments, lights, and a tree, then making them give it away, playing Santa Claus at all the parties, banning anything that hinted of holiday cheer in their home. *But the fucking bastard didn't give up* his *presents, the roast beef dinner he insisted Mom make, or his goddamn lectures on the spirit of giving.*

The brown-eyed man breathed heavily as the snippets from his fucked-up childhood ran through his head like a B-rated movie. *How could you have given him any presents, Mom? He treated you like shit. He treated all of us like we didn't matter.*

"I fucking hate you!" The pain from slamming the steering wheel shot up his arm as the car windows threw back the echoes of his voice. Resting his forehead on the steering wheel, he tried to sift through the decay of his life to find something salvageable. Nothing. His whole world was black.

"You fucking took in foster kids and lavished them with love and kindness, and you turned your back on your own flesh and blood, you bastard," he said aloud. An image he tried to keep hidden burst through: his sister dangling at the end of a rope she'd tied to the ceiling fan in her room.

His nose ran and saliva trickled from his mouth. "She was only four-teen years old. You made her believe she was ugly, fat, and unlovable. You bastard!"

The chime of his cell phone sounded distant, like it was from a different place and time. It kept ringing, dragging him out of the past. Sweeping his palms over his eyes, he inhaled through his nose. The ringing stopped. Picking up his phone, he saw his wife's name and threw the phone on the floor mat. The pictures from the past fled to the dark recesses of his mind. Spite resurfaced, pushing all other emotions into his soul's dark hole.

Coughing, he straightened in his seat and grabbed the list beside him. *Tomorrow night I'll hit the Montoya and Duggan houses.* Christmas was the one holiday he hated the most. All the yuletide and joyful feelings made him want to fucking puke. The look of anticipation on the children's faces when they went to see Santa or looked at their wrapped gifts under the tree made his skin crawl and his blood boil.

"Fucking brats," he muttered under his breath as he switched the defroster on high, grabbed the snow brush, and exited the car. Stretching gloves over his hands, he frowned at the multicolored lights twinkling through the white mist. Several inflatable angels and snowmen lay on their sides, having been blown over by the icy wind.

He'd come up with the idea to stamp out Christmas one inflatable at a time when he'd turned sixteen. With money earned from his part-time job at the hardware store, he'd bought a BB gun and snuck out of the house at night, canvassing the neighborhood and shooting inflated snowmen, penguins, snow globes, and nutcrackers. He'd hated them with a passion, and his mission was to rid his small Illinois town of all inflatables. On one of his nightly excursions, a policeman had caught him in the act, and he'd pled guilty to criminal mischief. Afterward, he'd made sure he was smarter and more alert the next time.

And there'd been years of next times as he moved around the country for his employment. He'd always been so meticulous with his hits, but the day at the outlaw biker's house, he'd lost his cool. He'd let a pretty woman turn his head. He didn't know what he was thinking by waiting in the house for her and Paisley. Not thinking he'd have the nerve to do it, he'd begun to leave when he heard the garage door open. If it'd been the Neanderthal, he'd have slipped out the first chance he had, but she and her daughter had come in and a rush of adrenaline shot through him.

In all the years he'd been stamping out Christmas, he'd never confronted the people in the houses he destroyed. He didn't want to; there was no fun in it. The pretty woman made him stay, of course, but it was the rush of knowing the house belonged to an Insurgent. He couldn't stand how they walked around town acting like they owned it, like they were hot stuff. In his opinion, they were nothing more than criminals and hoodlums, yet women flocked to them and the town tolerated them.

The bikers tried to act like they were good guys, putting on stupid toy drives, but in his eyes, they were a bunch of nobodies. So he'd enjoyed the rush of adrenaline as he destroyed property that belonged to one of them, and scared the shit out of the biker's wife.

Slipping back into the car, he banged the snow brush on the chrome door frame and then closed the door. Inside, it was toasty and the defroster had melted all the ice on the windshield. He shook his head; he hadn't planned on the pretty blonde to be a fighter. *I underestimated her. I should've figured the lowlifes would teach their women to defend themselves. But I bet their children can't fight me.* An evil smile began to slowly spread across his face. *What better way to ruin Christmas than to have your child snatched?*

A streak of excitement rode up his spine. If he could pull it off, it would be the best holiday season ever, but he couldn't rush into it. Making a mistake would be deadly, he was sure of that. He'd have to plan out all the details, though he didn't have much time. Christmas was only two weeks away.

Humming and tapping his fingers on the dashboard, he pulled away from the curb and drove down the quiet streets.

The phone rang again and he stopped abruptly, the back tires sliding. Looking down at the phone on the floor mat, his wife's name flashed on the screen. He pounded his fist on the dashboard. "What does that fucking cow want?" he yelled out. He knew it wasn't him. They'd stopped caring about each other years back. *Probably wants me to pick up something sweet for her at the convenience store. Well, fuck you, bitch. You can forget that.*

As he drove home, his wife's face filled his mind. *How did I ever think she was right for me?* The truth was, he'd never loved her; she was just there when he reached the decision to marry. They had similar backgrounds and they both liked traveling, but as the years rolled by, she'd become nothing but a nuisance in his life. She was like a gnat that just wouldn't go away, always buzzing around.

His fucking father had always called him a coward. If the bastard were still living, he wouldn't call him that if he knew what he was planning to do for his Christmas finale. Once he proved he could brazenly go after the Insurgents' kids, his next project would be getting rid of his wife. He was sick of her insults and sarcasm.

It's time to shut you up once and for all, you stupid cow.

The garage door closed and he went into the house.

CHAPTER SEVENTEEN

BELLE

"I STILL CAN'T believe Dale wants to be Santa at the fundraiser on Saturday. I was preparing for a huge argument, and he just said 'yes.' Just like that. 'Yes.' Amazing," Lindi said as she placed the pens and papers into a briefcase.

"I'm so glad he's doing it. Mitch didn't even answer me when I asked. His eyes just bugged out, he wrinkled his nose, and then went back to his crossword puzzle," Torey said.

Joseph rose from his chair. "I'm just happy I don't have to do it. Tell Dale thanks from me."

"And me," Evan chimed in.

"I asked Banger to do it, and he said he would as long as he could wear his cut and jeans. I didn't think he'd be a very approachable Santa Claus." Belle laughed.

"There's no way I was going to ask Rock. Can you imagine it?" Clotille said.

"Or Throttle," Kimber added.

"Or Axe." Baylee sniggered.

"Frankly, I can't picture any of the Insurgents down with playing Santa, so it's a good thing Dale volunteered." Glancing at his watch, Joseph gathered his laptop and file. "We all done here?" Everyone nodded. "Then I'll see you ladies on Saturday night."

Belle went over to the back table and put several of the mini Italian sandwiches Cara had made on a plate. Banger just loved the sandwiches Cara made, and he'd instructed Belle before she left that morning to make sure she brought some home for him.

"Take the whole tray," Cara said behind her.

"Hawk doesn't want any?"

"I probably won't see Hawk."

Before Belle could ask Cara what she meant, she scurried away. Wrinkling her brow, Belle pinched the skin at her throat. *Something's wrong.* She'd noticed that when she'd called Cara the night before, she'd seemed preoccupied and sad. When Belle had asked if anything was wrong, she'd said no, quickly making an excuse to get off the phone.

"Garret!" Cara's voice boomed.

Belle turned to the front of the room and saw Cara rushing out the door. She walked over to see what was going on.

"Garret!"

Cara's voice sounded hollow in the large hallway as it bounced off the concrete walls. Belle walked into the open hallway. "Who's that?"

Cara spun around, shaking her head. "I know he heard me. He just rushed off."

"Who?"

"That guy," she replied, pointing at a retreating figure with stringy brown hair. "He came into my office about a week or so ago. He gave me the creeps, and now he's here in the building."

"Are you suggesting he's following you?"

"No, not exactly. I don't know. It's just weird that he's here."

"Maybe he works here. Anyway, if you're freaked about it, you need to tell Hawk."

"Have a nice day, Belle and Cara," Evan said as he walked past them.

"Evan, do you have an employee working for you named Garret?" Cara asked.

"I don't think so. Lindi? Does someone named Garret work for us?" He smiled at the women. "I don't know all the seasonal employees."

Lindi and Torey came over, shaking their heads. "Not that I know of, but I can double-check with human services," Lindi replied.

"Could you?" Cara asked.

"Sure. I'll give them a call this afternoon. I have another meeting I have to go to." Lindi grimaced, then smiled as she scampered away.

Cara walked over to the floor-to-ceiling window that looked out at the parking lot. "He's driving away!"

Belle came over and saw a sun-faded turquoise blue van plastered with bumper stickers and duct tape leaving the parking lot.

"What kind of car is that?" Cara asked.

"It's a van, but I have no idea what make it is," Belle replied.

"Can you see the license plate number?"

"I can make out the last two digits—75. Kimber, can you please come over here?" Belle looked over her shoulder and saw Kimber walking toward them. "Can you hurry it up?"

"What's up? What're you two looking at?"

Cara tapped the window repeatedly. "That van. Do you know what make or year it is?"

Kimber nodded. "It's a 1975 VW van. Very popular. They were made from 1952 until 1990. A fuckin' great van. You thinking of getting one? Hawk could make it into a beauty for you."

The vehicle disappeared, and Belle turned away from the window.

"No, it's nothing like that. I just saw someone I thought I knew. Thanks."

"I wanted to ask you guys something, but I don't want to do it in the hallway. Voices travel around here," Kimber said.

Belle and Cara went back into the conference room.

Kimber closed the door. "Is Evan married?"

"Yes. Why?" Belle asked.

"It may just be a coincidence, but some horny bitch named Christiansen has the hots for Throttle. She has an account with his business, and she keeps wanting him to come by to talk about the work they're doing. Throttle told her he's too damn busy and they could talk by phone, but she's a persistent one. This damn bitch is the poster woman for bored suburban housewives."

"I hadn't heard that he and Britany were having any trouble. They seem to get along at the functions. Not like Torey and Mitch," Belle said.

"Or Lindi and Dale. I still can't believe he agreed to be Santa Claus. The last few years he didn't even show up." Clotille brought a glass of orange juice to her lips.

"It's probably a cousin or something. I just don't want to beat the shit out of someone he's related to because that's what I'm aiming to do to the Christiansen who keeps calling Throttle."

The women laughed, but Belle was a hundred percent sure Kimber wouldn't hesitate to do it.

"The name's sort of common. Maybe there's no relation at all," said Cherri.

"Talk about wanting to beat the crap out of someone, Chas's mean-as-hell ex is back in town," Addie said.

Kimber shook her head. "Fuck."

"Are you serious?" Belle said.

"That fucking sucks," Cara added.

"I'm so sorry," Clotille said.

"She's up to no good. Jax said she's an awful bitch," Cherri commented.

"And she works here, apparently. She's a damn receptionist. I'm here all the time helping out. I can't believe I'm going to run into her." Addie folded her arms on her chest.

Belle went over and patted Addie's shoulder. "Don't you dare let this stupid woman get to you. And don't make Chas think you question his loyalty. According to what Banger's told me, he went through the ringer with this woman."

"And didn't she abandon her son?" Clotille asked.

"She did. And before that, she was awful to Jack. He's already told me that I'm his mother forever. It was so sweet, I cried. He doesn't want to see her, but she's pushing it with Chas. I know she doesn't give a shit about Jack, she just wants to get back with my husband. The fucking bitch. She's acting like she's a changed woman, but a leopard can't change its spots."

"Chas knows that. Remember, he went through hell with her. She cheated on him and everything," Cherri said.

The door opened and Baylee came in wiping her mouth with a tissue. Belle took in her peaked appearance. "Are you feeling all right?"

Baylee shook her head. "I'm not. I went to the doctor last week, and you all were right—I'm pregnant."

Belle hugged her. "I'm so happy for you."

"I just knew it," Clotille said. "There's no mistaking morning sickness. I had it bad with Andrew and James, but it was worth it."

"Harley was a breeze. I was surprised because I was so much older than I was when I had Emily and Ethan. I'd sort of freaked myself out that it was going to be horrible due to my age, but it was a piece of cake." Belle brushed Baylee's hair from her damp forehead. "How'd Axe take the news?"

Baylee gripped the table, then flopped into a chair. "Not so good. We'd decided we didn't want kids, and now he acts like I broke that promise."

"*You* broke your promise? That sounds just like a man. They can be so goddamn selfish. What a jerk. All these bikers think they're not responsible for shit!" Cara turned away from the group and went over to the window, standing with her back to them.

Taken aback by her outburst, Belle made a mental note to speak with Cara after the other women left. She put her hand on Baylee's. "A lot of men freak out about being a father. It just took him by surprise."

"And me too." Baylee took another tissue and mopped her face.

"The important thing is to stay healthy and strong for the precious baby you're carrying. Axe will come around, but you both need to sit down and talk about it without blaming anyone."

"I know. I'm going to go home and rest. How long does this morning sickness last? My doctor said it can be the whole pregnancy. I'm not sure I'll survive it if it is."

"Mine was only the first trimester, and then I felt great after that,"

Clotille said.

"Same here," Cherri replied.

"What about you, Cara?" Belle asked.

Without turning around, she shrugged.

"If you need anything at all, let me know, okay? I've never been pregnant, but I can do food runs for you. I know the restaurants you love." Kimber slipped her jacket on. "I have to get back to the shop."

"I'll call you. We got to get you eating some healthier food than takeout every night," Belle said.

"Right now the thought of food makes me want to barf. Thanks, everyone. I'm headed home. I'll see you on Saturday night. I do feel better by the time evening rolls around, at least." Baylee slung her purse over her shoulder and walked out with Kimber.

"I have to get going as well. I want to get in some Christmas shopping before I have to pick Paisley up at school. Later." Cherri went toward the door.

"Wait up, Cherri. I'll walk out with you." Clotille waved at Belle. Pointing at Cara's back, she mouthed, "What's wrong with her?"

Belle shrugged and watched the two women leave. Closing the door, she went up to Cara. "Do you want to talk about it?" she asked softly.

"There's nothing to talk about. I better get going. I promised my mom I'd cook dinner tonight."

"You're staying at your parents'? Is Hawk good with that?"

Cara whirled around, facing her. "I don't give a damn what Hawk's good with." She crossed her arms. "We're going through a rough patch."

"Is this about the gossip Doris circulated this past Sunday? She was on the phone with me before I even took my shower. I didn't call you because I figured you weren't going to let her get to you."

"Hawk didn't come home this past Saturday night. We had a fight before he went to the club party, but he didn't pick up any of my calls or answer my texts. The asshole didn't even tell me he was going to crash at the club." Cara's voice hitched.

Belle grasped her hands, but Cara pulled them away. "Hawk not calling you was rude and inconsiderate, and I'd rake Banger over the coals if he did that to me. Banger said Hawk was really wasted. He could hardly walk. He also said that the new girl, Heather, kept trying to cozy up to him, but he pushed her away. When Hawk left to go upstairs, he was alone."

"Doris wouldn't make that shit up. She's a gossip, but she doesn't lie."

"I'm not saying she's lying. She probably heard some stuff going on around the club and blabbed it without finding out all the facts, or whether it was true or not. I don't know what happened, but I know Hawk. He's so in love with you, and he loves Isa and Braxton to death. I can't see him throwing all that away. What has he told you about what happened?"

"We haven't really talked about it. I was so pissed and upset. I didn't want to have a blown-out fight in front of the kids."

"You should've taken the kids to your parents' and stayed home and talked with Hawk. I can't believe he hasn't stormed over and dragged you and the children back home."

"He's called a ton of times and texted, but I think he's letting me cool down. Anyway, if he cheated on me, he's out. There's no way I can forgive him."

"But you have to talk to him first. Cara, you can't run to your parents when the going gets tough. Marriage is a lot of hard work, but you work through it together. You and Hawk have to figure things out on your own."

"I appreciate what you're saying, Belle, but I'm still very hurt and pissed off."

Belle inhaled deeply and slowly exhaled. "That damn Doris. She's always waiting for the married brothers to cheat on their wives like Ruben does on her, and Marlena's just as bad because Billy's always screwing the club girls at the parties. Misery loves company. Do you *really* believe Hawk cheated on you?"

"I never thought I'd even have to ask myself that question. Who knows when it comes to men? Years ago, I was engaged to a guy and found out right before our wedding he'd been cheating on me. I can't believe this shit is going on with Hawk. Men just can't be trusted to be monogamous. Whatever, I have to go. Thanks for being a friend."

"Talk to Hawk. Fight for your marriage. That's the end of my two cents. If you need anything, call me. I'll walk out with you."

On her way home, Belle couldn't get Cara and Hawk out of her mind. A woman had to be more secure than the average when she loved an outlaw biker. In the beginning, Belle obsessed about the club parties Banger attended, knowing that a bevy of young women threw themselves at him. It had been so bad that she'd have panic attacks when he was gone. The night Ethan rushed into her room when she was having a meltdown, fear and heartbreak etched on his face, was when she'd realized she had to stop torturing herself. After that, she'd watch a movie with Ethan or go out with the other old ladies. And then she made sure to show Banger how lucky he was that he'd come home after one of the parties.

Investing a ton of money in lingerie, sex toys, candles, and scented oils, she'd greet him as he came home with a big kiss that promised much more. In time, he started coming home earlier until he only went to one every couple of months.

When she arrived home, she opened the refrigerator. Staring at packages of ground beef, steak, and chicken, she sighed. For the past few weeks, she felt that her home life was on autopilot: make sure Ethan is on time for school, get Harley ready for school, make breakfast, pray that Emily goes through the day sober, clean the house, do laundry, make dinner. It seemed like it was the same day over and over again.

She closed the fridge and sent Ethan a text asking if he'd like to have an overnight at Jack's house. His enthusiastic *Ur awesome, Mom* made her smile. She then called Addie and asked if it was cool for Ethan to come over. Addie told her Jack would be thrilled. Emily and a friend were in Denver for a couple of days to do some Christmas shopping.

Harley. Picking up her phone, she tapped in Kylie's number. She was thrilled to have Harley spend the night with her and Jerry.

Since Harley had been born, she and Banger hadn't been alone together. If Harley stayed at Kylie's, then Emily was home, or Ethan. This was the first time all the children would be out of the house at the same time. She tingled all over. *This is exactly what we need.* From the deep lines crossing his face, the intense staring at the flames in the fireplace, and the intermittent sighs, Belle knew whatever was brewing with the club had Banger real worried. That night, she wanted him to forget everything except their love.

Bouncing on her toes as she waited for the Buckhorn restaurant to pick up, she practically jumped out of her skin when the back door slammed.

"I'm home, Mom." Ethan's voice drifted into the kitchen.

"Take off your boots," she reminded him.

"Aren't I going over to Jack's?"

"Yeah, but you have to pack an overnight bag, and I don't want you traipsing snow and mud through the house."

"May I help you?" the reservationist asked.

"I'd like to make dinner reservations for two at seven o'clock tonight. Is the table by the fireplace and window available?"

Ethan dashed past her, and she smiled when she heard his *thud thud thud* of running feet on the stairway. After confirming that their favorite table at the steakhouse was theirs, she waited for Ethan to come down. In less than twenty minutes, she'd dropped him off at Jack's house, waving at Addie as she'd pulled away.

THE JANGLE OF keys and heavy footsteps had shivers running up Belle's spine. Fluffing her dark hair with her fingers, she gave herself a once-over in the entryway mirror: hair free-flowing around her shoulders, simple makeup with a swipe of berry gloss, deep-V black dress skimming over her curves. Lacy black panties and bra along with silky thigh-highs made her feel dangerous and sexy. A low whistle made her spin around.

"You look damn good, woman." Banger's low baritone sent her mind reeling. "Are you going somewhere?"

"*We* are. I made reservations at the Buckhorn." Her stomach fluttered when she saw the lust in his gaze as it slowly caressed her body.

"Sounds good. Is Kylie coming over to watch the kids?"

"I sent them away. Ethan's spending the night at Chas and Addie's, Kylie came by a couple of hours ago to pick up Harley for a sleepover, and Emily's coming back tomorrow night. It's just you and me."

A big grin spread over his face as his gaze lingered on her breasts. "I fuckin' like that, woman. Come over here and let your man feel how soft and sexy you are."

Belle shook her head, curling her finger and gesturing for him to come to her. In one long stride, he snagged her around the waist and crushed her to him. "You got a real hold of my cock, woman," he rasped against her mouth. Pushing his tongue through her parted lips, he plunged it in hard and deep. "And that perfume you're wearing is driving me damn wild," he said between kisses.

Pulling his tongue into her mouth, she gently sucked it while caressing his neck. The low growl rumbling from his chest sent a long, pulsing quiver through her. His hand slipped under her dress, stroking the skin above her thigh-highs. "You're fuckin' killing me. I wanna see you in only these and those fuck-me heels you're wearing," he said thickly.

"When we get home we're going to make the most of being alone tonight." Running the tip of her tongue over his lips, she squeezed his firm ass hard.

"What time do we gotta be at dinner?"

"In fifteen minutes." She scratched the back of his neck as she rubbed her ample chest across his.

"That's enough time for a quickie," he rasped, his hand shoving down under her panties, pushing his fingers between her folds. A smile tugged at his lips. "So warm... so wet." Desire flooded her.

The phone ringing pulled her out of her sexual haze, and she glanced at the entry table to see Kylie's name flashing. Worry replaced desire in less than a heartbeat.

"It's Kylie," she whispered, bringing the phone to her ear.

Wrinkling his brow, Banger stiffened a bit and stepped back.

"Is everything all right with Harley?" Belle said.

"Yes. Fine. I didn't mean to disturb or worry you. It's just that he wants to have an ice cream cone. Jerry was going to go to Red Spot Creamery. Is it okay for Harley to have one? I know you watch his sugar and let him have some just on the weekends."

Belle leaned over and kissed Banger's cheek. "Everything's fine, honey. Harley's taking advantage of his night away and trying to get some ice cream out of it."

Banger bellowed and took the phone away from Belle. "Give Harley a big-ass cone. I know he wants chocolate chip. How's the little guy doing?" He pulled Belle close so they could both listen.

"Great. I'm so happy to have him over. We just finished eating and now we're going to get some ice cream. Jerry'll bring it back. It's too cold to go out. What are you two going to do tonight?"

"I'm going up to change. We got reservations at the Buckhorn. I'll give you to Belle. Talk to you later."

Belle took the phone and chatted for a few minutes with Kylie, and then to Harley. When Banger came down in a pair of black jeans and a fitted navy blue shirt with a tiny light blue diamond pattern, she sucked in her breath. And the way he wore his hair—slicked down and pulled back—coupled with the heady mix of frosted pinecones and mellow sweet applewood had her wanting to cancel their reservations and make passionate love instead.

"Ready?" He pulled keys from his pocket. Nodding, she put on her jacket, shivering when he placed his hand on the small of her back and led her out.

Dinner was fabulous and so relaxing. For once in a long time, they didn't talk about any of the children. The steak was so tender, it was like eating butter, and the stuffed mushroom caps topped with parmesan were to die for. Belle made a mental note to recreate them at home.

The dark woods, roaring fire, and delectable aromas of sizzling char-grilled steaks wafted through the restaurant. As they shared a slice of blueberry lemon cheesecake, Banger held her gaze, his eyes twinkling.

"It warms me real good to see the love in my woman's eyes." Grasping her hand, he brought it to his mouth and kissed it tenderly.

"You brought the love into my eyes and my life." She stroked the side of his face, tugging gently on his beard.

"I love you, woman. You came into my life and filled all the lonely places in my heart."

"You make me so happy. I can't wait to get home and show you." She ran the toe of her shoe up and down his leg.

Banger caught her foot and lightly moved his fingers over her calf. "Let's get out of here." He waved the waitress over and took out his wallet.

When they arrived home, Banger's phone went off, and by the way the muscle in his clenched jaw twitched, she knew it was club business. "Upstairs when you're done," she mouthed to him.

Hurriedly taking off her shoes and clothes, she wrapped a thick bathrobe around her naked body and went into the bathroom. Bending over the large Jacuzzi tub, she turned on the faucet and sprinkled some bath bubbles under the rushing water. The bubbles from the soap blended with the ones from the jets, and white lights inside the tub made the water shimmer and glow.

Taking out a lighter, Belle lit the ivory-colored candles sitting on the shelves next to the tub, and the rich, warm scent of vanilla curled around the room. Folding two large pale yellow towels over the warming rack, she looked around and smiled. *Perfect.* She slipped off her robe and climbed into the tub. The water flowed around her as she reached for a bottle of red wine she'd put on the shelf earlier that day and poured it into two glasses. Reclining against the smooth tub, she sipped the wine, gazing at the twirling snowflakes outside.

A low grunt came from the doorway, and she turned her attention away from the falling snow. "I didn't hear you come up. Everything okay?" She put her glass down.

"It is now." His smoldering eyes held hers as he kicked off his boots, then stripped off his clothing.

She licked her lips at his erection, tingles dancing on her skin. He eased into the tub and yanked her to him, the water lapping around them. Smooth and full, his lips molded over hers, nibbling and licking as her body strained closer.

"I love how your skin feels next to mine, babe."

"And I love kissing you. I'll be kissing you when I'm taking my last breath." She looped her arm around his neck and swirled her tongue over his lips and around his mouth. "Hmmm... you taste good." She pulled away, picked up another glass, and poured red wine into it. She slid back over to him and the water rushed around, making her buoy up. "Oh!" The wine spilled on her.

Banger caught her around the waist, then moved closer and dipped his head, his warm tongue lapping up the trails of wine on her wet skin. Throwing her head back, she pushed her breasts out and moaned deeply when his tongue swept over her hardening buds, delicately licking her hard nipples while he roughly squeezed her tits.

She gently pressed two fingers against his temples as she slowly glided her other fingers down his cheek, making tiny circles as she inched down his face. She drew a line along his strong jaw with her index finger, then traced around his mouth, dipping it inside through his parted lips. Raising his head, he captured her gaze with his and drew her finger deeper into his mouth, sucking it as he pinched her nipples.

Jolts of lust and desire shot from her aching buds straight to her pussy. "That feels real good," she said softly as she undid the tie in his hair, threading her hands through the golden strands.

"I could stay here all night playing with your sweet tits. Your body's so damn hot."

As he pulled her nipples, her arousal surged through her senses. Moving closer, she traced circles around his Adam's apple, loving the way his low, hungry moan echoed in the room. When she brushed her lips around the hollow of his throat and massaged the area softly with her tongue, Banger tangled his fist in her hair and yanked her head up, then seized her lips with a ferocity that took her breath away.

"The things you do to me, woman." His hand slipped under the water and cupped her aching pussy.

With both hands on his shoulders, she gently pushed his back against the tub. "I want to ride you. I want to feel your cock inside me, filling me up until I can't take any more."

"Fuck," he grunted, his gaze fixed on her as she kneeled, his legs between hers, and gripped his cock. "Fuck."

"You like that?" She moved her hand up and down and around, then guided him into her sex. "Damn, that feels good, honey."

He grabbed her breasts and stuffed one of them into his mouth, sucking vigorously. Water flowed around them as she rocked her hips back and forth. His fingers found their way between her folds, his thumb stroking her sweet berry as she rode him hard.

Faster and faster she went, water sloshing and splashing on the tiled floor as Banger stroked her nub with just the right amount of pressure. Up and down, back and forth. Faster. Harder. Their pants filled the room.

"Shit!" The coil inside her broke and a rush of pleasure took her away. She was floating on a carpet of rose petals, vanilla-scented candles lit all around her. She arched her back and his wonderfully strong hands cupped her tits. *He's so fantastic. He's everything to me.*

"I love you," she rasped as she gazed at him: eyes closed, face scrunched, low grunts as he pumped the last of his seed inside her.

"Fuck, Belle. That was… fuck." With a strong hand on her neck, he brought her down to him and kissed her passionately.

Her knees gave out and she collapsed on top of him, his arms wrapping tightly around her.

They stayed like that for a long time, and she'd thought he'd fallen asleep as goose bumps covered her and she shivered; the water had grown very cool.

"You cold?" His baritone voice washed over her.

"Yes. I can put some more warm water in." She reached for the faucet, but he pulled her hand back.

"Let's get out and have a few drinks."

He dried her off tenderly and she did the same to him; then they kissed passionately, clinging to one another, and finally went into the bedroom. He built a fire, then came over with the two glasses and the half-drunk bottle of wine.

Handing her a full glass, he clinked it against his.

"To us, baby. Forever." He smiled, the lines around his eyes fanning out.

"Forever plus one," she said softly.

They drank slowly, laughed heartily, and talked about whatever came into their heads. The hours spread before them. *We have all night.*

She knew he would make love to her and then in the morning before they picked up Harley and Ethan, he'd fuck her hard and rough.

The next day, she'd go back to doing the laundry, picking Harley up at school, helping Ethan with his homework, fixing dinner, and a slew of other things that made up her daily routine. Banger would go back to worrying about whatever the problems were with the club.

But that night was all theirs.

And she had every intention of making the most of it with her husband.

CHAPTER EIGHTEEN

HAWK

SITTING BEHIND THE counter in his shop, Hawk rubbed the back of his neck and stared down at his phone: fifteen unanswered texts. Clenching his jaw, he pushed the phone away. *This shit stops today.* For the past two days, he'd humored Cara, expecting her to come home and chew his ass out, but she hadn't. She'd taken the kids and left, running to her parents. His father-in-law had called him the day she'd come over, said she was upset and she'd probably cool down. Knowing his mother-in-law, Hawk wouldn't be surprised if she was encouraging Cara to stay longer. He sneered. *The bitch has never liked me.* But he put up with family dinners, charity fundraisers, and a host of other activities Cara's family did together because he loved her and wanted Isa and Braxton to be close to their grandparents. Cara was very close to her parents, especially her father, and Hawk didn't want to put her in the middle. He was cool with his father-in-law; it was Cara's mother who could be a pain in the ass. She never butted in except when they'd had a fight or Cara was upset with something. Then she would suggest that maybe Cara should've married someone from her background—her class.

I bet she's having a fuckin' field day with this.

"Is Kimber here?" Throttle asked, coming up to the counter.

Hawk jerked his head up. "I didn't hear you come in, dude. She went to Silverton to pick up some parts, should be back in an hour or so. When she gets back, I'm gonna cut out of here. I got some shit to do."

Throttle fidgeted in place, gripping the edge of the counter. "You got any beer?"

Hawk chuckled. "Starting kinda early, aren't you? I got some in my office fridge. Help yourself."

As Throttle left, one of his employees, Patrick, came in. "Sorry I'm late, Hawk. Uncle Banger wanted me to pick up some stuff for him in Mount Vista. He said you'd be good with it. Did he call you?"

"No, but it's cool. Take over the counter. I'll be in my office."

Throttle came back in and sat in one of the leather chairs, his legs stretched out and a can of beer in his hand. "Make yourself comfortable," Hawk said.

Throttle laughed. "I am. If it keeps snowing like this, Rags and I are gonna make a mint."

"Did you pick up Allard Food Mart? Rags was telling me a couple of weeks ago that they were interested."

"Yeah. I gave them a real sweet deal. So, you like being married?"

"Whoa, where the fuck did that come from?"

Throttle took a drink, then put the can on the desk. "I was just wondering. Do you ever miss being single?"

"No, but when your wife's pissed at you and won't fuckin' let you explain anything, it sucks."

"You still in the deep freeze? Cara didn't believe you about the club whore?"

"She hasn't even let me tell her about it. She believes Doris over me—her husband. Fuck, the woman is stubborn and really pisses me off sometimes."

"I guess my timing's off in asking how you like married life, then." Throttle swiveled around in the chair and took out another beer from the mini fridge behind him. "Want one?"

Hawk shook his head. "Why're you asking about marriage? You planning to hitch up with Kimber? Fuck, she's gonna give you a real run."

Throttle laughed. "I know, right? And… yeah, I'm thinking of asking her."

"Rags told me you bought a ring for her."

"Rags has a fuckin' big mouth. I didn't think you knew since you never said anything."

"I figured you'd tell me when you wanted to. It's a big step to ask a woman to spend the rest of your lives together."

"She's my old lady, so we should take it a step further. Anyway, I'd like a kid or two."

"Having kids rocks, brother. There's nothing like it. Is Kimber down for the whole package?"

"I don't see why she wouldn't be. I'm a great fuckin' catch." Throttle crushed the can and tossed it into the trash.

Hawk guffawed. "It's the other way around, dude. She's the catch."

Nodding, Throttle reclined in the chair. "Did you ever think we'd be this fuckin' conventional?"

"Never, but it's cool when you're with the right one."

For the next two hours, they talked about Harleys, business, women, and reminisced about the years they'd shared in the Insurgents before Cara and Kimber came into their lives. A rap on the door broke the flow of their conversation, and Throttle leaned over and opened it. A huge smile spread over his face, making Hawk snigger.

"I was waiting for you, babe," he said to Kimber.

She went over, dipped her head, and kissed him. "What a nice surprise." Clutching her waist, he pulled her onto his lap while she chortled.

"Everything go okay in Silverton?" Hawk asked.

"Yeah. Gary threw in some extras, said he was feeling generous. He's really just an old softie, and he likes and admires you a lot," Kimber answered.

"Gary's all right. You guys going out to lunch?" Hawk changed the subject. He didn't feel comfortable when people paid him a compliment. Maybe it was because his father never uttered a kind word to him, or the fact that his mother abandoned him. That's just the way it was.

"Did you come here to take me out to lunch?" she asked, stroking Throttle's cheek with the back of her hand.

"Yeah."

"You can be such a sweetie."

A deep ache throbbed in Hawk as he watched them. He missed Cara and the kids like hell. He stood abruptly. "I got some stuff to do. I won't be back, so I need you to close, Kimber."

She climbed off Throttle's lap. "Sure thing. Do you need me to stay here? I mean, Throttle and I can order out."

"Nah, go get some lunch. Patrick, Dwayne, and Bill are here. Anyway, it's slow. I'll see you tomorrow." He and Throttle fist bumped, and then he left the shop.

When he opened the garage door, Cara's maroon Land Cruiser was parked inside and warmth radiated throughout his body. Switching off the motor, he closed the door and went into the mudroom. Braxton's squeals and Isa's small voice made his heartbeat race, and he shoved his keys into his pocket and went into the kitchen.

From where he stood, he saw Cara cross-legged on the carpet next to Braxton, who knelt while he figured out a train floor puzzle. Isa sat next to Cara, putting colorful balls into a muffin pan. As he watched them, a grin he couldn't contain spread over his face. *I missed them so damn much.*

After several minutes, he crossed the length of the kitchen, his boots thudding on the hardwood floor. All eyes turned to him.

Braxton scrambled up with Isa following him and they ran over to him, Braxton grabbing hold of his leg while Isa raised her arms, saying, "Hold me, Daddy!" Hawk picked her up easily and pressed her close, and she nuzzled her face into his neck. "How's my sweet princess doing?" He kissed her.

Braxton tugged at his pant leg. "Daddy, come over and see the number train I'm doing. There're three dragons in the train car."

Hawk went over and knelt, setting Isa down on the floor. "Great job, little buddy. How many cars do you have in your train?"

Braxton held up five fingers. "And I have a hiptamanus, two monkeys, and… I have to see again." He bent over, looking at the puzzle pieces.

Picking up a red ball, he handed it to Isa, who put it in the muffin tin. He glanced at Cara who sat mutely, her head down and her fingers pulling at the fibers in the carpet.

"And four tigers." Braxton held up the piece. "See?"

Hawk took it from him. "How can four tigers fit in this small train car?"

Braxton took the piece back and stared at it, a small frown knitting his brows. He shrugged. "I don't know. But they do."

Hawk laughed and hugged him. Isa handed him a yellow ball and Hawk put it in one of the spaces in the tin. Cara still sat mutely, pulling at the carpet.

"Why didn't you come to Nana and Noni's with us?" Braxton pushed a puzzle piece into a space. "I did it, Mommy. See?"

"I was busy. Did you have fun?" Again he looked at Cara, and again she avoided him.

"Uh-huh. But I missed my bed." He yawned. "I finished." He clapped, then covered his mouth.

"Who was hanging out in the fifth car?" Hawk ran his fingers over Isa's hair as she lay on her side with her head on her arm, her eyelids drooping.

"Seals," Braxton laughed, rolling around the floor.

For a few seconds, it was quiet, and a strained tension crackled between Hawk and Cara. Braxton yawed again.

"Are you getting sleepy?" Cara said, uncrossing her legs.

"Yeah. I think Isa already fell asleep." Braxton kept rolling.

Hawk stood up and shrugged off his jacket as Cara picked Isa up and extended her hand.

"Come on," she said to Braxton, reaching for him. "Let's go to your room for your nap." Braxton held her hand and she climbed the stairs. Not once had she looked at him.

"Come down afterward, Cara. I wanna talk to you."

Without looking at him, she continued climbing the stairs, then headed down the hallway.

Hawk narrowed his eyes, knowing there was no way in hell she was going to listen to him. Shaking his head, he went upstairs and into their bedroom. *I'm not dealing with this shit anymore.* Standing by the window, he looked out at the falling snow clinging to the bare branches of the oak and maple trees. A group of neighborhood kids went by, dragging sleds behind them. Across the street, a few children threw snowballs at each other.

Warm, sweet vanilla drifted over to him. *Cara.*

"Oh," she muttered.

He turned around just as she started walking out of the room. Sparks of anger sizzled in his blood and he stalked over to her. Grabbing her arm, he yanked her to him as he pushed the door closed with his foot.

"Let me go," she said breathlessly, struggling in his arms.

"Don't you ever fuckin' take my kids away from me again."

She stopped struggling and looked at him. "What did you expect?"

"For you to act like a goddamn adult and talk about what the fuck's bothering you. We're together. This is our life, and if you're pissed at me, you need to talk to me about it, not run home to your mom and dad like you're a damn child. And you take my kids away from me? That fuckin' shit doesn't ever happen again."

"You cheated on me. How could you?" Her voice quivered and she looked down.

"Who told you that? That's right Doris, the club gossip, called you early Sunday morning to give you the fuckin' news."

"How could you do that to me… to us?"

"I didn't do shit."

"Ha! You're telling me *you're* the victim?"

They were standing so close he could feel the anger emanating from her. Her face was flushed, her eyes glimmered, and her nipples were hardening under her tight T-shirt.

"I'm telling you it was a setup. And if Doris would keep her god-damn mouth shut long enough to think with her brain, she would've known that. I was fuckin' wasted, went to my room and forgot to lock the door. One of the club whores concocted this shit, and when I found out, I threw her ass out."

"You didn't do anything with her? Not even touching?" Her bottom lip trembled slightly, and he wanted to slip it into his mouth and suck it gently.

"Nothing. When I woke up, I was shocked she was there, and then I got pissed."

For a long while, she was silent, but then she whispered, "You should've still called me and told me you weren't coming home. I was so worried."

"I fucked up. I own it. But you fucked up too by running away instead of hashing it out with me."

She lifted her chin and looked him right in the eyes. "Honestly, I couldn't stomach being in the same house with you."

"Doesn't fuckin' matter. We're a family and we deal with shit together. And you didn't even return my calls or texts. If your dad hadn't called me and told me you and the kids were at his house, I wouldn't have known where you were."

"Doesn't feel so good, does it? You didn't bother to answer my calls or texts either, and you didn't have the courtesy to tell me you were crashing at the clubhouse. It's okay for you to do that, but you don't like it when I do the same thing to you."

"I didn't come home for one night, and I came over the next morning ready to eat crow. You ran off for two days with my kids for fuckin' spite."

"I couldn't stand to see you. I was hurting and so angry."

"You could've left for a while to cool down and left the kids with me." They stood staring at each other, her body stiff, his neck aching. He leaned back on his boots. "How do you feel about seeing me now?"

She shrugged while glaring at him.

"You know something? Your skin glows when you're angry."

She placed two hands on his chest and pushed him away. Grinding his teeth, he put his hand on the small of her back and drew her firmly to him. Tangling his fingers in her hair, he pulled her head back and crushed his mouth against hers. She kissed back, biting his bottom lip hard and drawing blood. The taste of metal in his mouth was like a hot poker to his cock. Her nails clawed at his back and he slammed her against the wall, their kisses wild, erratic, and desperate.

Yanking at the hem of his shirt, she pushed it up and scratched his chest hard, drawing blood. He tugged her T-shirt up and pulled down her bra, grabbing her tits and twisting her nipples. She moaned in pain, but he felt her shiver beneath his touch. With one hand he unzipped his jeans, and her hot fingers curled around his cock. He roughly shoved up her skirt, then ripped off her panties and whirled her around so she faced the wall, bent at the waist, legs spread open. Craning her neck, she caught his gaze, and the intensity of desire brimming in hers made him wild with lust. With one fast movement, his hands smacked down on her sweet, rounded ass, and she groaned and squirmed under the attack. Burying his fingers between her swollen folds, satisfaction coursed through him when her juices covered them. She was dripping wet. Fire roared through his veins.

Primal desire overwhelmed and consumed him, and he slammed into her balls-deep. Cara cried out and then pushed back against him as if her pussy craved his dick to go even deeper. He pummeled into her, loving the way her heat pulsed on his cock, her juices covering him and dripping down his inner thighs. The sound of her wetness mixed with the slapping of his balls with each thrust filled the room, and sweat misted over their bodies.

"How the fuck could you even think I'd cheat on you?" he rasped as he pounded into her. "You're my everything."

"How the fuck could you not call me or return my texts?" she answered between pants. "I felt ignored and that hurt a lot. You treated me cruelly."

"I was so pissed at you. I might have let my anger take over my actions." Another hard, long thrust.

"*Might* have?" Her tits swayed with the force of his pounding, and he molded his hand around one of them, loving the weight of it.

"Fuck, babe. I'm gonna explode." He trailed his finger down to her engorged nub and flicked it as the back of his legs stiffened.

"Oh, Hawk." Her legs trembled against him and he knew she'd soon shatter into a million pieces.

He shoved his cock in and out a few more times, and then a rush of intense pleasure burst through, his hot seed filling her quivering pussy. He leaned down and covered her back with his chest, his arms wrapped snuggly around her waist to keep her up. She straightened and he walked her to their bed to lie down. They clung to each other, fused together by their raw passion and lust, never wanting to let go. Their breaths were still shallow and fast, and he could feel her heart beating rapidly against his skin.

"You know, I didn't *really* believe you cheated on me," Cara whispered as she placed her leg across his. "It's just that Doris sounded so smug and satisfied as if she were saying, 'See, your man is just as bad as all the others.' It pissed me off, and I took it out on you."

"Doris likes to make trouble. Banger's called her on it many times over the years. He's told Ruben numerous times that he needs to control his woman better." He felt her bristle under his touch. "Let's don't start a discussion about the 'control his woman' comment. Okay, babe?" He kissed the top of her head.

"We'll talk about that another time," she said.

He laughed. "Being married to a lawyer can be challenging sometimes."

"What does that mean?"

"It just means you have to always have the last word, and I think's it's fuckin' cute."

She tilted her head back and her gaze bore into his. "I love you so much. Even when you piss the hell out of me, I love you."

He dipped his head down and kissed her deeply. "I love you too. When you were gone, a piece of my heart was missing. Fuck, babe, you're the only one in my life and don't ever think for one second you're not. I should've called. That shit won't happen again." He wanted to tell her that he acted like a damn jerk and he was sorry he worried her, but it wasn't his style.

"Tomorrow night I'm going out with some of the women for our ladies' night. You and the kids will be on your own."

"Sounds good. I'll see if Banger, Jax, and Chas wanna come over for pizza and beer. The kids can play together, and Isa can hang out with us."

She chuckled. "I don't know if I want you guys corrupting her."

He ruffled her hair. "Fuck. It's gonna be hard when she gets to be a teenager and guys start wanting to go out with her."

"I feel so sorry for Isa. You're going to be impossible."

"Actually, babe, you should feel sorry for the boys who are gonna want to go out with her."

"Oh, I'm sure I will. They're going to be petrified of you." She giggled.

He chuckled and warmth spread through him as he pressed her closer to him. Everything was good now. He had his sexy wildcat in his arms again and his two kids back home.

He smiled when he heard her breathing deeply, and he pulled the blanket tighter around them. Staring out the window, he watched the ragged edges of stony gray clouds race across the leaden sky as a silvery mist licked at the treetops and neighboring roofs. Ice drops pelted against the window, and he was glad he was inside with the love of his life snug in his arms.

Chapter Nineteen

Sofia

OUT OF THE corner of her eyes, she watched Tigger as he walked warily into the bedroom, carrying a large bouquet of flowers in one hand and a small plastic bag in another. Closing her eyes, she feigned sleep, trying to ignore the sharp pains ripping through her body each time she inhaled. Blood leaked beneath her skin, making red and purple bruises on her pale flesh. There would be no doctors, no evidence, no mention of his cruelty, only a bouquet of flowers and perhaps a CD of her favorite group.

"Sweetcakes, are you sleeping?"

The touch of his hand on her shoulder made her cringe internally, though his cooing voice made her relax because it meant the cruel monster had been replaced by the groveling lover. The warm, smoky scent of hickory wisped under her nose. *He's pulling out all the stops this time.* He was cooking one of her favorite meals, baby back ribs, though the irony was that she'd never be able to eat through the pain that cut short each breath she took.

"I'm making ribs. I know how you love them. I picked up some coleslaw and have potatoes boiling." His lips pressed against her temple and she trembled. "Talk to me."

Cracking her eyes open, the light from the hallway pierced them. "The light. It hurts my eyes," she croaked, and he leapt up from the bed and closed the door, blocking it out. At that moment, he'd do anything for her. He'd treat her like he used to in the beginning. If the pain wasn't so acute, and her cheeks weren't swelling up, she could almost pretend that nothing had happened. Tigger always could. He was extremely adept at ignoring how his criticisms, punches, and kicks made her feel. For now, he'd make sure she knew she was his everything, but as she knew so well, it would only last until the next time he lost his temper.

"Let's go in the living room. I picked out one of those girlie movies you love. We can eat in front of the television."

Trying to sit up, her mind screamed out as pain seared through her chest and she fell back down, sweating and pulling her legs closer to her body. "I can't," she panted.

"Hang on, sweetcakes." Tigger ambled into their bathroom, and she heard the familiar squeak of the medicine cabinet opening. Soon he returned with a glass of water and two white tablets. "Take these. They'll make you feel better."

"What are they?" she asked as he put two pills in her palm.

"Pain pills. Let me help you." As he raised her up, she gritted her teeth, then popped the tablets into her mouth and swallowed them. "You'll feel so much better. You just gotta be better at not making me mad, you know?"

Over the years she'd learned to agree with him, so she nodded. She used to believe she was responsible for the anger, but since Wheelie started coming around, she felt differently. Thinking of Wheelie made her smile even though it hurt like hell. He was so attentive, so gentle, and the way he looked at her and kissed her made her feel like a woman again. Tigger hadn't made love to her in months. It was his way of punishing and controlling her. It used to bother her when he'd withhold sex; it made her think she couldn't satisfy him anymore. The longer he stayed away from her, the less she wanted him. Then Wheelie had come over when Tigger was away, and he made her feel special.

"What's going on in your pretty head?"

Her heart leapt in her throat. *I have to stop smiling. If he finds out I'm thinking of another man....* Like a true predator, Tigger could smell fear and sense weakness. She couldn't let her guard down. *I shouldn't have been thinking of Wheelie. Not with Tigger around.* She had plenty of time to think about him when Tigger went to the club, which was often.

"Just thinking about how we first met and how happy I am we're together." *Does he believe me? I think I sounded convincing.*

He bent down low and kissed her gently on the mouth. "I love you. You know I do. You're mine. All mine forever." She winced and then coughed, tears streaming down her face. "Aren't the meds helping yet?"

"They will," she whispered. The truth was they were already working, the sharp soreness having dulled to a constant ache. For the first time since she laid eyes on the handsome, buffed biker, Sofia wished she was with another man—Wheelie.

Wiping her wet cheeks, she mustered a small smile for him.

"That's my girl. I'll get you some dinner."

Biting the inside of her lip, nausea rolled over her, but she knew she'd make herself eat; otherwise, the doting Tigger she'd fallen in love with years before may very well transform into the raging beast from earlier in the day. She wouldn't survive a second beating so soon.

After they ate, he placed a pillow on his lap and put her head on it. Raking his fingers through her hair, he dipped down and kissed her forehead. "I love you more than anything. I'm never letting you go." He pulled her hair a little too hard.

Whispers of panic scattered inside her. "I don't want you to. I love you too."

Seemingly satisfied with her answer, he brushed the back of his hand over her swollen cheeks. "Want to watch a movie?"

"The meds are starting to work, so just put in a movie you'd like. I'll probably fall asleep."

"Good girl." He bent over and kissed her lips. "If you felt better, I'd fuck you, but we can do it another time. You'd like that, wouldn't you?"

"Yes."

He turned on the television and channel-surfed until he landed on a rerun of *Rocky*. She grimaced and closed her eyes. *There's no way I'm watching men beating each other up. Why do men love boxing?* Tigger was obsessed with it and won and lost plenty of money on the games.

As the voices on the screen grew more distant, the pain sensitivity lessened. Tigger ran his fingers up and down her upper arm as she let the little white pills do their job, giving into them. Drifting deeper and deeper, she welcomed the sleep. It was the place where there was no hurt, no fists, no cruelty.

Only dead-silent nothingness.

CHAPTER TWENTY

ADDIE

ADDIE PULLED CHAS back from the door and gave him a hard kiss on the lips. "Have a nice day," she said against his mouth.

"I can come back after I drop off Hope at school." He feathered her face with kisses.

"That'd be great, but Cherri and Belle are coming over to help make the gift bags for the fundraiser this Saturday."

"Do you need me to help?"

Laughing, she pushed him toward the door. "I can't picture you wrapping gifts and stuffing bags."

"I'm good at unwrapping clothes." Reaching around her, he patted her ass.

Rolling her eyes, she chuckled. "That was corny at best."

"What do you want at seven thirty in the morning?"

"Are we going, Daddy?" Hope stood by the car. Chas jumped down the two stairs and opened the car door.

Addie smiled as she saw him securing Hope in her car seat. Waving at both of them, she closed the garage door. Warmth spread through her, loving how great her life was with Chas. She had the family she'd always wanted, not the one Ian had wanted to give her all those years before. When she thought of the woman she'd been with Ian and the one she was with Chas, it amazed her that she'd let Ian distort her reality so much.

"I have band practice after school tonight," Jack said as he grabbed a breakfast bar she'd put out on the counter. "Belle's going to take us."

"What time do I need to come and get you guys?"

"Around six."

Jack, Ethan, and three other friends of theirs had started a rock band the previous summer. Jack played bass and Ethan was the rhythm guitarist. She and Chas had gone to their first gig at the school talent show in the fall, and she'd thought they were pretty good. Chas accused her of being biased, and she supposed she was, but the boys definitely had talent, and she liked that they had something to do other than getting into trouble.

After Jack left for school, Addie made sure everything was ready for the women when they came over in an hour. Lighting an apple cinnamon candle, she inhaled deeply, loving the warm, robust scent. Cinnamon, nutmeg, and vanilla were the candle scents she loved most, and if she was having a bad day, all she had to do was light one, stir a generous helping of hazelnut creamer into her coffee, sit back, and look out the window, watching life unfold.

An hour later, Addie opened the door and Cherri and Belle walked into the house.

"Did you make apple pie?" Belle asked.

"It's the candle I lit. I love the aroma," Addie replied.

"It gives off a cozy feel. I love candles, but Jax's freaked about fires, so I have to use flameless ones. It's just not the same as the real deal." Cherri handed her jacket to Addie.

For the next two hours, the women worked steadily on wrapping, stuffing, and decorating a hundred gift bags. The bags would be given out on Saturday night to all volunteers and the mothers of the children who would be at the event receiving gifts. Brighter Lives selected sixty-five children to attend the event and receive their gifts that night. The other toys collected would be distributed to other families the following week.

The chime of the doorbell interrupted their workflow, and Addie jumped up and went to see who it was. Opening the door, she cursed herself for not checking the peephole first. Brianna, decked in a white faux fur coat and thigh-high leather boots, stood on the porch.

Addie sucked in her breath and opened the screen door. "Can I help you?"

Wrinkling her nose as her gaze wandered up and down Addie, Brianna clutched the jacket collar with her gloved hand. "Is Chas here? I need to talk to him. I saw him last night at the hospital and I forgot to ask him something."

Typical Brianna. "Chas isn't home, but there are such things as phones, you know."

Brianna laughed. "How's Jack? Is he home?"

"He's fine, and he's in school. Look, some friends of mine are here and I have to go. I'll tell Chas you stopped by."

"Actually, I'd like Jack to spend the weekend with me."

What fucking gall! "That's not going to work out. We're all going to a big charity event on Saturday, and on Sunday we have family plans.

Brianna narrowed her eyes. "I'm family too."

"It's just not going to happen. As I said, we already have plans with Jack."

Brianna stepped closer to Addie, who still stood in the doorway, holding the screen open. "I'm Jack's mom. So stop acting so fuckin' high and mighty."

Licks of anger rose inside her. "You're the one who gave up your parental rights. I adopted Jack, and I'm more of a mother to him than you ever were."

"I was using and drinking back then. Things have changed. I've cleaned up my act."

Even though it was cold outside, Addie was burning up. "That's great, but we still have family plans this weekend. I really have to go."

"You self-righteous bitch! It doesn't mean shit that you have a piece of paper saying you're Jack's mom. I'm his *real* mother. He's got my blood flowing through him. My blood and Chas's, and no fuckin' piece of paper will ever take that away. Chas will *always* be tied to me."

Remembering an article she'd read about stress and anger management, Addie counted to ten while inhaling and exhaling deeply. "I have to go."

Brianna put her foot in the way and pulled the screen door open wider. "I hired a lawyer and now that I'm clean and sober, I'm going to take your fat ass to court and challenge it. You fuckin' turned my son against me!"

"This is ridiculous, Brianna. Do what you want to do, but I'm done talking to you."

Brianna sneered. "Chas must be hungry for a sexy woman with a good body because he couldn't take his eyes off me. I've known him longer than you, and I know what he craves." She brought her face in closer. "And flab and a big ass aren't it."

A bolt of white-hot anger ripped through her, and she didn't count to ten, take deep breaths, or think of a peaceful place. She raised her hand and walloped the smirk right off the evil ex's face.

Staggering backward, Brianna's arms flailed before she gripped the potted tree next to the door. "Bitch!" she yelled, straightening up.

"There's more where that came from unless you take your skinny, bony ass out of my sight."

In that frozen second between disbelief and reality, Addie saw Brianna's face transform from shock to pure hatred. At lightning speed, she flew at Addie, her hands over her head, long sparkly nails clawing. Addie yelled out and pushed Brianna back, then stepped out onto the porch. The fight was on. Clumps of hair, broken nails, sharp kicks, and a few well-placed punches had both women red-faced and breathing heavily.

"What's going on?" Belle asked from behind Addie.

Not answering, Addie jerked Brianna's long hair hard, and the woman lost her balance on her high-heeled boots and slammed face down on the porch. The area beneath her stained darkly from the flow of blood. Pushing up, she wiped the back of her hand over her mouth. Streaks of crimson painted the white leather gloves.

"Fuck you!" she cried, lunging toward Addie.

"Get the hell out of here and leave us alone!" Addie cocked her head and her disheveled hair dangled, swinging slightly in the icy breeze.

Belle and Cherri ran out and grabbed Brianna's arms. The woman twisted and jerked in a vain attempt to get free. "Leave me alone. Let me go!"

"You need to go. Now," Belle said as she turned Brianna so she faced the stairs. "You shouldn't be coming over and upsetting people."

Brianna pulled away and looked behind her. "If I broke a tooth, your fat ass is paying for it." Cherri handed her a handkerchief, but Brianna swatted it out of her hand. "You're all fuckin' bitches." Grabbing the handrail, she clomped down the stairs and stalked away.

"Are you okay?" Cherri murmured as she went over to Addie.

"What the hell happened?" Belle asked, her gaze still on the woman as she drove away.

Addie wiped her nose. "I let her get to me, dammit. It's the one thing I didn't want to happen. She just pissed me off. I can't believe we fought it out on my front porch in front of the neighbors." She groaned.

"Let's go inside. It's freezing out here. And with a skank like her, you have to fight it out. That's all she'll understand. I got into plenty of fights when I stripped. That was the only way I earned respect. Believe me, she'll think twice before dragging her ass over here again." Cherri handed Addie a tissue. "She scratched you pretty good under your eye."

The face looking back at Addie from the entryway mirror appalled her: long, red marks on the left side of her cheek and neck, dried specks of blood under her eyes, tangled hair, and blotchy skin. *This isn't who I am.* Covering her face with her hands, she bent her head down. A hand softly squeezed her shoulder.

Addie looked up to see Belle's soft face reflected back at her. "Cherri's right. Don't beat yourself up all over again. You have to show her you're not going to put up with her shit. This is your house and family, not hers."

"I know, it's just that I acted so out of line with who I am."

"She came over here wanting to fight. You gave her what she wanted. No reason to feel bad about it." Cherri gripped Addie's arm and tugged her into the kitchen.

"What did she want, anyway?" Belle asked as she poured a fresh cup of coffee for Addie.

"Jack… and Chas. She's a horrible person. She's threatening to take me to court and undo the adoption."

"Can she do that?" Cherri asked, passing the creamer to her.

"No, and I know that, but I still let her get under my skin." She stirred the flavored cream into her coffee. "What really gets me is that I let her bring out my insecurities. She said Chas was checking her out and was getting tired of being with a big woman."

"That's nonsense. He's with you and not her." Belle sat across from her, reaching for her hand.

"I know, but it hit my insecurity button, especially since I never lost all the weight I gained when I was pregnant."

"I haven't lost all the weight I gained when I had Emily, and that was twenty years ago. Banger loves every inch of me, and that makes me feel sexy. It doesn't matter if another guy doesn't think I'm sexy, or some woman thinks my hips are too big. All that matters is that my man loves me just how I am and that I do too. I love my curves and the way I look in a pair of jeans."

Cherri nodded. "You do have to love yourself, but it's so damn hard. I've been working on it for years. It's helped a lot to go to therapy, but old insecurities are hard to get rid of. I'm not sure if a person ever does. When I was in school, I was skinny as a pole with no tits, and there was a group of girls and boys who never let me forget how ugly I was. People can be so damn cruel, and when they've moved on, you still have all the mean things they said to you catalogued in your head. It's hard to forget it."

"That's why we have each other, to remind us how wonderful we are," Belle said.

Addie set her coffee mug down. "It's true. It seems that together we can pull through anything. It's like when I'm down, others are there for me, and when someone else is down, I'm there for her. I really appreciate our friendship."

Cherri smiled. "I never had a good friend. My background is littered with shit I never want to think about, but one of the best things in my life besides Jax and Paisley is knowing I have a group of friends who really care about me, and that I can count on all of you. It means the world to me."

"When I married Banger, I had no idea that a wonderful group of ladies was part of the biker world. And it's great because none of my friends outside of the club *really* understand what living with a one-percenter is all about, but you all do."

"Do we ever." Addie laughed.

"I love having such a close-knit relationship with all of you. It helps me understand the love the brothers have for each other," Belle said.

Cherri and Addie bobbed their heads in agreement. Cherri sat back and stretched her arms over her head. "I wish we could get through to Sofia," she said softly.

"Me too," Addie said.

"We can't stop trying even though Tigger makes it hard by not letting her socialize that much. I talked to Banger about it, and he said that he'd tell Tigger that one of Sofia's duties as an old lady is to help out and be active with club events. I know she wants to be a part of the group, but the sonofabitch won't let her," Belle replied.

"I'm so glad you talked to Banger about her, Belle. I know she wants to get out, but she's feeling trapped. I can understand that." Cherri cast her gaze downward.

Addie's heart went out to her. From what Cherri had shared with them over the past few years, Addie gathered that she'd had a lot of horrible things happen to her. The fact that Cherri was still standing spoke volumes about her strength.

"We better finish up these bags. Before you know it, school will be letting out." Belle picked up several bags from the chair next to her. "Did you all hear that stupid rumor Doris was spreading about Hawk and Cara?" Addie and Cherri shook their heads. "No? Well let me tell you what she told Cara...."

THE SCRATCH UNDER Addie's eye was red and swollen. Pulling open her makeup drawer, she took out her concealer and dabbed it on, wincing with each stroke. She didn't want to field any questions from Jack, especially since she'd gone on and on about him getting into a fight at school. Groaning inwardly, she brushed on a thin layer of foundation, then examined her reflection—the welt was barely visible. A swipe of lipstick and gloss made her skin shine, and as she ran a brush through her hair, she saw Chas come up behind her.

"Thanks for picking Jack up after band practice. It took longer than I expected making up all the gift bags."

"Especially since you took time out for a boxing match." He nuzzled up to her.

Her shoulders curled forward. "You heard?" *I asked Cherri and Belle not to say anything.*

"Brianna called me, cussing up a storm. She said you decked her for no reason. Knowing you and her, I'd say she must've really pissed you off."

"I can't believe I hit her. I shouldn't have done it, but she just touched a nerve and all reason went by the wayside."

"It's fine, precious. Brianna can get under your skin. Believe me, I know. I found it incredibly sexy that you defended your turf."

"What did she say?"

"That she came over to see Jack and you went all defensive and jealous. I knew that was a crock of shit. She got super pissed when I told her that she probably deserved the beatdown you gave her." He chuckled.

Addie moaned. "Don't call it that."

"Then the wallop."

"No, it was a beatdown. I succumbed to that on the porch in front of our neighbors."

"I fuckin' love it." He whirled her around and kissed her deeply.

She giggled. "Your lips wear my lipstick nicely." Even though fighting was a part of Chas's world, she never considered it a part of hers, so she wasn't proud of the fact that she'd kicked Brianna's butt. She could only imagine what would've happened if Cherri and Belle hadn't been there to break it up. "She said she's going to take me to court."

"She's not gonna do shit. She's always had a big fuckin' mouth. I told her she's not to come over to our house ever again."

"I mean, if Jack wants contact with her, I don't want to forbid it."

"Jack doesn't want anything to do with her. She was a shitty mom and he knows it. He adores you, and he's been happy ever since she went away and you came into our lives. She's just doing this shit because she thinks it's gonna get her and me back together. That'll never happen, babe. You're stuck with me for life."

"And you're stuck with me." Placing her hand on the back of his neck, she drew him close and kissed him deeply.

"Let's take the kids and go out to dinner," he said as he cupped her ass.

"I can't. Tonight's ladies' night out, remember?"

"Fuck, I forgot."

"I made a casserole and salad for you and the kids. You just need to warm it up and put some dressing on the salad."

"I'm gonna miss you."

"I won't be late. Make sure Jack finishes his book report."

"Okay. You wearing a new perfume?" Chas tugged her to him.

"I bought a gingerbread latte spray at the drugstore. It was cheap, but I really like it."

"So do I." Chas began to slip his hand under her top. "You smell good enough to eat."

Addie smiled while gently pushing him away. "I have to get going."

Nipping her neck, he said, "You can't leave me like this." Taking her hand, he put it on his erection.

Shaking her head, she chuckled. "We can have some fun later on, but I have to go." She swept her lips across his, then turned back to the mirror to reapply her lipstick.

On her way out, she gave Chas the instructions for heating up the casserole, told Jack to finish his homework, and kissed Hope goodbye. She opened the garage door and the icy air swirled around her. Cranking up the heater in the car, she backed out and headed to the restaurant.

Country Kitchen was a newer restaurant that served home-style cooking with a Southern accent. Delectable fried chicken and melt-in-your-mouth buttermilk biscuits were what kept diners waiting over an hour for a table.

Entering the eatery, Addie was grateful for the roaring fire in the brick fireplace filling the back wall. The smoky scent from the logs blended with the warm hickory aroma seeping from the kitchen. Framed paintings of rolling hills, small shelves stacked with homemade preserves and spices, and random farming tools adorned the wood-paneled walls. Blue gingham tablecloths gave a pop of color under the low lighting from brass lanterns that hung from overhead wood beams.

Addie saw Clotille, standing up and waving at a large table toward the back of the packed restaurant. She waved back and went over to the table, joining Cara, Belle, Cherri, Baylee, Kimber, Kylie, and Bernie.

"Long time no see." Belle smiled.

The women ordered several bottles of chardonnay and toasted each other on getting everything together for the upcoming fundraiser. They placed their dinner orders and settled back. After the day Addie'd had, she guzzled her wine and refilled her glass. Turning to Baylee, she asked, "Has Axe come around to having a baby?"

"A little. He's not as sulky as he's been, and he mentioned we should probably move out of the apartment. It's not like he's ecstatic and beaming all the time, but he's beginning to talk about it. That's good, right?"

"It's huge, especially for a young guy who didn't expect to have a baby. Add in the outlaw factor and he's definitely coming around," Belle replied. The other women murmured their agreement.

Kylie picked up her wineglass. "I'm in a different situation. Lately, all Jerry can talk about is wanting a baby. Actually, several babies. We agreed we'd wait before we started a family. I'm not that old, and I really don't want a baby right now. I do want a family, but I'm only twenty-three and I have time. I want to finish grad school and teach for a while before starting a family."

"Did you tell Jerry that?" Baylee asked.

"Yeah, but it's like he doesn't hear me," Kylie said.

"That's a man for you," Kimber added. Sniggers circled around the table.

"The thing is I'm not sure if he's saying he wants to start a family because he really does or because he wants me to quit school. My gut's telling me it's all about my studies. He was cool when I was in college, but me being in grad school has sorta flipped him out. It's like he's threatened by it. I don't know. It's weird."

"A lot of men are threatened by the unknown. Maybe he's afraid you'll go in a different direction from him, meeting new people, and the two of you will drift apart," Cara said.

The waitress placed a plate of steaming fried chicken in front of Kylie. Her blue eyes lit up. "Yum… this smells delicious. I'll be hitting the gym harder tomorrow, but tonight, calories don't exist."

"Amen," Bernie agreed as she picked up a chicken leg.

All the women but Cherri ordered fried chicken, mashed potatoes, green beans, and baskets of biscuits. Cherri opted for the pot roast and a side salad.

Addie wiped the corners of her mouth with a napkin. "This is awesome. Good choice of restaurants, Clotille."

"When we came here for dinner, we were blown away. Rock and Andrew said it was the best fried chicken they'd had since they moved west. I had to agree with them. I have to admit that we come here a bit too often."

Kylie looked ready to burst before she blurted, "I'm not sure how to handle Jerry's insecurity about me and school. He's been accusing me of being bored with him and wanting a guy who's gone to college. He tells me I never have time for him anymore. I try and juggle everything, but it's damn hard. It'll be cool during the winter break, but when school starts back up, it's tough to party all the time. Grad school is a million times harder than college, and he just doesn't get it. And my dad getting in his face about it didn't help."

"The minute your father told me you were upset, I knew he'd get in Jerry's face." Belle shook her head.

"He knew what he was getting into," Kimber said, pouring wine into Addie's, Cara's, and her wineglass.

"I know, but I wish my dad would back off a little. It just causes more friction between me and Jerry." Kylie frowned.

"Then don't tell Banger about it," Bernie offered.

"Easier said than done. My dad knows when I'm upset. He knows me too well. Besides, I'm not sure how to convince Jerry that I don't want anyone but him. I love him so much. Why can't he see that?"

"He does, but a man likes to feel like they're the first focus in their woman's life. Sometimes life gets in the way, like problems with the kids, work, school, whatever, and we become so focused on those issues that we don't realize we're not in tune as much as we should be with our man. Take a break from your studies and plan a romantic evening where Jerry has your undivided attention," Clotille answered.

Kimber nodded. "Clotille is so right. When I became manager of Hawk's shop, Throttle was such a pain in the ass about it. I had to pull in some late hours, and he was feeling like I wasn't as into him as I used to be. So I told Hawk that I had to leave early two nights a week, and he was cool with it. When Throttle came home from work and found me wearing nothing but knee-high boots and a thong, he forgot about everything that'd been bugging him. He was just so happy that I'd made it a priority to come home early just for him. The whole night was all about him, and he fuckin' loved it. I still surprise him on my early nights. It keeps him guessing and eager to get home."

Bernie bobbed her head. "I've been hitched to PJ for twenty-five years. We hooked up when I was eighteen, had four kids, and have had a rough-and-tumble life with a lot of fucking and loving. Men think they got all the control, but it's really the women. You just have to let a man think he's calling the shots, and make him feel special in a way that has him running to get between your legs, forgetting all about them club whores. It also helps to let him know you'll castrate him if you find out his dick was in anyone else's pussy but yours." She cackled.

"You're so bad, but so right." Belle laughed.

"Changing the subject, I'm scared to death to open the curtains and show off our Christmas tree. It's fuckin' ridiculous." Cherri crossed her arms.

"I don't blame you. I'd be terrified too. Has Jax found out anything about the guy?" Addie asked, buttering her biscuit.

"No, and it's killing him that he can't. I just make sure the alarm is on at all times when Paisey and I are alone in the house. This whole Christmas vendetta this fuckin' psycho has is the freakiest thing I've ever heard of."

As the evening wound down, they talked about the toy drive and how happy they were when Evan had contacted Cara, telling her the event was sold out. They'd hoped to double the amount they'd raised the previous year, and they were well on their way.

They said their goodbyes in the parking lot and climbed into their cars to head home to their men. While Addie waited for the defroster to clear her windshield, she leaned back and hummed the chorus to "Jingle Bells." A sense of weightlessness settled over her as it always did after one of their ladies' nights out. The friendship she had with the other old ladies was the kind that bloomed in the center of the heart. They all knew they could get together and spin their hearts out without worry of judgment or mockery. They gave each other advice, shoulders to cry on, and the warm feeling of belonging.

Ping. She looked down at her phone and swiped.

Chas: *U coming home soon? Hope & Jack r in bed.*

A large grin broke over her face.

Addie: On my way now.

Chas: Drive safe.

Addie: See u soon. ♥

She sat up, placed her hands on the steering wheel, and drove out of the parking lot, heading home as fast yet safely as she could.

When she came into the living room, a full glass of white wine and a glass of whiskey were on the side table. In front of the dancing fire was a large Sherpa blanket, and playing softly through the stereo speakers was her favorite CD—a collection of ballads from Guns N' Roses, Poison, Metallica, Avenged Sevenfold, Iron Maiden, Pantera, and Killswitch Engage.

"What's this?" she asked as Chas came into the room and headed over to her. He nuzzled his face into her neck and she cocked her head to the side, giving him better access.

"Picking up where we left off." He licked the inside of her ear with the tip of his tongue.

"I'm glad you didn't forget," she said, shivering as she let him guide her down on the blanket.

"That's all I thought about," he replied huskily, his eyes fixed on her mouth.

She stroked the side of his face and brought hers closer to his. When their lips met, an electrifying current skipped across all her nerves.

Pulling away, she held his gaze as she slowly lifted her top over her head.

"Fuck," he growled as her sheer bra came into view.

The side of her mouth tugged into a smile as she reached back and unsnapped her bra, letting it fall from her. The exposure to the air made her nipples harden. When he dipped his head and sucked one of them into his mouth, she closed her eyes and let herself feel the arousal taking hold of her body.

"We've got all night, precious." He grasped her nipple between his teeth and pulled on it while his fingers trailed down her chest.

She moaned and arched her back, pushing her nipple deep in his mouth.

Yes... we have all night to love each other.

Lying down, she pulled him closer.

CHAPTER TWENTY-ONE

AXE

PICKING UP A shot of Jack, Axe waited for Hawk to come in and give the word that they were ready to head out to Chad Bridgewater's place. He'd had some time to kill after working at the club's restaurant that day, and he wasn't ready to go home. For the past two days, Baylee kept telling him they needed to talk, but he didn't want to just yet. He felt like a pussy, but the thought of their life changing so drastically still weighed on him. The club offered him a respite from reality, and he needed that in the worse way at that moment in his life.

"Give me another," he said to Brandi who was subbing for Rusty. The three prospects were busy loading the SUVs with guns and grenades. When the prospects weren't available, the club women picked up the bartending duties.

"Here you go, sweetie. You look like you lost your best friend. Do you wanna talk about it?" Brandi leaned over and smiled when Axe glanced at her tits.

"I'm good." He swiveled on the stool, his back to her. *Baylee's overjoyed about the baby. Why the fuck can't I be? Maybe it's different for a woman because the baby's growing inside her.* For him, everything felt the same way as it did when she first told him she was pregnant. His mother's face floated in front of him. He couldn't remember how many times she'd told him during his growing years that she hadn't wanted him but his dad had insisted she had him. And then his dad had blown and his mom had acted like it was Axe's fault she was stuck with him. *Why am I thinking about* her? He wasn't anything like his mom, or was he?

He placed his empty glass on the bar. Baylee just didn't get it because she had two parents who loved each other and were crazy about her. *She has no idea how it felt to be around parents who didn't give a damn about you.* So how in the hell could he tell her he was scared of being like them? He was an Insurgent and being afraid wasn't okay.

"Another one." He looked behind his shoulder at Brandi who smiled and winked while pouring him a double.

"You better take it easy. We got some serious shit going down tonight," Jerry said, taking the stool next to his.

"I'm fine."

"What's up with you? You've been off for the past week." Jerry brought the beer bottle to his mouth.

"I just got some shit going on at home right now."

"Yeah me too, but when I got shit going on it's a double pain in the ass because I gotta always deal with Banger too. Fuck. Every time I say or do something that upsets or pisses Kylie off, she runs to Daddy and tells him. Then Banger gets up my ass. I fuckin' hate that."

Axe nodded. "That sucks for sure. Are you sure Kylie's telling Banger shit, or is he just picking up on it 'cause she's his daughter?"

Jerry shook his head. "I'm not sure if she tells him all the time, but he fuckin' knows it. Either way, it's a pain in the royal ass."

"What's the problem you got going on now?" Axe asked.

"I'm pissed that Kylie's in grad school. She didn't even ask me how I felt about her going on with her studies. I missed her like hell this past semester so she said she'd do the classes online so we could be together. Now she's basically telling me she can't do much for the next four months. And I think she's gonna go to summer school. It sucks."

"What's she studying?"

"Something in education. She wants to work with kids that have problems. I don't even know why she had to go to grad school. She doesn't need it because we want a family and she'll be home with the kids, so what's the point of it all? I wanna get going on starting our family soon."

Axe leaned back against the bar. "Maybe she doesn't want a family just yet. Just because you do doesn't mean she wants it to. Maybe she wants some time before she gets saddled down. Kids change everything." He drained his glass.

For a few seconds Jerry didn't say anything, and then he nodded. "That's right. You're gonna be a dad. Why the fuck didn't you tell any of us? Kylie told me."

Staring straight ahead, he shrugged. "Didn't really think about it, and I don't want to talk about it." Jerry gave him a funny face, and Axe stood up, his head jerking to the front door. "Hawk's telling us to come over. It's time for us to fuck up some assholes real bad." He sauntered to the door with Jerry following behind.

Once outside, he and Jerry joined the other men huddling near the cars. The wind was bitter as it sliced through Axe, and he zipped up his leather jacket and stomped his feet on the frozen ground. Cruiser handed him a joint, and he cupped his hands and lit it, capturing the frosty air as he inhaled deeply.

"Rock and Tiny have been surveying the compound for the past couple of days. As they tell it, the fuckers are cocky as hell and don't have anyone standing guard," Hawk said.

"That's 'cause they don't think we know it's them. They did a good job making the network think it was bikers." Banger took the joint Cruiser handed him.

"The way we see it, they got only eight people max staying at the farm. They don't have anyone watching the warehouses. We figured a couple of them are for growing weed, a smaller one looks like a meth lab, and the rest are for storing dope and guns," Tiny said. The six foot three man built of muscle and grit made citizens move out of his way when he walked the streets of Pinewood Springs. With tats covering every inch of his arms and most of his chest and back, he was an imposing figure, and the average citizen who heard his road name didn't dare snigger or ask where it'd come from.

"Any women or kids at the compound?" Hawk asked.

"Not that we saw," Tiny answered.

"They got cameras watching the shit, but Blade's gonna take care of that when I give him the signal," Rock said.

"You gonna tell us where you want us to be? I was looking at the layout of the area again before I came, and it seems if we can cover it on all four sides, we'll be good, especially since no one's at the warehouses," Throttle said.

"And it being ten fuckin' degrees out helps us. I'm sure the lazy motherfuckers will all be inside warming their asses," Helm added.

Chas chuckled. "We'll warm them even more when we blow the fuck outta them." The brothers laughed, their breaths rising above them and mingling with the night air.

"Hawk, Bear, Wheelie, Axe, and me will go in to have a talk with the assholes. The rest of you will follow Rock's direction on where to be. Split up into two groups with Tiny heading one and Rock the other. If you hear shooting inside, you'll know to attack. Let's head out." Banger opened the door on a black SUV and several brothers jumped inside the vehicle. The club had several dark-colored Chevy Tahoes and Ford pickups and used them in covert operations.

Axe slid over to make room for Jerry, Throttle, and Wheelie. Hawk looked over his shoulder. "Is everyone in?"

"Yeah," Rock replied.

Hawk backed out and followed Banger out of the parking lot. Conversation was minimal which was normal before a hit. Preparing the mind and eliminating all thoughts and feelings were essential in confronting whatever lay ahead. Each time the Insurgents went out on a mission, it could be one of the brothers' last time. Life and death were interwoven, and in the violent outlaw world, death was omnipresent. In the honor-obsessed outlaw biker world, disrespect took on a life-or-death significance, and the result was usually death to the offenders. The Insurgents were highly skilled warmongers, plotting, surveilling, and studying rivals. They learned where they lived, worked, and played, and then they'd silently enter their world and destroy them.

After a half hour, the vehicles slowed down and killed the headlights. They went off the road and drove a small distance before the engines turned off. The night was dark. The Insurgents used the darkness to shield them on one of their missions. Since Chad Bridgewater's residence was outside of town, there were no streetlights, and the closest neighbor was a good quarter of a mile away.

The snow crunched under the men's boots as they walked toward the farmhouse. In the distance, the howls of wolves and coyotes pierced the night air, and the wind whistled through the pine and evergreens. The faint pattering of small animals through the brush made several of the brothers whip out their guns. When they realized it was wild rabbits, foxes, and rodents, a hushed chuckle cracked the tension and they put away their Glocks and continued on their way. Axe glanced upward: stars glittered through the gaps in the trees.

"There it is," Tiny said in a low voice.

Up ahead, a ranch-style house with a large porch greeted them. Wisps of smoke rose from the chimney, and the lights in the front part of the house cast yellow squares on the glistening snow. The six metal warehouses stood off to the left side of the main house. They weren't huge buildings and perched on the front sides of them were security cameras. The buildings creaked in the wind.

"Do they have a camera at the house?" Banger asked.

"Nope," Rock replied.

"Fucking unbelievable," Throttle said.

"What a bunch of dipshits." Helm spat on the ground.

"This is too fuckin' easy," Ruben said.

"We should take the shit from the grow building and the guns," Axe said.

"That's what I was gonna suggest." Banger turned to Rock. "You and Tiny know which is which, so we won't strike those until after we take the stuff. Rusty and Skinless are bringing the trucks. When we kick the front door in, give the signal to Blade to cut the cameras. Let's go."

In a flash, they were on the front porch, Wheelie carefully opening the screen door and jerking his head at Axe. Axe raised his leg and, with his full strength, kicked the door. It groaned and splintered, and the rush of excited voices told him he had less than a second to break it open. Another kick and the door flew open. He rushed in with his gun drawn and saw two men run to the back of the house. Knowing Jerry, Chas, Cruiser, and Helm would be waiting, he let them go and moved over quickly to let Hawk, Wheelie, Banger, and Bear in.

"What the fuck?" a tall man with red hair said. "Banger? What the fuck are you doing?"

"I came over to visit," Banger replied, his hand inside his jacket.

"Why the fuck didn't you just knock? You broke my fuckin' door. You gonna pay for that?" From where Axe stood, he could see the red blotches on the man's face, and the vein in his temple pulsing.

"Brothers, this here is Chad," Banger said. Turning to two other men who stood near Chad, he laughed. "How in the hell did you get mixed up in this shit Randy?"

"I needed the money," Randy blurted out.

"Shut the fuck up!" a skinny man said.

"Let him talk if he wants, Beau. It figures you and Calvin are working with Chad." Banger shook his head. "But Randy? It's too damn bad you didn't go to the bank for a damn loan."

"I'm not involved with any of this, Banger. Honest. I was just helping with some of the plants." Sweat beaded up on the dude's forehead.

"Banger's here because he's pissed we're doing meth. What the fuck can I say? I need the money. I couldn't get the grow license, so I had to do something. The farm hasn't been doing that good. Hard to get good help." Chad smiled but it was one of the most insincere smiles Axe had seen in a long time. "Do you and your friends want a beer?"

Beau started to move away. "Don't fuckin' move, old man or I'll put a bullet through your head," Axe said.

Chad snorted. "No reason to be so serious. Sit down. Tell me what's on your mind. We can reach an agreement. The fucking cops don't even give a shit what I'm doing. I'm not a big honcho. I'm not threat to anyone's operation. Really."

"This isn't about the weed or meth. It's about Sketcher," Hawk gritted.

"Who? I don't know him." Chad looked at Beau, Calvin, and Randy. "Do you guys know who he's talking about?" They shook their heads, but Randy looked like he was going to have a heart attack.

"I'm not asking if you knew him. I'm telling you why the fuck we're here." Hawk took a step forward.

Chad snorted. "Banger? Tell your friend that I don't know who he's talking about."

Banger shook his head. "You fucked up, man. You killed one of ours."

Randy's eyes bugged out. "He was an Insurgent? Fuck. We didn't know."

"I told you to shut the fuck up." Beau slammed his fist in Randy's face.

"Both of you shut the fuck up! Sketcher was part of our family. We don't like it when someone messes with someone in our family. It doesn't matter if they're brothers, club girls, or on the payroll, they are in the fold." Banger took out a joint and lit it.

"Go check the other rooms," Hawk said to Axe and Throttle.

Axe went into one of the rooms and saw a small girl sleeping on the bed. "Fuck," he muttered under his breath. He checked the other rooms and met Throttle in the hallway.

"All clear," Throttle said.

"Same here except for a girl who's sleeping. She looks about five or six. Shit." Axe replied.

"I thought Rock and Tiny said there were no kids?"

Axe shrugged. "Stay here. I gotta tell Banger."

When he went past the kitchen, he nodded at Jerry and Chas who had the two guys who'd tried to run on their knees with their hands behind their backs. He went into the living room. "There's a kid sleeping in one of the rooms."

The vein in Chad's temple throbbed. "That's my granddaughter. Don't hurt her."

Banger went over to Chad and slammed his gun into his head. "Don't tell me what the fuck to do." Chad cried out and brought his hands to his head.

"You want me to take her out?" Axe asked.

"Yeah. How old is she?" Banger said.

"She's only five. Please don't hurt her." Chad's voice broke.

"Put something over her eyes and take her out." Banger went over to Randy. "Now you're gonna tell me the truth because we're done fuckin' around here. If I don't hear the truth from you, I'm gonna make you sorry you ever heard of the Insurgents."

Axe chuckled and walked back into the room with the girl. He went over to her and stared down. Her lips were parted in an "O" and with her blonde hair and fair skin, she looked like one of those angels he'd seen in books. He turned away and rummaged through some drawers until he found a scarf. He went back to the bed and picked her up, blanket and all. She moaned slightly then wrapped her arms around his neck. He walked to the kitchen.

"What the hell?" Chas asked.

"She's the fucker's granddaughter," Axe replied.

"You practicing for when you're a daddy?" Jerry chuckled.

"Fuckin' lame, dude. I gotta get her outta here. I can tell by the way Banger and Hawk are standing that shit's about to hit the fan." He went outside.

The cold air woke her up and she cried out, "Poppa. Where are we going?"

Axe's heart twisted. "Your poppa's busy. I'm helping him out. We're going to play a game. Have you played pin the tail on the donkey?"

"Yeah, but I don't wanna play."

He kept walking to the SUVs. He wanted to get her out of there before the gunfire and the explosions started up. Jerking his head at

Skinless, Axe opened the door of the vehicle.

Skinless tossed his cigarette to the ground, stubbing it out with the toe of his boot. "Just got the word to move in."

"Shit's about to get real." Axe handed the prospect the scarf. "Put this around her eyes."

"I don't want that," the girl cried, trying to wiggle out of Axe's tight clasp.

"It's just for a little bit. It's a game." He pulled the driver seat back and slid in, the girl still in his arms. Skinless went over to the truck and took off toward the farmhouse. After turning on the ignition, Axe cranked up the heat.

The girl rested her head on his shoulder. "How long we gonna play the game?"

"Not long. How old are you?"

"Five. Do you know Poppa?"

"Yeah. Where's your mom and dad?"

She shrugged.

"Do you live with your poppa?"

"No. I sometimes sleep over. I don't like too, but Mama takes me sometimes." She yawned.

"Why don't you like to stay over?"

"I don't know. I don't like Uncle Beau and Poppa makes me be nice to him." She buried her face in his jacket.

Axe clenched his jaw as threads of fire wove around his spine. "You tell your mama you don't like staying over?" She shook her head, her face still buried in his leather jacket. "Why not?"

"I'm not supposed to. Please don't tell Poppa I said anything. I don't wanna talk."

He took a deep breath and exhaled slowly. "I won't say anything. What's your name?"

"Charity."

"It's a pretty name." He wrapped his arm around her a little tighter, listening to her breathing. Seconds turned to minutes, and from the way she relaxed in his arms, he could tell she'd fallen asleep. On high alert, his eyes darted all around, making sure no one lurked among the trees or the underbrush.

Crack! Pop! Pop! Boom! The gunshots and explosions split the night. Charity jumped and whimpered in her sleep, not fully waking up. Billows of gray then black smoke mingled with the frosty air as streaks of orange-yellow flames illuminated the darkness. Axe wished he could be in the thick of the action instead of watching it as he babysat the asshole's granddaughter. Happy the girl slept through the melee, he stared straight ahead, watching for Skinless and Rusty to come by in the pickups.

After a long while, wavering headlights made him squint as the two trucks came toward him. Then several brothers jumped out and made their way to Axe and the other SUV. A few brothers stayed in the pickups with the prospects, lifting their chin to Axe as they drove away.

"You driving?" Hawk asked, opening the driver door.

"I can. You wanna take her?" Axe replied. Hawk nodded and Axe started to hand her over when she woke up screaming.

"I don't want to. Stop it." Tears rolled down her face as she tried to tear off the blindfold.

"Charity, it's me. I'm not gonna hurt you. Calm down. We're almost done with the game. Remember?"

"You're not Uncle Beau?"

"No."

"I wanna stay with you." Her voice broke.

"Take her in the back and take off her blindfold. She's freakin' out," Hawk said.

"She's gonna see us," Throttle said as he settled in the front seat.

"It's dark. It'll be fine," Axe replied, slipping in the back seat. "Everything go good?"

Hawk glanced behind his shoulder. "Yeah."

They rode back in silence, and Axe turned his body so that Charity could look out the window and not at the brothers. No one dared say a word about what had happened at the farmhouse. The less the child knew, the better it would be for her and for them.

By the time they arrived at the clubhouse, the girl had fallen asleep again against Axe. He covered her head with the blanket and went into the clubhouse.

"Take her to my room," Hawk said, handing him the key. "We gotta figure out what we're gonna do with her. Have Kristy stay with her."

The rest of the brothers came in, and Rusty and Skinless pulled the trucks around back to unload the marijuana plants and the guns. The other prospect, Hog, had drinks lined up and ready for the brothers when they were ready for them.

Axe climbed the stairs to the third floor and opened the door. Illuminated by moonlight, he gently placed her on the bed and covered her with the blanket then slipped out to find Kristy. Once Kristy was in place, he went down to join the others in the great room.

Banger motioned him over. "A goddamn mess with the kid. Did she see or hear anything?"

"Not really. She seems pretty tired. I'm damn surprised she slept through the noise. Sorry I missed it."

"The only bastard we didn't get was Reggie. We checked everywhere and the asshole wasn't around. If he takes up where his dad left off, we'll get him." Banger grabbed the beer on the bar.

"I thought the pussy was the one who cut off Sketcher's balls."

"That's what Randy said before we put a bullet through him, but we don't know for sure. Let's see what he does. The fucker still needs a beatdown and he's gonna get it for sure. Is the kid his?"

"Not sure. She didn't say too much about her parents. Seems like the fucker Beau was messin' with her from some of the stuff she said, and grandpa didn't seem to give a damn." Axe shook his head.

Banger jerked his head back. "What a bunch of sick perverts. Well, the little one doesn't have to worry about that shit anymore. Glad we took them out. They deserved it."

Axe bobbed his head as he brought his shot to his lips.

"We gotta take her back to her parents. Find out who they are so we can bring her back before morning. We're gonna have enough shit to deal with when the fuckin' badges start snooping around. A kidnapped child will take all this to a new level."

Jerry came over and sat down on the barstool. "We took the money and drugs, so it'll look like a robbery. They'll probably think it was Los Asesinos. We did find out Chad was cheating them. They had a whole stash of cash and drugs in a safe he'd put behind a false wall. We made it look like it was a hit."

"That's why we gotta bring the girl back to her parents right away," Axe said. "I'll go up and see what I can get out of her."

A few hours later, Kristy, decked in a wig, glasses, and heavy makeup, rang the doorbell of Paige and Eddie Bridgewater. It turned out that Chad was Eddie Bridgewater's grandfather and Charity's great-grandfather. Kristy told them she'd found Charity wondering in the streets. She rushed away as the two confused parents hugged their daughter. It seemed that the news about Chad's death hadn't reached them yet. It'd probably take a few days before the badges received a call. By then, Kristy would be back at the clubhouse—her safe haven.

Axe dropped her off and drove home. It'd been a night of mixed emotions for him. Holding and comforting Charity had sparked something inside him he couldn't explain. He didn't know the child, but he'd been concerned for her safety and the way she felt. He hadn't wanted her to be afraid of him. And when she'd said she didn't want Beau around her, anger had flared up inside him and he'd wished he could've beaten the shit out of the man before Banger had put a bullet into his skull.

Axe went quietly into the bedroom and slipped out of his clothes. Slipping between the sheets, he smiled when Baylee mumbled something in her sleep. He scooted close to her and rested his hand on her belly. *She's got our kid growing inside her.* For the first time since she'd told him the news, a thread of happiness unfurled inside him. He actually *wanted* this baby, and that thought blew him away. And something deep inside him assured him he'd be nothing like is mom or dad; he'd love his child no matter what.

"What time is it?" Baylee's sleepy voice startled him.

"Almost four."

"You're back real late. Is everything okay?" She turned around and faced him.

"Yeah. Everything's good." He dipped his head down and kissed her tenderly. "I love you, baby."

A smile flicked across her lips, and she brought her hand to his cheeks and stroked it. "I love you too."

Rubbing her stomach, he kissed her again. "I'm happy about the baby," he muttered against her lips.

"You are? Really?"

"Really, babe."

Hugging him, she kissed his throat. "I've waited to hear you say that. Even though we didn't plan it, this baby is a wonderful gift."

"Yeah. You gotta hurry with the house plans. I want the best for our son."

"Or daughter." She chuckled. "I'm almost done with the plans, but we can wait until the spring to start building. The baby won't come until July."

He squeezed her and pressed her closer. *Fuck. I'm gonna be a dad. Life can be so damn unexpected.* He hadn't expected to fall in love with Baylee and now he couldn't imagine his life without her in it. He hadn't planned on being a father, but now he was going to be one.

Yeah… sometimes life can be pretty fuckin' awesome.

Holding her close, he shut his eyes and let sleep take him away.

CHAPTER TWENTY-TWO

GARRET

I HATE NEEDING a fix so badly that I'm breaking into Brighter Lives to steal shit. Garret cut the glass easily, slipped his hand inside, and unlocked the window. He hoisted himself up and climbed through. Moving the flashlight around, he made his way down the stairs to the basement. He was supposed to steal the toys, but when he saw the sheer volume of them, he figured it'd take him hours to drag them upstairs and load them into his van.

"Why the fuck didn't *he* come and help? He's the one who has the problem with Christmas." His heartbeat raced as sweat coated his body. He needed a fix real bad, and he couldn't wait anymore. The money promised to him after he stole the toys was just a few miles away.

Licking his lips, he paced the length of the room. Stopping, he rammed his hands into his pockets, digging for any loose change or bills. Nothing. He was dead broke. Mostly every dollar he earned or panhandled went to support his meth habit. Two days before, he'd gone to Bridgewater's farm to buy a few bags, but the whole damn place had been destroyed, and there was yellow tape and cops swarming the grounds. He'd high tailed it out of there. He didn't need any trouble with the cops.

He kept pacing, thoughts whirling through his mind. The memory of seeing the lawyer at Brighter Lives the week before made his head throb. She'd called out his name a few times, but he'd pretended he hadn't heard and got the hell out of there as fast as he could. He'd been shocked to see her. And driving to Durango and Pueblo to sell the shit *he* gave to him made him sweat even more.

Garret had become a slave to a demented person who enjoyed watching children cry. The madman had taken a good holiday and twisted it into something evil and painful. Even though Garret hadn't been home for Christmas in a few years, his mom and sisters always sent him gifts, and he always called them to wish them a Merry Christmas. *The bastard's sick as hell, but he pays well.* So, Garret pawned items in neighboring town and cities, got rid of what wouldn't sell, and found himself in the basement of Brighter Lives contemplating on what to do with all the toys. If he didn't destroy them, the man wouldn't pay him and he needed a fix so badly he could taste it.

Abruptly, he stopped. He took out his lighter and went over to a pile of dolls in shiny boxes. Ripping them open, he threw the cardboard on the floor. He lit the dolls' dresses and then the cardboard boxes and smiled when they caught fire. He systematically did that with all of the toys and boxes. As the fire caught, he rushed around the basement looking for paper, gathering it in his arms and throwing it on the fire. Soon the smoke began to grow thick and he rushed up the stairs and climbed out. As he pulled away from the building, the alarms screamed. In his rearview mirror, he saw the golden glow from the basement windows, and he turned into a dark alley when he heard the wail of fire truck sirens in the distance.

Garret drove slowly down the alley, not wanting to draw any attention to him. Driving farther and farther away from the sirens, he made his way to their meeting point. He'd get the money first then tell the man how he'd ruined Christmas for the needy boys and girls. After that, he'd call Reggie and see if he had some meth he could buy. He couldn't wait until he was back in his room, the rush of crystal surging through his body. There was nothing like it.

And the man knew it.

It was how he controlled him.

CHAPTER TWENTY-THREE

CARA

"I CAN'T BELIEVE someone would set fire to Brighter Lives. What's wrong with people?" Lindi asked.

"The good thing is it was after hours and no one got hurt," Joseph said.

Cara went around her dining room table pouring coffee in the board's mugs. Joseph had called an emergency meeting, and Cara offered to host it at her house since the building had been closed down by the fire department.

"It looked like whoever did it was targeting the toys. The fire chief said that's where it started. It's appalling." Torey stirred sugar into her mug.

Evan shook his head. "With the benefit only a day away, it's going to be a sad affair for the children we invited to come. We don't have any toys to give out, and we don't have the budget to replace them. It took us weeks to get what we had."

"No worries. I spoke to Banger and he and the other guys are madder than hornets. He said that they're going to take care of it," Belle said.

"What does that mean?" Joseph asked.

"It means there will be toys for all the kids we invited to the event and plenty more for the others next week," Addie replied.

"How is that possible?" Lindi asked.

Cara laughed. "Don't ask how. Just know that if the Insurgents say it'll happen, it will."

"What a relief," Torey said. "Since we have that solved, I'll grab myself a sweet roll. When I came over, my stomach was in knots. Knowing that the kids will have their toys makes me very happy. Tell the men thank you so very much."

"Yes, tell them we are very grateful and appreciative," Joseph added.

"We'll let them know. They've been doing this for many years, and there was no way in hell they were going to let someone ruin it for the kids," Belle said.

"I hope they catch whoever did this. It's despicable," Addie replied. The others nodded in agreement.

"Since we have that settled, let's just go over the mechanics of Saturday night, and then we'll let you ladies get on with your day," Evan said, pulling out a folder from his briefcase.

The next hour they reviewed everything connected to the event. Cara's mind kept wandering back to the arson. In her gut, she knew it was the crazy person who was destroying Christmas decorations in people's houses. *What better way to ruin the holiday than to destroy the toys for the children. It has to be Garret. I saw him at Brighter Lives the week before.*

"Are you zoning out on us, Cara?" Joseph asked. A smile tugged at his lips.

"I was. Sorry. I was just thinking about the fire. I can't help but think that guy, Garret, is involved in it. I know you told me he doesn't work for Brighter Lives, Lindi, but what was he doing in the building when I saw him?"

"Maybe he's after you. Have you seen him since?" Evan asked.

Cara shook her head. "No."

"Or he could've been there applying for a job." Joseph turned to Lindi. "Did you check out the applications?"

"No. I just checked out our employee roster. I can go through the applications if you want me to."

"It wouldn't hurt," Torey added.

Joseph stood up. "I have to meet with the board of directors about what happened last night. I'll see you all on Saturday." The other employees of Brighter Lives rose to their feet and said their goodbyes as they followed Joseph out of the house.

Belle and Addie helped Cara clean up before they left, and after they'd gone, Cara went to the computer and plugged in everything she knew about Garret. Nothing came up. Frustrated, she rubbed the back of her neck and picked up a file she'd been working on for a preliminary hearing the following week.

When she heard the patter of running footfalls, she smiled right when Braxton ran into the study. "Mommy!" He rushed up to her and she settled him on her lap.

"Did you have a good day at school?" she asked.

"Ya. We made Christmas stuff. I made something for you and Daddy but you can't see it until Christmas."

"How sweet you are." She kissed his cold cheek. "You're frozen. Let's go in the kitchen. I'll make you some cocoa. Where's Nana?"

"She's still taking Isa out of her car seat. I'm big so I'm faster."

She went into the kitchen and saw her mother and Isa coming in from the mudroom. "Mommy!" Isa toddled over to her and she picked her up, kissing her soft cheeks.

"Hi, Mom. Thanks for picking up the kids. I'm making hot chocolate. Do you want some?"

"I'll have a cup. It's so cold outside. Do you have anything sweet?"

"Do I. There's a ton of sweet rolls and cookies that the ladies brought for the meeting. Help yourself. They're in the cupboard next to the stove."

"That's awful about the toys being burned. What're you going to do for Saturday?" Her mother took out a tin of Christmas cookies and placed one on a plate and handed it to Braxton.

"Thanks, Nana." His eyes sparkled and Cara and her mother laughed.

"Hawk and his brothers are taking care of it. They'll buy all the toys. I'm sure there are several Insurgents and a few old ladies buying out some of the stores in Denver."

"How can you stand being called an 'old lady'? I'd die if your father said that to me." Cathy shook her head and placed another cookie on Braxton's plate.

Ignoring her mother's comment, Cara mashed a banana in a bowl and placed Isa on her lap. "Can you watch the cocoa on the stove, Mom? Anyway, I think it's great that the Insurgents are making sure the needy kids have a great time on Saturday."

Before her mother could answer, the back door slammed shut and the thud of heavy steps had Braxton sliding out of his chair and rushing toward the mudroom.

Hawk walked in with Braxton in one arm. Cara looked at him and desire curled inside her, making her tingle. Wearing tight blue jeans and a long-sleeved T-shirt pulled tight across a thickly muscled chest, he held her gaze, a smile twitching on his full lips. She ran her eyes over his big mound and licked her lips before returning her gaze to his. The recessed lights made his ebony hair shine, and the dangling sword earring he wore gleamed under the lights. *He's so gorgeous. I'll never tire of looking at him.*

"Hey, babe," he said in a gravelly voice; his eyes smoldering with intensity.

"Hey," she said softly as Isa grabbed her hand for more fruit.

Her mother standing up broke the lusty haze between them. "I better get going," she said.

"Hiya, Cathy. Don't leave on my account." He went over and kissed Isa then Cara. "I missed you, babe," he whispered, his hot breath fanning over her face. Setting Braxton down, he walked out of the kitchen.

"Where're you going, Daddy?" Braxton asked. "We're having cocoa."

"I got some work to do, little buddy. Save me some."

Cathy sat back down. "I guess I can stay for one cup."

"I wish you'd be nicer to Hawk, Mom. He's a great father and guy. It isn't fair that you always act like he has the plague when you see him,"

Cara said under her breath, not wanting Braxton to hear.

"He just makes me nervous. I don't know why, but he does. Anyway, we have absolutely nothing in common." Cathy came over and poured the hot chocolate in two mugs and Braxton's plastic cup.

"You have me, Braxton, and Isa in common," she replied as she reached for Braxton's cup. "Grab me an ice cube from the small ice tray. It's too hot for him."

Her mother placed a small cube inside the mug and sat down. Changing the subject, she talked about her upcoming trip to Europe with two of her friends. They talked until raspberry red and blackberry violet embraced the edge of the clouds as a brilliant white patch slipped behind the mountain peaks. Cathy glanced out the window then at the clock. "It's later than I thought. I better get home and start dinner." She stood up.

"Dad's easy. He's good with a sandwich and soup. Take some cookies for him. I'll pack up the sweet rolls. I'm the only one who eats them in the house, and I don't want to be tempted." She rose to her feet and Isa smacked her lips, her eyes fluttering open.

"Your father doesn't need them either."

"He can bring them to the office tomorrow." She pulled out the box from the cupboard and handed it to her mom.

She walked her mother into the garage. "Drive safely." She kissed her on the cheek.

"I will." Cathy ran her finger over Isa's cheek. "Tell Braxton bye for me. I'll see you and the children on Saturday." She went into the garage, and Cara waited until she'd backed out and headed down the road before she closed the door.

"Brrr... it's cold, sweetie," she said to Isa as she closed the door and went back into the kitchen. Hawk stood in front of the open fridge. She came behind him and patted his firm butt. "Looking for something?"

He turned around and pulled her into his arms, Isa chortling. "I just found it." He squeezed her ass cheeks.

Isa squirmed and held out her arms. "Daddy." Cara handed her over to Hawk.

"Hey, princess." He rubbed his face against her and she giggled.

"Leftover lasagna sound good? I'll make salad and garlic bread."

"Sounds great, babe."

"The people from Brighter Lives were blown away today when Belle told them the Insurgents were replacing all the toys. They were very happy and grateful."

"Of course. We're not gonna let a pussy-ass fuck with the toy drive."

Cara sighed. "Honey, please watch your language around Isa. Okay?"

He went over to her and swept his lips across hers. "Okay, babe." He swatted her ass and went into the family room.

As Cara prepared dinner, Hawk played with Isa while watching *The Muppet Christmas Carol* for the twentieth time with Braxton.

"I think you should look into this Garret guy who came to my office. Remember I told you I saw him when I went to a meeting last week at Brighter Lives? Lindi said that he doesn't work there."

Hawk looked over his shoulder: a line etched between his brows. "You didn't tell me he was there. Have you seen him since?"

She shook her head. "I just have a gut feeling he's the crazy guy who's destroying Christmas things."

"You think he started the fire last night?"

"I do. I don't know why I do. It's a feeling. I have a description of his van and two numbers from his license plate. Remember I told you I couldn't read his last name on the ID he gave Asher when he came to my office."

"Yeah. You didn't make it sound like this fucker was dangerous." He got up from the couch and came over to her. "Has he threatened you?"

"No. Nothing like that. I just don't have a good feeling about him. I wish you'd check him out."

"Give me the details and it's done."

Cara gave the description of the van and the two numbers and Hawk took out his phone and went to the mudroom, closing the door behind him. As she was setting the table, Hawk came into the kitchen and went over to her.

"Did you find out anything?" she asked.

"I will. Don't worry about anything. I'll take care of it. Dinner smells good. I love your lasagna." He spun her into his arms and kissed her. "And I fuckin' love you, babe."

She kissed him back. "We have to make sure the kids are safe on Saturday. All the Insurgents will be there, right?"

He nibbled her neck. "Yeah, and the prospects too. We got this, babe."

While they ate dinner, Braxton told them what he did at school, and Hawk kept throwing sultry glances her way. By the time the food was put away and the dishes were in the dishwasher, she was a quivering mess of lust and desire.

When the clock struck seven thirty, Cara took the children up to bed. Isa fell asleep almost immediately after rocking her in the chair, and Braxton was already in bed waiting for his bedtime story when she went into his room. She and Hawk took turns reading to him, and she cherished the nights when she held one of his favorite books in her hands and transported her son to the world of make-believe.

Switching off the lamp, she smiled as she watched Braxton sleep, his ratty teddy tucked under his chin. As she went down the stairs, electric heat moved through her as her need for him intensified. Her body had been craving his touch since he'd come home.

He was on the couch, his feet propped up on the coffee table, the lamps turned down low, and a fire spitting in the fireplace. A show with a lot of zombies stumbling around was on the screen, the sound turned down so low she couldn't make out any of the dialogue.

She came up to him from behind and put her arms around the front of him. He tilted his head back and she bent down and kissed him deeply. He reached behind him and grasped her waist, lifting her off the ground and bringing her over the couch to him. They didn't say anything, just grabbed onto each other: their lips fusing together, his hands sliding under the hem of her top, her arousal rising within her like a flaming torch. The space between them was supercharged with the electricity of lust and desire. He plunged his tongue deep inside her mouth and hers tangled around his in a tantalizing dance, stoking that fire.

The way he kissed her, touched her made it seem like the earth beneath her melted away and all time stopped. She only felt.

"Fuck, babe. You're the spark to my flame. I can never get enough of you. Never," he rasped against her skin as he pinched her nipples and moved his lips down her neck.

A wave of warmth filled her up, spilling out from her heart and rushing to every corner of her body: her curling toes, her aching nipples, her throbbing mound. Every inch of her was saturated with desire. "Oh, Hawk," she moaned. Her arms reached up and tangled around his thick, strong neck. In an instant she'd pulled away and arched up into his broad chest, moaning in the contact of body heat against her own, before she drew back into his lips.

"Let's get on the floor, babe," he whispered, pulling her up. He moved the table out of the way, and she grabbed a blanket strewn over one of the cushy chairs, laying it out on the floor. He lifted his shirt over his head, the fire's glow illuminating every ripple in his amazing chest and arms. His tats danced as he reached out and yanked her to him, his mouth crushing against hers.

As he eased her down on the plush blanket, desire, love, and joy spread through her. She loved and desired Hawk so completely that she knew no matter how long she lived, she'd never get her fill of him. He was her world and she was his, and no matter how tough things got, they always had each other.

She grabbed a fist of his hair and brought his face to hers.

Chapter Twenty-Four

Banger

THOUSANDS OF TWINKLING white lights welcomed guests to the Brighter Lives' Toy Drive Fundraiser. The Insurgent men looked out of place amid the dangling snowflakes, glittering trees, beaded and sequined cocktail dresses, and designer suits. Round tables with chairs draped in white and secured with red satin bows filled the large room, and servers balancing large silver trays filled with a variety of hors d'oeuvres maneuvered through the labyrinth of people.

Popping a stuffed jalapeño into his mouth, Banger snagged a glass of champagne with his free hand as a waiter walked by carrying a tray full of flutes.

"Never thought I'd see you drink piss water," Hawk said, coming up to him.

"I was fuckin' thirsty. And I can't catch one of these people to get me a Jack."

As if on cue, Throttle and Axe came over with four glasses full of amber liquid. Banger took one from Axe and drank a big gulp. "I needed this, brother."

"Thought you would," Axe said as he brought his glass to his mouth. "This is a kickass turnout."

"Cara said it's gonna double last year's profits easily. Good to see people helping out the kids." Hawk took a few bacon-wrapped shrimp and gave one to Throttle.

"Hear you're gonna be a daddy." Banger cupped Axe's shoulder.

"Yeah. Fuck, how the hell am I supposed to know what to do? I never had a real dad."

"It just falls into place, I guess." Throttle took a bite out of the appetizer.

"Just make sure you love him and are there for him no matter what," Banger said.

"I still can't believe we're going to have a baby, but it's going to be okay. Baylee's designing our house. Do we have a clue who destroyed the toys?"

Banger narrowed his eyes. "When we catch the sonofabitch, I'm gonna kill him. I'm sure it's related to the shit that's been goin' on in the town."

"He's probably the same asshole who broke into Jax's house and scared the shit outta Cherri," Throttle replied.

"Cara gave me the name of a guy she suspects. She just knew his first name but got a partial plate number and description of the car. I gave it to Blade and he got a match this morning. He went over to the dude's place, but he wasn't around. Looks like he owns some property outside of town." Hawk motioned a waiter over and ordered four more whiskeys.

"We'll head out there tomorrow and pay this fucker a visit. Tonight I have all the brothers and the prospects on high alert. If the asshole's gonna pull something tonight, we're gonna nab him," Banger said.

"Why don't you guys circulate a bit?" Belle asked as she came over.

The dark green evening dress showed off her figure, and Banger loved the sheer top that hinted at something only he had the right to see behind closed doors. Pulling her to him, he kissed her and patted her ass. "We don't fuckin' 'circulate,' woman."

"Especially with citizens," Throttle added.

"Yeah, babe. We're good." Banger winked at her.

Rolling her eyes, she held up her hands. "You guys are impossible. Do you know where Cara is, Hawk?"

"Last time I saw her, she was on the stage fixin' some shit."

"I bet she's making sure everything's set when Santa comes out."

Belle rushed off toward the stage.

"Remember when we had ribs and slaw and the event was at Steelers? That was a blast. None of this fancy shit, just good food, whiskey, and a whole lot of people coming out to raise money for the kids." Throttle shook his head.

"That was before we got old ladies who wanted to kick it up a notch. What can I say? I'm guilty of bringing a rich girl into the fold." Hawk spread his arms out. "This is all my woman knows. She wouldn't have a clue how to have a laid-back fundraiser."

"You better keep her outta the bike rallies," Axe said, and the men chuckled.

"But we never raised the money like we are now for some of our charities." Banger clasped his hand on Hawk's shoulder. "Your woman has done good."

Hawk nodded, his lips twitching.

Wheelie and Rags came over and fist bumped with Banger and the others. Rags jerked his head toward a pretty woman in a formfitting red dress covered in beads that shimmered under the lights. "Our horny client is here."

Throttle glanced over, his eyes widening. "Damn. Mrs. Christiansen. There's no way in fuck I want her to see me. If she starts shit, Kimber will belt her one, and Cara will fuckin' kill me."

"You got something with her?" Hawk asked, looking over at her.

"Nah. She's a bored housewife who wants some cock. We got a lot of those. This one's just more persistent than the others."

"Did you give Kimber her ring?" Wheelie asked.

"Tonight." Throttle downed the rest of his whiskey.

When Tigger and Sofia joined in, Banger saw Wheelie run his eyes over the petite woman, and then he stiffened when Tigger high-fived him. As they talked, Banger saw Sofia and Wheelie steal glances at each other, smiles whispering on their lips. Coldness ran through him, and he made a note to talk to Wheelie in the morning.

The dinner was catered by Gourmet Bites, and Banger had to admit the steak was fucking great. Kylie sat across from him, and she looked all grown up in her sleeveless ice-blue dress. He watched the way Jerry leaned in close to her, stroked her cheek, laughed at her jokes, and looked at no one but her, and he knew she'd found the right man to take care of her. It didn't mean Banger wasn't still going to give Jerry shit— he had to make sure the brother kept in line—but a large part of him relaxed knowing his little girl would be taken care of.

"I like this," Harley said as he shoved a forkful of mashed potatoes in his mouth.

Banger laughed. "You fixin' to see Santy Claus tonight?"

Bobbing his head up and down, tendrils of hair fell over Harley's forehead. "Ya. Brashton and me are gonna get there first."

"You have to let the other kids go first, honey. Remember we talked about it at home?" Belle wiped his face with her napkin.

With his bottom lip out, eyes narrowed, and jaw clenched, Harley crossed his arms without saying a word. *He's Insurgents material.* Banger's chest expanded.

A woman came up to Belle while they were finishing their food. She glanced at Banger, then bent down and whispered something in Belle's ear that made her brow crease.

"What's going on?" Banger asked.

"Lindi's husband wants to leave. Oh… Lindi, this is my husband, Banger, and this is Lindi."

Banger shook her hand. "If you need a ride home afterward, we can take you."

Lindi gave a weak smile. "That's not it, but thanks. Dale, my hus-band, said he'd play Santa tonight, and now he's trying to back out. I really don't know what his problem is. I guess it stems back from when he was a child. He never talks about it, but he's told me the holidays were a nightmare." She shrugged. "He just hates Christmas, but he promised he'd be Santa. What're we going to do, Belle?"

As the women talked, Banger's mind went back to his Christmas past when his mother would slave for days making food for their holiday dinner, then sit glumly and pick at her meal while his dad would whisper things into his mistress's ear and feed her. To this day, he hated his father for humiliating his mother that way.

"Daddy, can I go over to Brashton's table? I'm finished eating," Harley said.

Jerking his head back, the past fled and he looked at his boy. "Okay, but I'll walk you over."

"You don't have to. I'm big now."

He chuckled. "I know you are, but there are too many people, and most of them are bigger than you. That's the deal. Take it or stay here with Mommy and me."

Scrunching up his face, Harley pushed against the table. "Okay. But I still could go alone."

Banger walked Harley to Hawk's table and watched his son run over to Braxton. "Keep an eye on him for me," Banger said to Hawk, then went back to his table. "What the hell's going on with Lindi's pussy-assed husband? You want me to make him get his ass in the fuckin' red suit?"

Belle leaned in close, and the scent of her perfume lit a fire in him. "Shh… people may hear you. Dale came over while you and Harley were gone, and he told her he was just joking. Something's terribly wrong with him."

"Sounds like he needs someone to set him straight."

"Well, at least he's going to do it, so we've avoided that catastrophe."

Chimes rang out from an overhead speaker and the lights dimmed a few times. All attention focused on the stage where Joseph stood with a microphone. He thanked all the volunteers and the Insurgents for making the event such a success. Congregated in the front were groups of children who fidgeted in place in anticipation of Santa Claus coming on stage to hand out the toys.

"I'm gonna watch Harley," Banger said as he leaned in to kiss Belle's cheek. He walked over to Hawk who was standing behind Harley and Braxton. The two men chatted until the trumpets rang out and Santa

Claus came onto the stage. The children went wild, and the applause from the audience was deafening. Harley jumped up and down in place while looking behind him at Banger.

"Cara's motioning me to come over. I'll be right back," Hawk said. Banger nodded and focused on the stage.

Fifteen minutes into Santa calling children up on stage and giving them their gifts, Hawk came back over, his brows snapped together.

"What's up?" Banger asked.

"Cara spotted that Garret fuck. She said he was standing by the stage."

Banger scanned the area but didn't see anyone besides a few Insurgents and volunteers. "What does he look like?"

"Not too tall, wiry, longish unkempt hair. She said he's around thirty. She's positive she saw him. Hang tight. I'm going backstage to take a look." Hawk disappeared into the crowd.

There were so many children crowded in the front, and an uneasy feeling took hold of Banger. Placing his hands on one of Harley's and Braxton's shoulders, his eyes darted around the room searching for anything that was amiss. Nothing seemed out of place. *Why is the fucker here? Cara's not the type to imagine shit.*

Hawk came back over. "Nothing in the back or around the area. I told Bear, Helm, Tiny, Rags, Cruiser, Klutch, and Bones to watch out for anything that doesn't look or feel right. I gave them a description of the jerk."

"I feel something off. What about you?" Banger asked.

"Yeah." Hawk turned his head from side to side.

"You've all been so good this year. Ho. Ho. Ho," Dale said as he tugged on the white beard.

Banger jerked his head toward the stage. "He's not too convincing, is he?"

"No. Next year we'll pay for a professional," Hawk answered.

Then the lights went out and the room was plunged into blackness. For a second, it was quiet as a tomb and then frenzied voices rose to the surface, children cried, bodies rushed and bumped, and chairs toppled over.

"What the fuck?" Banger said out loud as he reached in front of him. "Harley! Braxton! Call out." He whipped is cell phone out and turned on the flashlight. Soon the room was lit with an eerie white glow as people held up their phones to guide them to their tables.

"Where're the boys?" Hawk asked.

"I don't know. They were right in front of us before the lights went out. I should've kept my hands on them. Fuck!"

"Braxton! Harley!" Hawk yelled as he and Banger pushed through people.

"Everyone remain calm. There's been an outage. Power will be restored soon." Lindi stood on stage and Banger glanced over and noticed Santa's chair was empty. *That's strange. I gotta find Harley. Fuck!*

"Maybe they went backstage," Hawk said, rushing ahead.

Banger caught up to him and as they approached Tiny and Bones, the room was flooded with light. The patrons cheered and applauded and children scrambled over to their parents.

"Did Harley and Braxton come this way?" Banger asked the brothers.

"It was so fuckin' dark, I couldn't see a thing, but when I turned my flashlight on, I didn't see them," Tiny said.

"I heard some kids screaming and I tried to see what the hell was going on, but by the time I took out my phone, I didn't see anything. I ran out of the room but didn't see shit. Are the boys missing? Tiny asked, his forehead creasing.

The sound of his heartbeat thrashed in his ears. He'd been a one-percenter for thirty years, and he'd been faced with all kinds of danger, but he never let it affect him. But at that moment, terror seized him, squeezing every nerve in his body, splintering his heart.

"Banger!"

Belle's voice made his stomach knot. *What the fuck am I gonna say to her? I shoulda never let him out of my grasp. And Braxton. Fuck!* He whirled around and saw Belle approaching him. He clenched his jaw.

The festivities of the night resumed with one major change: Santa Claus had vanished. Lindi stood on stage, her eyes swimming with tears, and read off the names of the children while a few volunteers handed them their toys.

"Where's Harley?" Belle asked, her face glistening with sweat.

"He's not with you?"

Fear crossed her face. "No. He was in the front with you, Hawk, and Braxton. Where's Braxton?"

He placed his hands on her shoulders and held her gaze. "We don't know where the boys are, but we're gonna find them. You gotta be strong and let me do what needs to be done to find them."

She jerked away from him. "What do you mean you don't know where they are? Weren't you and Hawk watching them? My God, what if some sicko kidnapped them?" She covered her mouth with her hand. "This can't be happening," she mumbled as terror overtook her face.

"Don't fuckin' freak out on me. I got shit to do. We're gonna find the boys. I need to know you'll be okay."

"How can I be okay? I'm petrified!" Her voice broke and he drew her close to him and held her tight while he ran his hand up and down her back.

"It's gonna be fine. I'll make it fine. You gotta believe in me," he said in a low voice.

All around them, people laughed, children ran, and Christmas music filled the air, but they were in their own private hell. Ethan and Emily came over.

"What's wrong, Mom?" Emily asked.

Banger pulled away and guided Belle over to Emily and Ethan. "Take care of your mother. I got something to do." He knew that every second he did nothing was a second that took his son farther away from him.

"Where's Harley?" Ethan asked.

Belle covered her face and shook her head. Banger gently shoved her closer to Emily. "It's gonna be fine. I have to go." He walked away and went over to Hawk. "The boys are missing. Belle's a fuckin' basket case and I don't blame her. I gotta get a grip. We both do. We gotta focus or this isn't going to turn out good." He knew he had to put a wall between his love for his son and his determination to find him. If he let emotions enter into it, he'd slip up and it may cost his son his life.

With a face of stone, Hawk nodded. "We need to focus on getting our boys back. Cara's convinced this fucker Garret is involved. I agree with her."

"How's your woman doing?"

"She's trying to stay brave. She doesn't want her parents to know anything's wrong. But I know she's dying inside and it's fuckin' killing me." Hawk pounded his fist on the nearby table.

Rock ran up to them. "Throttle, Axe, Tigger, and Chas were outside talking to people and several of them said they saw two men rush out of the community center dragging two boys behind them. A couple of them said that the boys were telling them to stop."

"What the fuck did they look like? Did they see where they went?" Banger asked.

"When I went out to question them, they said one was medium height, kinda looked like a dirtbag, and had stringy brown hair. The other guy was wearing a suit. They said the two didn't look like they fit together."

"Did they get into a car?" Hawk said.

"A van. It's the fucker your woman pegged."

Banger kicked the table over and people jumped out of the way. "We fucked this up. *I* fucked this up! We had him. He was here, and I fuckin' handed my boy and yours to him. Fuck!"

Hawk place a hand on his shoulder. "No use blaming yourself or me blaming myself. We don't have time for that shit. We gotta find them. Now."

Banger let out a harsh breath. "You're right. Get Blade over here."

As he waited for Rock to find Blade, he tried to focus on finding his son, but Harley's face kept flashing in front of him, and Banger knew he'd be scared. A weight settled on his heart.

Hang on, Harley. I'm coming to get you.

Not finding him wasn't an option.

And when he did find him, Banger would tear apart the bastard who took his precious son.

CHAPTER TWENTY-FIVE

THE CRAZED GRINCH

"WE HAVE TO get out of here," Garret said as he paced the length of the room. It was dank and smelled of stale cigarettes.

"You need to calm down. No one knows who we are. We're good." The man pinched the bridge of his nose, hating the whine in Garret's voice. He preferred working alone, but he had to enlist the help of the druggie to unload the merchandise he'd stolen at all the houses he'd broken into and to help snatch the Insurgents' brats. He'd shown Garret where to pull the breaker switch the day before the fundraiser. He hadn't trusted him to snatch the kids. He was afraid the dirtbag would lose his nerve, so he made sure he was the one to do it.

And it worked out perfectly. *What do you think about that, Dad? Who's the loser now?*

"I didn't know you were planning to take the Insurgents' kids. You've fucking gone insane. There's no way they're not gonna find us, and when they do, we're dead." His face blanched and he ran his hand through his stringy hair.

"They're not going to find out. Anyway, I'm just messing with them. I don't want their brats. I just wanted to make them sweat. I bet they are too." He chuckled.

"You're fucking crazy, and you dragged me into this. Damn. They're gonna kill us." Garret resumed pacing.

Taking out a baggie, he waved it in front of Garret. "Want something for your nerves?" He had to get the sonofabitch to stop pacing. Garret stared at the bag dangling from his hand then came over and snatched it from him. Without saying anything, he went to the corner of the room, dragging a small table behind him. Sitting on the concrete floor that had mildew cracks snaking across it, he opened the baggie.

What a scum bag. His whole life is about getting high and finding the next fix. Pathetic. He glanced over to where the boys slept on a stained mattress against the back wall. *Still knocked out.* The last thing he'd wanted to hear was them whining about wanting to go home. In the morning he'd take the rascals back to town and dump them somewhere, and then he'd place an anonymous call to Cara or Belle and let them know where their sons were. He didn't want to hurt them, he just wanted to prove he could dupe the hotshot bikers. At that moment, he was enjoying the rush of accomplishment.

He stretched out his legs on the mismatched couch and rested his head on the arm. *I'll bet the bikers haven't told anyone about the missing kids.* At the event, he'd made his apologies to everyone, telling them he must've eaten something that didn't agree with him. It was his way of slipping away without drawing any suspicion. His wife didn't give a damn about him leaving. She'd been flirting all night with one of the members of the big board. *They'll probably fuck in his car before he drops her off home.* That thought only stirred disgust and contempt in him. He was over caring about who she screwed and what she did. As long as it didn't tarnish his name, he could care less what she did.

That night, he'd proven to himself that he could step over the line and execute a detailed plan well. He now knew that he'd be able to snuff the life out of his wife. Just thinking about it gave him an erection—something his wife hadn't stirred in him for a very long time.

Excitement skated through his body. That night was the turning point for him, and he intended to make the most of it.

With a contented sigh, he closed his eyes while visions of his wife's limp body danced in his head.

CHAPTER TWENTY-SIX

HAWK

B LADE RUSHED UP to Hawk who stood outside the community center with several brothers.

"What do you have?" he asked Blade.

"I mounted a GPS tracking device to the bottom of the asshole's van when I saw it on the street."

"Why the fuck didn't the prospect tell us he'd driven over here?"

"Banger called on all the brothers and prospects to be at the event. No one was watching him."

"Where the fuck is he?"

"At a location outside of town. It's the unincorporated part of the county. The van's been stopped there for the last twenty minutes or so."

"Let's go. I'm gonna grab Banger and some of the brothers." Hawk motioned Banger to come over. "Blade got a reading on where this fucker is. I'm gonna grab Rock, Tigger, Tiny, and Throttle. We'll all go in one car."

Nodding, Banger pulled at his beard. "Let's roll."

Settled in Hawk's SUV, the brothers sat stone-faced and silent as he steered the vehicle over the icy backroads. Inside his nerves sizzled and snapped threatening to explode, but he'd have to keep his cool in order to save his son. Thoughts of what Braxton and Harley may be going through had to be kept at bay. If he started thinking about how scared they probably were, he'd lose it, and fear and rage might make him do something stupid. He had to cool the fire in his veins with ice cold hate. Emotions had to be replaced with steely calculations. After he made sure the boys were safe, he'd let the smoldering fire in him wreak havoc on the sonofabitch who dared to kidnap his son.

"It's coming up," Blade said, his voice breaking through Hawk's concentration. "It must be down the road to the right. Do you see the dirt road over there?"

Hawk spotted a narrow break to the side. If Blade hadn't pointed it out, he would've driven right past it. Out in this part of the county, there weren't any streetlights and blackness filled the space under a waning moon. He turned sharply, killed the headlights, and slowed way down.

"Do you know how many are involved in this?" Banger asked.

"No. I just know the van is here," Blade replied.

"We better be prepared for a battle. Maybe Chad's pussy-assed son's behind this," Throttle said.

"Reggie? I don't think he'd have the know-how to pull this off," Tigger answered.

"Revenge makes you figure out a lot of shit. We offed his old man. I'm sure he wants retaliation. I know I would," Rock said.

Hawk gripped the steering wheel harder. "I agree with you. To be sure, four of us will go in the back and the other four will stay guard in the front. We don't know what's inside the house."

The tires crunched on the snow as they drove down the long road lined with gnarled, leafless tree limbs. In the distance, the outline of a small house came into view. As they approached, two windows in the front cast weak pools of yellow that barely lit up the ground beneath them.

Hawk stopped. "We'll walk from here," he said as he switched off the engine.

The men filed out and headed to the house. As they came up to the dilapidated abode, the van came into sight. It was parked off to the side. Banger went over to it and tried the door. It swung open. Tiny jumped in and Banger followed. Hawk stood watching them, his pulse pounding in his ears.

A couple of minutes later, Banger and Tiny exited the vehicle. Banger rolled his shoulders. "Nothing." His voice was tight with rage.

"They must be inside," Tiny said.

"Throttle, Banger, Rock, and I will go in through the back. This place is small so I don't think there are that many rooms. The rest of you be ready to come through the front when we call out," Hawk said.

"There's a basement, but I don't think anyone's down there." On his knees, Tigger looked through the windows.

"I think they're in the front room. It's the only one with lights on." Tiny pulled out a gun from the inside of his leather jacket.

"We gotta play this slow and cool. We don't want our kids hurt." A sharp pain lanced Hawk's heart, but he pushed it away and focused on getting into the house and confronting his opponent.

Hawk and the three men walked softly toward the back of the house, his small flashlight providing the only illumination. Placing his gloved hand on the doorknob, he slowly turned it, and to his surprise, the door swung open.

"You gotta love careless people. It makes it easy as fuck for us," Throttle said in a low voice.

"These stairs are damn loud though," Rock replied.

"Let's wait for the heater to kick on. I'm gonna bet it's not a new, quiet model. When I was growing up, the heater would be so fuckin' loud when it turned on and off, and the transformer would be so damn noisy the whole time it was running," Banger said.

They stood waiting on the porch for several minutes and then the click and thump of the furnace pilot light catching filtered to their ears, and a loud humming noise replaced the quiet.

"Time to roll," Hawk said as he crossed over the threshold, Banger, Throttle, and Rock following behind him.

A blast of heat smothered them as they stood in the middle of the small kitchen. To the right, a mouse scurried across the linoleum floor. Jerking his head toward the hallway, Hawk quietly walked out of the room. As he neared the only room with a light on, he pressed his body against the wall and inched closer toward it. Banger was next to him, his 9mm in his hand. Stopping just short of the doorway, he craned his neck and glanced inside the room. A bare bulb with a pull string was the only light in the room. Damp spots on the dingy walls, a jumbled row of what looked like paint cans, and a stack of cardboard boxes under the windows were the first things he saw from his vantage point. Extending his head a bit farther, he saw a man matching the description Cara had given him of Garret leaning against the wall rubbing and scratching his arms as his legs twitched. On the table next to him, Hawk saw an empty baggie and a rolled up bill. He glanced at Garret again, and a bolt of rage shot through him. *The fucker is high. If he hurt Braxton, I'll make sure he dies a real slow and painful death.*

Against one of the walls, he noticed a mattress. His heart pounded: Braxton and Harley lay on their sides. A chill went through him. *Are they dead?* The thought froze his soul.

"See anyone?" Banger asked.

"Yeah. I see the boys. The fucker's tweaking out. Probably meth. Let's go in."

When they entered the room, he immediately saw the mismatched furniture shoved over to the right-side of the room. A man sat up, surprise and then panic lacing his face. Hawk rushed over to him and grabbed him by the front of his shirt and yanked him to his feet.

"What the fuck did you do to my boy?"

Banger rushed over and without warning, punched him hard in the back near the kidneys. The man howled and Hawk let go of him, satisfaction coursing through him as the man fell down on his knees, sweat pouring down his face.

"I didn't know they were your kids," a high-pitched voice said behind Hawk. He whirled around and saw Rock slam Garret against the wall a few times.

Pointing at the man on the floor, Hawk turned to Tigger. "Watch the fucker." Banger and he rushed over to the mattress, a huge sense of relief washing over him when he saw Braxton's and Harley's small chests rise and fall.

"Hey, little buddy," he said as he knelt down and picked up Braxton. The boy's head flopped forward and his eyes remained shut.

"They fuckin' drugged them," Banger hissed as he held Harley close to him.

Lying Braxton back on the mattress, Hawk rushed over to Garret. "What the fuck did you give them?" He bounced the wiry man against the wall.

Tears streamed down Garret's face. "Nothing. I swear. I didn't know they were your kids. I'm not fucking around with you." Pointing his finger at the man on the ground, he shook his head. "It was all his idea. I didn't wanna do it. He's done all this shit. He thought it'd be funny to take your kids. I didn't know they were Insurgents." He spoke fast and kept repeating himself.

"I'm gonna get the other guys in here. We need to call Doc," Banger said as he went to the front door.

Hawk and Throttle went back over to the man crumpled on the soiled carpet. Hawk grabbed him by the collar of his dress shirt and yanked him up. "What the fuck did you give our kids?"

"I..." He stumbled on his words. Hawk shook him hard. "Benadryl," he mumbled.

"What the fuck?" Throttle said.

Hawk look behind him and saw Throttle jerk his head back. "What?" Hawk asked.

"That's Mr. Christiansen. He's one of my clients. What the fuck, dude?" Throttle came next to Evan, who hung his head down.

"Aren't you one of the fuckin' head honchos at Brighter Lives? *You* took my son?"

Evan Christiansen shrugged as he slowly raised his head.

"That's all you have to say, asshole?" His fist collided with Evan's cheekbone, snapping his neck backward like a pine tree caught in the wind.

"I can't fuckin' believe it's you. Why the hell did you do it?" Throttle rubbed his hand over his chin.

"He's the one breaking into people's houses and destroying their Christmas." Garret wiped his nose on his shirt sleeve.

"You're the one who attacked Cherri, you sick bastard?" Hawk sunk his fist into Evan's belly.

Gasping for air, he shook his head vigorously. "I didn't know she was home," he sputtered.

"Bullshit!" Hawk whacked him on the jaw, knocking him out. He gave Evan a hard kick on the side and went back to the mattress, picking up Braxton. The young boy stirred and his eyes fluttered open. Hawk kissed his cheek. "How're you feeling?"

"Tired," Braxton's lids closed again.

"Don't fall asleep on me. I'm gonna hand you over to Tiny. He'll take you outside for some fresh air, okay?"

"Okay, Daddy." He yawned and rested his head against Hawk's shoulder. He handed his son to Tiny. "Did Banger get a hold of Doc?"

"Yeah. He's talking to him now. Doc's on his way over here."

"Good. If Braxton's breathing gets slow or his heartbeat races, get me. I need to finish up in here." Tiny lifted his chin and left the room.

"Please don't hurt me. I swear I didn't mean for any of this to happen. I won't tell anyone what happened. I just needed some extra money. I didn't know they were your kids." Garret stood against the wall, scratching his arms until they bled.

Hawk believed him: he was a junkie and Christiansen fed his habit. He felt a twinge of regret that they'd have to kill him, but they couldn't leave any witnesses. Besides, junkies were the worst. Hawk had no doubt that Garret would try and blackmail the club once he needed money for his next fix. They couldn't have a loose thread like Garret. *Junkies can never be trusted.*

Looking at Rock, he shook his head. "You know what to do," he said in a low voice.

Rock quirked his lips and pulled Garret into a choke hold. The man struggled and gasped as Rock's arm tightened. Hawk turned away and went over to Evan who had come to and was sitting on the couch, his head between his hands.

"Now I know why his wife's so horny for me," Throttle said.

Evan looked up at him. "So you're the one she keeps talking about?"

"Shut the fuck up! How much Benadryl did you give the boys?" Hawk loomed over him, and a surge of pleasure zipped through him when he saw fear in the Crazed Grinch's eyes.

"About four capfuls. I wasn't going to hurt them. I intended to call Cara and Belle and have them pick the children up. It was a stupid joke. I apologize for it."

"Yeah… it was a fuckin' stupid thing to do. The problem is I don't like jokes. What about you, Throttle? Are you a joke man?"

Throttle scrunched his face while he slowly shook his head. "Nah. I don't go in for them. Seems like no one's laughing here, ass wipe."

"I didn't hurt them. Ask them. I just had a stupid moment. I shouldn't have done it."

"I'd say giving them a shit load of Benadryl is hurting 'em. What do you think, Throttle?"

Nodding, he rocked back on his boots. "I'd have to agree with you, Hawk. I'm fuckin' pissed about it so I can only imagine how you must feel."

Evan's eyes darted from Hawk's face to Throttle's and back to Hawk's. "How can I make this up to you? I really like Cara and Belle. I can't believe I did something so stupid."

"Stop saying my wife's name or I'm gonna punch you in the throat to shut you the fuck up." Anger roared through him.

"Okay, okay." Evan tried to stand, but Throttle shoved him back.

"Doc's here." Tiny's voice broke through Hawk's fury.

"I'll be right back." As he walked out of the room, he saw Garret's body in a heap on the floor and Rock bending over it.

The frosty wind made Hawk's eyes water and he blinked several times as he walked over to Doc's car. Banger sat in the front seat and Doc was in the back.

"How the hell are they?" Hawk asked as he slid inside the Land Rover.

"Do you know how much cold medicine they took?" Doc asked.

"The fucker said four of those cups that come with the medicine."

"That's a little over one tablespoon. It's double the dose."

"Fuck!" Banger yelled as he pounded the dashboard.

"It sounds worse than it is. If they were younger or if they weighed less, it could be a real problem, but they'll be fine. They're going to sleep for about ten hours or so. Any adverse reaction to the medication would've occurred by now. When they wake up tomorrow morning, they'll be very dehydrated, so give them water. Keep them hydrated for sure. If they start acting confused, complain of stomach pain, can't go to the bathroom, or just stay groggy, call me. I don't think that'll happen, but just letting you know what's normal and what's not."

"Thanks, Doc," Hawk said, and Banger nodded. "I got some stuff to do. Take Banger and the kids back to Pinewood." He turned to Banger. "Call Cara for me and let her know Braxton's good. I'm sure she's going through hell. Tell her I'll be home as soon as I can."

"Will do. You taking care of it?"

"Yeah. I'm already halfway finished." Hawk slid out of the vehicle, went to the back and kissed Braxton's cheek, clasped his arm on Doc's shoulder, and walked back into the house. He waited until Doc drove off then he went back into the room.

"How're the children?" Evan asked.

It took all of Hawk's strength not to kill him right then and there. "I can't believe you fuckin' work for a charity for kids and you hate them. You're a goddamn psycho."

Evan smiled weakly. "It is a dichotomy, isn't it? What can I say? My wife likes a nice life, and the pay is quite good. Anyway, it was a clever cover. No one will believe that I'm the Crazed Grinch. The only thing enjoyable about this whole damn thing will be my wife's embarrassment. Brittany won't be able to hold her head up in town." He chuckled softly.

"Do you believe this motherfucker?" Throttle asked Hawk.

Hawk shook his head. "Too bad you won't be able to see her shame. I'm tired of this shit." He grabbed Evan by the collar and dragged him up.

"You need us to help?" Tiny asked. Tigger came over to them.

"Yeah. Don't make it messy," Hawk said.

Evan shook his head. "Please. Don't. I'm sorry. I know it was a huge mistake. I didn't hurt the children. I don't want—"

"Take him out of here before I slit his fuckin' throat," Hawk gritted. With Blade and Tigger following, Tiny and Rock dragged a sobbing Evan out of the room.

For the next hour, Throttle and Hawk smoked pot and talked while they waited for the brothers to return. He kept tabs on Braxton and Cara via texts to Banger. Belle and he were staying with Cara until Hawk returned home. Evan's cries bled into the night unheard by anyone but the brothers. And then it was quiet—still as a graveyard at midnight.

Hawk rose to his feet. "Time to head out." He made sure the front door was locked then he and Throttle walked through the kitchen and out the back door into the inky blackness. As he walked to the front of the house, his boots slipped on the icy ground beneath them. The wintry wind's harsh bite tore through him making the hair on his arms raise. As the brothers made their way to the SUV parked down the road, puffs of vapor rose above them, mingling with the icy air.

"Fuck it's cold," Hawk muttered.

"Were you able to get rid of the two assholes with all this fuckin' snow and ice?" Throttle asked.

"Everything's good," Rock said as he swung up into the SUV.

Hawk switched on the ignition and turned the heater to full blast. Soon they were back on the old highway. Hawk would drop off Tiny, Blade, and Tigger at the clubhouse, and then drop Rock and Throttle at their houses before he went to his home.

It was another hour until he pulled into the garage. The door flew open and Cara ran out, throwing herself into his arms. She wrapped her arms around him and buried her head in his jacket, her body trembling like a flame blown by the wind.

"Shhh, baby. Don't cry. Everything's okay." He pressed her close and guided her into the house where warmth blanketed them.

"I was so scared. I'm glad you're safe," she said between quivering gasps.

As she struggled to catch her breath, he tilted her head back and wiped the tears from her cheeks with his fingers before he brushed his lips over hers.

"Oh, Hawk," her voice hitched and she clung to him tighter.

"How's Braxton?"

"He's still sleeping but Belle and Banger said that's normal. Is it?"

"Yeah. Is he breathing okay?" She nodded. He gripped her around the shoulders. "Let's tell Belle and Banger they can take Harley and go home."

"Why would anyone do something like this to our sweet boy? Did he abuse Braxton?" The tears slipped down her face again.

"No. He just drugged him and Harley. He said it was a joke."

"What a sicko. Did you call the police?"

Hawk led her into the family room where Belle and Banger sat with Harley curled in their lap. "How's the little guy?"

"He's doing okay," Banger answered, his eyes fixed on Hawk.

"Good." Hawk lifted his chin and the president's face relaxed. Sprawled on the loveseat was Braxton with a fleece blanket tucked around him. He went over and ran his fingers over his cheek.

"Did you find out who did this?" Belle asked as she threaded her fingers through Harley's hair.

Taking Cara by the hand, he led her over to the couch and eased her down. "You'll need to sit for this one." Clearing his throat, he crossed his arms. "The fucker who endangered our boys is Evan Christiansen."

Belle and Cara looked at each other, then at Hawk. As the reality of his statement sunk in, Cara's mouth dropped and she quickly covered it with her hand while Belle stared at Hawk incredulously.

"Isn't he the guy you've been working with at Brighter Lives?" Banger asked. Belle nodded slightly, her gaze still on Hawk.

"I don't believe it," Cara whispered. "Evan? Why would he do something like that? I stupidly thought it was Dale since he was gone when the lights came back on. Lindi was freaked out about him not being there, and she had to finish giving the gifts out to the kids. I later learned that he was in the back room, drinking up a storm and making out with Evan's wife, Brittany. But I never thought Evan would do something like this. He always seemed so nice. Can you believe this, Belle?"

"No, I can't. Are you sure, Hawk?"

"Yeah. Throttle recognized him because his wife's always calling Throttle to come over."

"So Kimber was right. It was Evan's wife who was making a play for Throttle," Belle said.

"Your Mr. Fuck's been busy this holiday season. Not only was he plotting to take Braxton and Harley and pretending he gave a shit about the Toy Drive, he was also breaking into people's houses and smashing up their Christmas decorations. He's the one who paid a visit to Cherri. Jax's gonna be pissed he didn't get a chance to confront him."

"Evan's the Crazed Grinch? What the hell? How did we not pick up he was a total lunatic?" Cara glanced at Belle who sat shaking her head with her fingers touching her parted lips. "What about Garret? Was he involved at all?"

"He was Evan's stooge. You didn't tell anyone about Braxton and Harley being kidnapped, did you?" Hawk looked at Cara and then Belle. Cara shook her head.

"No," Belle whispered.

"Keep it that way." Hawk went over to the couch and sat next to Cara.

"My head's spinning. I can't believe any of this. Why did Evan do all those things? Why did he ruin people's homes like that?" Cara leaned her head on Hawk's shoulder.

"Who the fuck knows? He's a psycho," he answered, squeezing her shoulders.

"But there must've been a reason," Belle mumbled. "It's just too crazy. And to take our sons. We spent a lot of time with him. I can't believe he'd do this to us."

"Those are the worst kind of fuckers," Banger said. "They pretend to be your friend, take you into their confidence, and then do shit behind your back. You never suspect them because you think they're your friend." He ran his hand up and down her arm.

"Did he tell you why he took Braxton and Harley?" Cara asked.

"He said it was just a joke," Hawk replied.

"A *joke*? How can taking two innocent boys away from their parents and drugging them be a joke? Belle and I were beside ourselves wondering if they were hurt or killed." Her voice broke and Hawk tucked her head under his chin.

"It's okay, babe. It's over."

"What if he does this again?" Belle asked.

"He won't," Banger replied.

"How do you know that?"

"I just do." Banger grasped her hand.

"Did you call the police?" Cara asked.

"Badges and us don't mix," Banger said gruffly.

"All you two need to know is the fucker won't hurt the boys again. The rest is club business." Hawk stood up and went over to the wet bar in the corner. "I need a shot. Who else wants a drink?"

A half hour later, Hawk closed the front door and turned off the porch light. He went over to the loveseat and cradled Braxton in his arms. "I'm beat. Let's go upstairs. Braxton can sleep in our bed." He waited until Cara switched off the lights and turned on the alarm then he followed her to their room.

With Braxton cocooned between them, he lay back on the pillow and stared at the ceiling. That night was the worst one in his life. He'd done four tours of duty in Afghanistan before he joined up with the Insurgents. He'd seen his best buddy get blown to bits. Once he joined the Insurgents, he'd been shot at, gotten into fights, did a short stint in the pen, and almost lost Cara, but nothing had prepared him for the cold terror he felt when he'd found out his son was missing. Glancing over at Cara, he smiled when he saw her arm resting over Braxton as they both slept. Shaking off the covers, he shuffled over to Isa's room, picked her up from the crib, and went back to the bedroom. He placed her next to Braxton and slipped under the covers. Content that he had his family close to him, he let the tension, anger, and fear melt away and welcomed the refuge of sleep.

CHAPTER TWENTY-SEVEN

THROTTLE

A BLAST OF arctic air poured into the clubhouse as Detectives McCue and Ibuado opened the door. Throttle shifted in his chair and gestured for another shot of whiskey. The last thing he wanted to do was field questions from the fuckin' badges. He doubted they were here about Christiansen or Garret, but the little problem the Insurgents had taken care of at Bridgewater's farm was another story. Before McCue could reach him, he downed his shot, the smoky flavor and bite warming him.

"How's it going, Throttle?" McCue asked as he took out a stick of gum.

"I can't complain," he answered, his gaze fixed straight ahead.

"It's like the damn North Pole out there." McCue moved into Throttle's field of vision.

"You didn't come here to give me a fuckin' weather report."

Ibuado chuckled. "No, we didn't. We have some questions we wanted to ask you and the other club members."

"The women as well," added McCue.

"I don't know anything you'd want to know, so you're wasting your time," Throttle replied as Hog placed another shot on the table and ambled away.

"That's the thing with people. They never think they know anything, but when they start thinking about it, they actually know a whole lot of things. Where were you last Tuesday night?"

Throttle picked up his glass, sipped slowly then put it back down on the table. Stretching his legs in front of him, he looked pointedly at the detective. "I was home with my woman."

"You weren't at Chad Bridgewater's place?" McCue's jaw moved incessantly.

"No reason to be there. Chad and me aren't close."

"What about the other guys around here?" Ibuado asked.

"Don't know, but if I had to guess, everyone was where they were supposed to be."

"What the hell does that mean?" Ibuado said.

"Hitched brothers were with their old ladies and single ones were enjoying themselves at the club with the club women. Just an ordinary night."

"We need to speak with the club women. How many you got living here?" McCue took out another stick of gum.

Throttle held the detective's gaze for several seconds and the tension between them hissed. "Six."

McCue shoved the stick of gum into his mouth. "We need to speak to them. Get them."

Anger bristled inside him. "They're resting."

"You guys wear them out?" The detective's lip curled.

"The brothers leave them satisfied."

"McCue, what the hell are you doing here?" Banger's voice broke through the tension.

"Just asking Throttle if we can talk to the club girls."

"Why do you wanna talk to them?" Banger turned to the bar. "Two shots over here."

McCue and Ibuado shook their heads. "We're on duty, but thanks," said Ibuado.

"Don't sweat it. The shots aren't for you." He took the two glasses from Hog and gave one to Throttle. After downing it, he put the glass on the table. "You didn't answer me."

"We're the ones asking the questions," Ibuado replied.

"They're not available. We're busy around here." Banger pointed to the door. "You can let yourselves out."

"Where were you last Tuesday night?" McCue asked.

Banger scratched his head. "Tuesday," he muttered under his breath. "I was with my old lady and kids."

"You weren't at Chad Bridgewater's farm?" Banger slowly shook his head. "Are you sure about that?" McCue took a tissue out of his pocket and spit his gum in it.

"Yeah, I'm sure. I have nothing with Chad. I haven't seen him in a long time. Why you asking?"

"Didn't you threaten him to stop selling drugs in the county a couple of years ago?"

Banger laughed and Throttle joined in. "We don't threaten. We ask nicely."

"That's right," Throttle added.

Ibuado leaned against the table. "What happens if someone doesn't listen when you ask nicely?"

"Then we keep asking nicely." Throttle shifted in his chair. "We got shit to do around here. You guys done?"

"Hardly," Ibuado answered.

Banger cleared his throat. "I don't know what more to tell you. I haven't seen Chad in over a year. Have you seen him around town, Throttle?" Throttle shook his head.

"He was killed late last Tuesday along with Beau Larker, Randy Lyon, and Calvin Schwind. His farmhouse was set on fire and several large metal containers were destroyed. Do you know anything about that?"

Banger scratched his beard. "Fuck. Chad must've really pissed someone off."

"His great-granddaughter was spending the night at the farmhouse." McCue narrowed his eyes.

"Damn. That's terrible," Throttle said.

"She was taken away before Bridgewater was murdered. She said a man with a leather jacket took her away. He blindfolded her."

242

"And you think it was one of us because we wear leather jackets? I don't think we're the only ones in Pinewood Springs wearing them." Banger laughed.

"A woman dropped her off early in the morning at her parents' house." McCue took out another stick of gum.

"So that's why you wanna bug our club women? You think one of them dropped her off? What the fuck are you smoking? Our club women are busy early in the morning. Every morning." Throttle sniggered and bumped his arm against Banger who chuckled.

"Check with my old lady and Throttle's. Neither of us was near Chad's place."

Ibuado flipped through his notebook. "We already did. We checked with all of the members' wives and girlfriends. They corroborate what you're saying."

"There you have it. Like I said, we're busy." Banger turned away and walked toward the hallway leading to his office.

Throttle stood up. "I got shit to do." He walked away and went over to the bar where Wheelie and Tiny sat and took the stool next to them, his back to the detectives. When the cold blast of air coiled around him, he knew they'd left.

"What did the fuckin' badges want?" Wheelie asked.

"Wanted to find out what we were doin' on Tuesday night. Seems like some people torched and killed Chad Bridgewater and his loser cohorts." The three men guffawed.

"Feel like a pool game?" Tiny asked.

"Sure. I got time. Kimber's coming home late tonight." Throttle picked up his glass of whiskey and sauntered over to the pool table with Tiny and Wheelie following close behind. Taking out three joints, he handed one to each of them and they lit up, enjoying the weed they stole from Chad's place the week before.

Grabbing a pool cue, he walked to the table, bent down low, and took the first shot.

THROTTLE PUT THE ribs he'd picked up at Big Rocky's into the oven. Kimber would be home soon and he wanted to surprise her with dinner. He'd planned on asking her to marry him after the charity event a couple of nights before, but with the snatching of Braxton and Harley, all focus was on getting the boys and making the dirtbags pay.

He wrapped the twice baked potatoes in a second layer of aluminum foil and popped them in the lower oven. The chef at the restaurant prepared a Caesar salad kit for him, and he placed it in the refrigerator. Glancing around, he made sure everything was neat and tidy. Kimber was obsessed with keeping things in order and could get easily distracted if she saw something out of place. That night, he wanted her focused totally on them.

The jiggle of the doorknob signaled she was home. He leaned against the kitchen island waiting for her to come in. When he saw her, she smiled and he swept her into his arms.

"You're so cold," he murmured, rubbing his face against hers.

"It's fucking cold out there. And I stepped in a puddle of water that one of the new idiots we have working at the shop made with his hose. My feet are soaked."

"I can warm you up real good, babe."

"I know you can, but I don't feel that sexy in my coveralls. I need to take a warm shower." She pulled away and cocked her head. "I smell barbecue sauce."

"I picked up dinner from Big Rocky's."

Her eyes lit up. "Really? You've never done that before. What a great idea." She gave him a quick peck on the cheek and ambled away.

The scent of roses and patchouli wound around him as he stared at the television screen, and a slow smile spread across his face.

"Feel better?" he asked as she sank down next to him on the couch.

"Much. My feet are still ice though. I should've put on a thicker pair of socks."

He rose. "I'll be right back. You want to eat?"

"Yeah. I'm starving and ribs sound so good right now."

He went into the kitchen and turned on the ovens and then headed to the bedroom. Coming back with a pair of pink fuzzy socks, he went over to the couch and sat down. Tugging her legs toward him, he placed them in his lap and took off her thin socks. He blew on his hands and rubbed them over her cold feet. He glanced up. Her eyes had that smoky, languid look sending warm ripples of desire through his body, thinning the air in his lungs.

The sound of her shallow breathing, the soft rose in her cheeks, and the parting of her full lips filled him with a fierce longing. "Kimber," he whispered as he bent toward her, gripping her shoulders, pulling her into him, pressing himself into her. His hungry mouth melded into hers, the tip of his tongue brushing against the seam in her lips, and she opened to let him in, moaning with each urgent thrust. Desire licked through him as she slipped her arm around his neck, melding her body to his. Groaning low in his throat, he circled his arms around her, fusing them even closer, easing her down on her back, still kissing.

"Throttle," she smothered against his lips as his hands moved under her fleece top.

"You consume my heart and my thoughts. You fuckin' rock and I love you so much."

"I adore you. You're my soul mate, and you know when to say it's okay and when to just listen to me when I just need an ear. I'm so connected to you."

"Our bond is like steel, babe." He crushed his mouth against hers, swallowing her words, loving the small whimpers coming from her.

An ear-splitting sound sliced through their sensuous haze, and Throttle leapt up, his body tense and ready to fight. He glanced at the door and looked down at Kimber who was laughing her ass off.

"What's so funny?" he asked.

"It's the timer on the oven. You must've set it when you turned it on to warm up dinner."

Jerking his head toward the kitchen, he saw the green light flashing intermittently, and he joined in laughing. "Fuck. I thought someone was messing with me. That's an annoying sound, and it's so goddamn loud." He shuffled over to the oven and turned it off.

After dinner, they sat on the couch, him holding her close, the fire dancing in the fireplace, and the soft strains of Queensryche's "Silent Lucidity" filling the room. Throttle traced his fingers on her arm, the side of her neck, and her throat. "I love your skin."

"Tonight's wonderful. I was so pissed and cranky about the fucking cold and stepping in the puddle of water, that all I wanted to do when I got home was to change, have a bowl of soup, and veg on the couch. You lifted my shitty mood. Thanks." She tipped her head back and smiled at him.

He swept his lips across hers. "I bet I can make it even better."

She lightly ran her fingers over his cheek. "I know you can."

Capturing her hand, he brought it to his lips and kissed each finger. "I'm not talking about that right now, but it's definitely gonna happen later. I picked something up for you." Stretching, he glided his hands into his pocket and pulled out a black velvet box. Wide-eyed, she darted her gaze from the box to his face and back to the box. "Open it." He could see her hand tremble as she took the box from him.

"What is it?"

He chuckled. "Open it up and find out." She slowly opened it and stared at the ring. "Do you like it?"

"Yeah. It's beautiful. I love black diamonds. Are these pink tourmalines?"

"Sapphires."

She whistled softly. "This must've cost you some bucks."

"You're worth it. I want us to get married. Do you wanna marry me?"

A tear spilled down from her brimming eyes and she wiped it away quickly. Without speaking, she bobbed her head.

"You okay?"

Wiping her eyes, she nodded again.

"Let me put it on your finger." He slipped the ring on her finger. "It looks good on your hand." Sniffling, she held her hand out and moved it around, the stones catching the light.

"You okay if I hug you?"

Another nod.

He pulled her close and she buried her head in the crook of his neck, her body shaking, his skin damp with her tears. "Are those happy tears, babe?" With women, he couldn't be too sure.

"Yeah." She sniffled. "I'm so damn happy I don't know what to say except I love you and want to be with you forever," she sputtered.

He raked his fingers through her hair. "That's cool 'cause I want to spend the rest of my life with you. Have a few kids too."

Laughing, Kimber pulled back a little. "I just got engaged. Don't have me barefoot and pregnant too soon." The glow from the fireplace lit up her face and made her blue eyes sparkle.

Heat stirred within him as his gaze traveled over her, taking in every bit of her. She'd never been so vulnerable and sexy as she was at that moment, and he loved her for trusting him with her forever.

"I just love this ring. I can't believe you picked it out by yourself. Did Cara or Belle help you out?"

Throttle poked her playfully. "What? You don't think I have good taste?"

"I know you do. You chose me." She winked at him.

"I'm gonna smack your ass for that. And no one helped me pick out the ring. I knew it was perfect for you the minute I saw it. Now give me your lips."

Kimber pressed into him and he devoured her mouth with his. That night he'd give it to her rough and nasty, the way he knew she loved it. Warmth spread through him. *I'm getting married. Fuck.* He never figured he'd be hitched, but since Kimber had come into his life, he couldn't picture it any other way.

And that suited him just fine.

CHAPTER TWENTY-EIGHT

WHEELIE

WHEELIE STOOD IN the corner of the living room at Hawk and Cara's house, sipping a glass of whiskey while he watched Sofia talk with Cherri. Tigger's arm snaked around her waist and the glow from the colored lights around the Christmas tree brightened her pale skin. Dressed in a red dress that hugged her body just right, Wheelie thought she'd never looked prettier as she did at that moment. Every few minutes, she'd glance sideways at him, but she never made eye contact. She couldn't.

"Dude, you're fuckin' obvious," Throttle said as he passed by him.

Wheelie took another drink from his glass and kept staring at the woman who'd been the main feature in his thoughts for the past few weeks. A couple of times he saw Banger's brows furrow when he looked his way, but Wheelie didn't give a shit. He just couldn't keep his eyes off Sofia, she looked like an angel.

"Do you want something to eat or are you gonna stand in the corner sulking like a goddamn teenager?" Throttle asked.

"I'll get something. Did Kimber like the ring?"

A grin cracked over Throttle's face. "She fuckin' loved it."

"When's the wedding?"

"She wants to have a summer one so we decided on next June. Remember Brenda from Ruthie's?"

"Brenda? Who's she?"

"The waitress with the big tits."

"The one Tigger's always got a hard-on for?"

"Yeah. Anyway, Rags and me were in there a few times last week and each time we were there she came over to the table and asked about you. She's got a thing for you, dude. You need to go over there and sit at her station."

"She's not my type."

Throttle exhaled loudly. "You gotta move on. Sofia's taken. You haven't been with the club girls for the last few weeks. I know what you're feeling, but she's a brother's old lady. You—"

"Fuck, man. Will you leave it alone? I know the damn score." He pushed away from the wall and walked into the kitchen.

"Do you want a plate?" Kimber asked as she handed him one.

"Thanks. Nice ring."

Kimber's face shone. "I think so too. I love it."

"You guys know how to make our hearts soar," Addie said as she placed two deviled eggs on her plate.

"Do you want me to fix you a plate?" Cara asked, placing a pot of tomato sauce down on the counter.

"Thanks, but I'm good." Wheelie placed some food on his dish, his eyes reverting back to Sofia. This time she was in front of him, and their gazes locked. Tigger was talking with Jax, and for the space of a held breath, it was only them, a heated longing in her green eyes.

"You need me to refresh your glass?" Hawk's deep voice broke their connection.

Wheelie shook his head. "I'm good." The ice clinked as he brought the amber-colored drink to his lips.

"I'll take some more," Tigger said, holding out his glass. He turned to Wheelie, his gaze unfocused. "I heard Brenda's got the hots for you. What a lucky sonofabitch. She's totally stacked."

Wheelie glanced at Sofia's taut face. Licks of anger rode up his spine and he clenched his fists. *If the fucker doesn't shut up, I'm gonna deck him.*

"That's not a very nice thing to say with your wife standing right next to you. Show her some respect," Cara said, her hands on her hip.

Redness mottled Tigger's face. "You show me respect. You don't tell a brother shit." Sofia stepped away, fear etched on her face.

"You've had too much to drink, so I'll forget I heard what you said to my wife," Hawk said. "This is a get-together for the brothers and their old ladies. I'm not gonna tolerate any disrespect in my house. What you said was shitty to Sofia. Cara called you on it before I had a chance to."

Tigger stared intently at Hawk then at Cara. Sofia stood stiffly off to the side. From the way she watched the situation, Wheelie knew she didn't want it to escalate because she'd feel the brunt of Tigger's anger and frustration later on when they were alone.

"This is a damn party. Crank up the music," Jax said, his hand clasping onto Tigger's shoulder.

Tigger turned to Wheelie. "Where's your old lady?"

That's it. Before Wheelie could react, Banger said, "Some of the single brothers are here 'cause they're friends with Hawk. I'd like some more of your spiked eggnog, little lady." He handed his glass to Cara.

"I wanna show you some pictures of the new Harley I'm thinking of buying," Jax said to Tigger.

The mention of a Harley lessened the strain between Tigger and Wheelie. He pulled his focus away from him and smiled at Jax. "When you buying it? I'm gearing up to get a new one." He followed Jax to the study.

"Me too. Mine's been acting up too much. Kimber suggested I look into getting a new one," Axe said as he joined them.

After Tigger left, the tension lifted, and Wheelie went over to Cherri and Sofia.

"I just don't want him to be pissed when he leaves tonight." Sofia's soft voice fell on his ears.

"Jax will get him talking about motorcycles, and you know how these guys love their Harleys," Cherri replied.

Sofia chuckled. "Yeah. That should put him in a good mood. He's been talking about getting another one for quite a while."

"Harleys always put a biker in a good mood," Wheelie said, injecting himself into their conversation. Sofia glanced at him and smiled, her eyes sparkling. "How've you been?" he asked softly.

"Good. What about you?" She brought her drink to her lips.

"Not bad. I'm thinking of starting a business."

"That's cool. What kind?"

The scent of violet swirled around him. "Car wash and detailing. Diesel and I are going into business. I'll start it up and he'll join me when he gets out of the pen. You remember him, right?"

"Yeah. He's been doing time since Tigger and Skeet got out. Is he going to get paroled?"

"Nah. His sentence is finishing up. Should be out in about eight months or so. Remember the car wash on Alameda Street?"

"Of course. I took my car there a lot. It's been closed for a while."

"The landlord's giving me a sweet deal on the lease. All the stuff is still in good working condition. Old man Jenkins just split and left everything behind." He chuckled. "I guess he wanted to get away from his wife real bad."

Sofia giggled. "I can't say that I blame him. Rogina's a real bitch. Each time I went into the car wash, she'd give me the evil eye and was so rude to me."

"That's because you're pretty. She was jealous the old man would hit on you."

A soft pinkish-red blush painted her cheeks. "Thanks. You always say real nice things to me."

He brushed his fingers across her hand. "I mean everything I say."

"Did Jenkins take off with another woman?" Cherri asked.

Wheelie had forgotten Cherri was there. "Uh… no one knows for sure, but the rumor is he did. Him leaving just made Rogina meaner. She didn't want any of the car wash's equipment which is good for me and Diesel. I'm gonna meet with the landlord after the first of the year."

"I hope it all turns out," Cherri said.

"I know you'll do great." Sofia squeezed two of his fingers then quickly moved her hand away.

Desire ribboned through him as his cock stirred. "I need to talk to you. Meet me in the laundry room. It's just for a few minutes," he said in a low voice. Her eyes flicked to the hallway. "Don't worry. He's still in the study with Jax and Axe. They'll be there for another hour looking at Harleys. I'll go first and wait for you." When she nodded slightly, he smiled and walked away.

What the fuck are you doing? He leaned against the washing machine feeling like a damn teenager who was afraid of being caught by his dad. In his case, it was Banger. The president had just given him a talking to the day before, and here he was, desire and excitement weaving through him as he waited for Sofia. *Fuck! This is so damn lame.* But the truth was that he wanted to feel her soft lips against his one last time. As crazy as he was about her, she was a brother's wife, and until she changed that, she was off-limits. The brotherhood had always come first in his life—in all his brothers' lives. He couldn't betray another member, and he didn't want to throw away the brotherhood for an affair.

The door opened slowly and then Sofia came in, closing it behind her. She smiled and walked toward him.

"I can't stay very long. I don't want Tigger to come looking for me." She brushed the stray hairs off her face. "I keep thinking about that night you came over when Tigger was out of town."

He cocked his head. "Me too." He reached out and stroked her cheek with his fingertips. "You look amazing tonight."

She looked down at the ground, her face turning soft shades of pink. "Thanks." She clasped and twisted her hands as if washing them under an invisible faucet.

"You don't need to be nervous around me." He stepped forward and placed his hands on hers, stopping their constant motion. Sofia glanced up at him. "I got something for you." He reached inside his cut and pulled out a silver box.

Staring at it, she brought her fingers to her collarbone. "I didn't get you a Christmas present."

He put the box in the palm of her hand. "You don't have to."

As she opened the lid, her fingers shook and he wanted to pull her into his arms and press her close to him, making her feel safe and cherished, but he just stood there watching as she stared at the sterling silver necklace.

"It's so beautiful," she murmured as her finger brushed over the open ring pendant. Taking it out of the box, she held it up to the light. "'You've got a friend in me,'" she read. She clasped it in her hand.

"Do you like it?"

"Yes," she whispered. "It's the most beautiful thing I've ever received." Wetness dampened her cheeks.

"If you ever need me, I'm here for you. Don't ever hesitate to call me. You got that?" She bobbed her head. "Just remember that you're a special woman, and no one can take that away from you."

"Oh, Wheelie." She wrapped her arms around him, squeezing him tightly, and he rubbed his hands up and down her back, inhaling her sweet scent and loving the way her body molded into his. She tipped her head back and he bent down and traced the soft fullness of her lips with the tip of his tongue, then his lips pressed against hers and gently covered her mouth. They stood kissing, holding each other as though it was the end of the world. After a few minutes, Sofia pulled away. He swept a callused thumb over her lips. They were warm and wet from the kiss.

"Where's Sofia?" Tigger's voice shattered their moment. Sofia jumped away from Wheelie as though he'd caught on fire.

"She's in the bathroom," Cherri said.

Sofia looked at the closed door then back at him. "I've gotta go. How does my lipstick look?"

Quirking his lips, he shook his head. "You need to reapply it." He watched as she rummaged through her purse, took out a tube of shiny red, and ran the wand over her lips.

"I'll have to hide the necklace," she said, shoving it into her purse.

"I figured as much."

She gave him back the silver box. "I love it. I really do."

"I'm glad. When you decide what you want to do about Tigger, let me know."

"What do you mean? It sounds like we won't see each other again."

"We'll see each other at the club and at family functions."

Sadness crept into her eyes and he hated that he was responsible for it.

"We won't see each other alone?"

He shook his head. "You know we can't. I'm an Insurgent. The club's my life. It's the blood in my veins. I can't betray a brother. And if I see you alone again, I'm not gonna stop at a kiss. You're too tempting. We'll end up doing something we'll both regret." He scrubbed his face with his fist. "We can't see each other as long as you're still with him. And why the hell are you with him after everything he's done to you?"

"He's been real nice lately. Last week he made me ribs. He's trying. And I understand about the brotherhood. I don't want to be responsible for getting you in trouble with Banger or the others. I'd never forgive myself." She brushed her hair back behind her shoulders. "I have to give my marriage a chance. Tigger's really trying."

"That's good. You better go back to the party. Just remember I'm here if you ever need me to help you out." She came over and kissed him on the cheek and then she was gone.

For a long while he listened to the gaiety of his brothers and their old ladies as a surge of anger, sadness, and emptiness raged inside him. Sofia had made her decision. Had he really expected her to denounce her husband and run gleefully into his arms? He shook his head. Life was a series of disappointments so one more wasn't going to break him.

Exhaling a breath he wasn't aware he'd been holding, he switched off the lights and went back to the party.

CHAPTER TWENTY-NINE

CARA

*P*OOR *WHEELIE. HE has it bad for Sofia. I wish she'd do the right thing and kick Tigger's ass out and hook up with Wheelie. She looks miserable except when she looks at him. I bet they were together. I hope they were. I know Hawk will be pissed if he even knows what I'm thinking, but I've got to talk to her and set her straight. She has to dump her asshole. Pronto.*

"Babe, can you hand me the bottle of Jack in the cupboard by the sink?" Hawk broke through her thoughts.

"Sure." She bent down and took out the bottle of whiskey and handed it to him.

"I tried making your pizzelles and they came out too thick and tough. Yours are like clouds of goodness. What did I do wrong?" Clotille said as she picked up one of the cookies and nibbled on it.

"Pour the batter until it is half full in the pizzelle maker. It took me a long time to master it. My grandmother's pizzelles were the best. Mine are getting there, but they're still not like hers even though I use her recipe."

"I think they're delicious. Maybe you can come over one day after the holidays and I'll make them while you're there so you can guide me."

"That sounds good." Cara stacked more cookies on the platter. "How's everything going with Andrew?"

"Better. We've got a ways to go, but he hasn't skipped any more school since he began therapy, and he and Rock seem to interact better. They seem to listen before arguing. Believe me... that's a huge step."

"I'm glad. He doesn't scowl as much." Cara poured some sweet dessert wine into glasses. "I love dunking these in wine." She picked up an almond-studded biscotti and dipped it into her wine glass.

"I'll have to try that. And who are you talking about? Andrew or Rock? Both of them scowl." Clotille laughed and picked up one of the crunchy cookies and dipped it into her glass.

"Good point. I think one of the prerequisites of becoming an Insurgent is that you have to scowl." She laughed. "I was talking about Andrew. He seems less brooding."

"He is. He's a good boy. Hard-headed and macho like his dad, but he'll grow up to be a wonderful man. Just like his father." She glanced at Rock and smiled warmly when he looked back at her.

"So did Evan just ditch his wife?" Baylee asked as she came over to the dessert table.

"That's what they're saying. Joseph told me that after that night when he took Harley and Braxton, he just disappeared," Addie said.

"And Torey told me they think he was behind the break-in and fire at the Brighter Lives building. She said they can't prove anything, but the whole thing just seems really strange." Cherri picked up a brownie bite and popped it into her mouth. She handed a sugar cookie to Paisley.

"The really weird thing is that there hasn't been anything in the paper about any homes being broken into by the Crazed Grinch. I mean, you'd think the past few days would be prime time for the whack job. It makes you wonder if Evan was involved in it. I just can't believe he was the one who snatched your kids. Why the hell did he do it?" Baylee asked, pouring carbonated water into her glass.

"He's a fuckin' psycho. It's a good thing he left town. Throttle was ready to go over and beat his ass," Kimber said.

Cara watched the brothers as the ladies spoke and they didn't comment or offer any funny quips, they just hunched together, their faces serious, their jaws locked. In that instant, she knew Evan would never snatch another child.

As the night grew darker, Addie picked up a yawning Hope and hugged her close. "We better head out," she said to Cara. "This one's dead tired. She'll be up early tomorrow to see what Santa brought her, won't you, sweetie." Hope nodded and rested her head in the crook of Addie's neck.

"We should go too. James has overloaded on sugar and he needs to calm down before he goes to bed. As always, it was a wonderful Christmas Eve, Cara," Clotille said.

Banger came over with a sleeping Harley in his arms. "It's time we go, woman." Belle nodded and slid off the stool.

Emily came over and held out her hands. "I can take Harley." Banger handed him over to her and went over to Ethan.

"How're things going, Emily?" Addie asked.

"Good. I got a job at the pet store. I love working with the animals."

"And she's enrolled to take a few classes at Pinewood Springs Community College," Belle added, her face beaming.

"I went there. I really liked it. They have some good profs," Kimber added.

"I'm excited but scared. I'll be working fulltime so I can only take a few classes. I'll see how it goes."

"You'll do great," Kylie said as she leaned over and snatched a lemon bar. "It's so much fun to learn new things. What're you interested in?"

"Animals. I'd love to be a veterinarian. Maybe a vet tech to start. You know… small steps." Harley stirred in her arms. "Do you want to go out to lunch next week? I'd love to get some pointers from you about college."

Kylie bobbed her head. "Totally. What about next Monday?"

"Sounds good. Let's go somewhere the club doesn't own." Emily smiled.

"Getting tired of barbecue and burgers?" Kylie laughed. "No problem. I'll Facebook you and we can decide where we want to go." She jumped when Jerry came up behind her.

"Ready to go, baby?" he asked and she nodded.

Cara loved watching Jerry and Kylie together; the young couple had fought hard for their love and relationship. "Are you guys going over to

Banger's for Christmas?"

"Yes. Dad wanted us to spend the night, but we want to open one gift tonight."

"I can't wait for you to open mine," Jerry replied, and the women chortled. "Let's get going."

"How're you doing, babe?" Hawk asked as he curled his arms around her waist and nuzzled her neck. "You're so soft."

"I'm pretty beat. Did you put Isa to bed?"

"I did that an hour ago. She was sleeping while I changed her. She was so damn tired." He laughed then kissed her neck. "I can't wait to put you to bed."

She placed her hands on his. "Do you want me to be naughty or nice?"

"Fuckin' filthy," he whispered as his teeth grazed her ear.

Shivers tingled through her. His presence, his scent, his touch made her feel like she was going to melt. Everything about him ignited deep feelings of love and lust inside her.

"It was a lovely party. We had a good time as always. Thank you," Baylee said as Axe helped her with her coat.

"Dude," Axe said to Hawk, bumping fists with him.

"I'm so glad you and Tigger could make it," Cara said to Sofia, hugging her warmly. "We're planning a birthday lunch for Belle in two weeks. You have to come."

Sofia glanced at Tigger who narrowed his eyes. "She'll let you know. She's got a lot of things to do in the house."

"She's an old lady and needs to be at my woman's birthday lunch," Banger said. He looked at Cara. "Sofia will be there."

Tigger nodded. "Yeah. Of course. I thought you meant tomorrow."

What an idiot. Kudos Banger. "I'll put you down. I can pick you up or Cherri can if you don't want to drive." *The asshole doesn't let her drive anywhere without him. Drop his ass, Sofia!*

Sofia looked at Tigger. "Thanks, but my husband will take me."

When Tigger nodded his approval at her, Cara wanted to kick him in the balls in the worst way.

"We had fun. Merry Christmas," Sofia said. Tigger walked out and Sofia followed, but for a split second, she paused, looked over her shoulder, and threw a warm smile at Wheelie. "Merry Christmas," she mouthed, and then she took Tigger's hand and walked down the porch steps.

Cara watched Wheelie from her peripheral vision as he stared out the front door, watching Sofia as she slid into the car and drove away into the snowy darkness. He looked like he'd just lost his best friend, and her heart went out to him.

"Do you want to come with us tomorrow to my aunt Teresa's house?" she asked.

Surprise flashed across his face. "Thanks, but I'm going to the club and hang out with the brothers. The club women will make dinner. Have you seen Rags? We drove over together. He's crashing at my place tonight."

Cara clapped her hands. "I'm so glad you won't be alone tonight." Wheelie gave her a funny look and ambled toward the kitchen.

"What the hell was that all about?" Hawk asked, closing the front door.

"What do you mean?" Cara tried to brush past him, but he grabbed her arm.

"Cara, stop thinking what I know is in your mind. Leave Wheelie alone. Leave Sofia alone. And definitely leave Tigger alone. Don't get involved with any of it."

"I don't know what you're talking about. I just asked one of your single friends if he wanted to share Christmas with us. I wouldn't call that getting involved. I'd call it being nice and thoughtful."

"Don't act so innocent. Remember how you were obsessed with hooking Banger up?"

"And it worked. He and Belle are very happy. What's your point?"

Hawk scrubbed his face. "Just stay out of it. Anyway, Tigger's a brother and if Wheelie crosses the line, he's out of the Insurgents. I doubt he'd give up the brotherhood. Loyalty runs deep for us."

"I know. Stop getting all bent out of shape." Cara turned away and plastered on a huge smile. "Rags, Wheelie, I'm going to pack up some food for you." She scurried into the kitchen, giggling softly as she pictured Hawk's scowling face.

As she closed the front door, she heard Hawk's heavy footsteps on the stairway. She looked over and saw him carrying a sleepy Braxton and a deep, warm love spread through her. After switching off all the lights and setting the alarm, she went upstairs to their bedroom. She grabbed the red teddy with all the ribbons and cut-outs that Hawk had given her for Valentine's Day a couple of years before and went into the bathroom.

When he came into the bedroom, he closed the door and looked intensely at her, the glow from the fire shining on them. He glanced at the lampshades covered in red scarves and slowly unbuttoned his shirt. She held the sheet under her chin and watched him, mesmerized by the way his hard muscles flexed with every move. Looking at his deep V, she licked her lips, knowing where it led. Still holding her gaze, he kicked off his boots and then unzipped his jeans. Stepping out of them, he paused and her eyes fixed on the pulsing hard bulge in his boxers. With deliberate movements, he tugged them down, his erection springing out, pointing at her.

"Come over here," he rasped.

"What if I don't?" she breathed.

"I'll come and get you, and I won't be gentle."

A long pulsing quiver ran through her. "Then come and get me."

Hunger shone in his eyes as he walked slowly to her, and each step made her shiver in anticipation. When he reached her, he tangled his fist in her hair, yanking her head back. He dipped his head and took her mouth in a deep, wet, claiming kiss. The sheet fell away as she circled her arms around his neck, drawing him closer. All thoughts slipped from her mind and there was only sensation, sizzling sensation. Steamy, like the sweltering heat of July. They were kissing fast, hard, deep, and frantic. Cara put her hand on Hawk's face, loving the roughness of his day-old shave. He rubbed his face against hers—sweeping the cheeks, the nose, nuzzling the ear, finishing with feathery kisses on the forehead. Her passion ignited and gripped her.

"You're so sexy. I'm on fire, honey," she whispered, pressing even closer to him.

He pushed back and his gaze devoured her. "Fuck, you look tempting." He reached out and took the satin ribbon tied over her tit between his fingers. "I can't wait to unwrap you, babe," he leaned in again and kissed her hard, gliding his hand under her ass and squeezing it.

His scorching tongue heated the skin on her throat, the swell of her breasts, dipping down into her cleavage before he took the end of one of the ribbons between his teeth and pulled it, revealing a hard rosy bud.

Desire burned in his eyes. "Luscious." He untied the other ribbon, revealing the other bud. He rolled her pink nipples, and she squirmed. "So fuckin' delicious," he said hoarsely. Bending his head down, he licked her hard nipples while he squeezing her tits.

She arched her back and let out a moan. "That feels so good, honey," she said in a soft voice as she pulled the tie out of his hair. Spilling down over his shoulders, the ends of his hair tickled her skin.

Slowly, his hand inched down to the last ribbon on her teddy. She held her breath as he ran his fingers over the satin fabric, touching her inner thighs, and running his fingers back over the ribbon. Her sex throbbed like crazy and she pivoted her hips so she could rub against his hand. He chuckled, his hot breath ghosting over her breasts, and then he pulled one of her reddened nipples into his mouth.

He kept teasing her until she thought she'd go mad, and, at last, he tugged at the ribbon, and she spread her legs wide. Hawk's fingers curled between her legs, slipping in. She bucked and groaned. Still feasting on her tits, he pushed in and out of her vigorously until she cried out, her voice bouncing off the walls, her body blasting off into a cloud of euphoria.

"Hawk," she murmured as pleasure coated every inch of her.

He swept his tongue over her clit and she jumped at the touch. Dragging his tongue up over her, he met her lips and kissed her deeply. "Did you like that, babe?"

"It was so good. I can't believe how fast I came." She pulled him down next to her and placed her head on his shoulder. Enveloped in his arms, happiness, desire, and love washed over her like a wave of warmth. Every inch of her was saturated with love and pleasure. Hawk was the anchor in her life, he'd shown her how to love and trust again, and he'd given her two beautiful children. He was her everything and she was his. They were connected together in a way she'd never thought would've been possible with a man.

She glided her hand down his smooth chest and chuckled when she grasped his erection. "I need to do something about this."

"Yeah," he rasped.

"Would you like to feel my tongue around your dick before you shove it into my warm mouth?"

"Fuck, babe." He pinched her nipple.

"Let's get on the floor. There's a whole lot more I want you to do to me."

"Damn, woman." Hawk grasped her arms and jerked her on top of him, his hand pulling her hair. He kissed her roughly. "I love you, babe."

"Me too. Merry Christmas. We have about six hours until Braxton rushes downstairs to see what Santa brought him."

"Let's make every minute count."

She rolled off him and he helped her up. Dropping to her knees, she wrapped her hand around his hard dick and looked up at him. With his eyes locked on hers, she moved her mouth closer to him.

That night she'd be his sexy wildcat, his wicked vixen, and the following day, she'd be the proper wife and mother at Christmas dinner. Tenderness spread through her as she saw desire and love shining in his eyes. *I'll love him until I die.*

She opened her mouth and slowly took her husband inside.

Make sure you sign up for my newsletter so you can keep up with my new releases, special sales, free short stories, and other treats only available to newsletter readers. When you sign up, you will receive a FREE hot and steamy novella. Sign up at: http://eepurl.com/bACCL1.

Notes from Chiah

As always, I have a team behind me making sure I shine and continue on my writing journey. It is their support, encouragement, and dedication that pushes me further in my writing journey. And then, it is my wonderful readers who have supported me, laughed, cried, and understood how these outlaw men live and love in their dark and gritty world. Without you—the readers—an author's words are just letters on a page. The emotions you take away from the words breathe life into the story.

Thank you to my amazing Personal Assistant Natalie Weston. I don't know what I'd do without you. I value your suggestions and opinions, and my world is so much saner with you in it. You make sure my world flows more smoothly, and you're always willing to jump in and help me. I appreciate the time you took in reading and offering suggestions with the book and the cover. And a big thank you for watching out for me when I'm in writer mode and live life with blinders on. I'm thrilled you are on my team!

Thank you to my editor, Kristin, for all your insightful edits and excitement with *Outlaw Xmas*. I truly value your editorial eyes and suggestions as well as the time you spend. Thanks also for your patience with me as I tried to meet all the deadlines. You're the best!

Thank you to my wonderful beta readers, Natalie, Jeni, and Barbara. Your enthusiasm and suggestions for *Outlaw Xmas* were spot on and helped me to put out a stronger, cleaner novel.

Thank you to the bloggers for your support in reading my book, sharing it, reviewing it, and getting my name out there. I so appreciate all your efforts. You all are so invaluable. I hope you know that. Without you, the indie author would be lost. And thank you to the bloggers who have been with me from my very first book, "Hawk's Property: Insurgents Motorcycle Club." Your continued support for my books is beyond awesome!

Thank you ARC readers you have helped make all my books so much stronger. I appreciate the effort and time you put in to reading, reviewing, and getting the word out about the books. I don't know what I'd do without you. I feel so lucky to have you behind me.

Thank you to my Street Team. Thanks for your input, your support, and your hard work. I appreciate you more than you know. A HUGE hug to all of you!

Thank you to Carrie from Cheeky Covers. You are amazing! I can always count on you. You are the calm to my storm. You totally rock, and I love your artistic vision.

Thank you to my proofreader, Ellie, whose last set of eyes before the last once over I do, is invaluable.

Thank you to Ena and Amanda with Enticing Journeys Promotions who have helped garner attention for and visibility to my books. Couldn't do it without you! Also a big thank you to Book Club Gone Wrong Blog.

Thank you to Paul Salvette of BB Books for the awesome job he does in formatting my books. You always come through for me, and your work is stellar. You make it so much easier for me to be an indie writer. Glad you're part of my team.

Thank you to the readers who continue to support me and read my books. Without you, none of this would be possible. I appreciate your comments and reviews on my books, and I'm dedicated to giving you the best story that I can. I'm always thrilled when you enjoy a book as much as I have in writing it. You definitely make the hours of typing on the computer and the frustrations that come with the territory of writing books so worth it.

And a special thanks to every reader who has been with me since "Hawk's Property." Your support, loyalty, and dedication to my stories touch me in so many ways. You enable me to tell my stories, and I am forever grateful to you.

You all make it possible for writers to write because without you reading the books, we wouldn't exist. Thank you, thank you! ♥

OUTLAW XMAS: Insurgents Motorcycle Club (Book 10)

Dear Readers,

Thank you for reading my book. The Insurgent men keep wanting their stories told, so I had to do a Christmas story and revisit Pinewood Springs. I have to confess that I loved getting back together with all the Insurgent men and their women. Many of them have families now, and I loved writing about each of the couples. It seems that Insurgents have more to say, so look for a few more books to come out in the coming year.

Romance makes life so much more colorful, and a rough, sexy bad boy makes life a whole lot more interesting.

If you enjoyed the book, please consider leaving a review on Amazon. I read all of them and appreciate the time taken out of busy schedules to do that.

I love hearing from my fans, so if you have any comments or questions, please email me at chiahwilder@gmail.com or visit my facebook page.

To receive a **free copy of my novella**, *Summer Heat*, and to hear of **new releases, special sales, free short stories**, and **ARC opportunities**, please sign up for my **Newsletter** at http://eepurl.com/bACCL1.

Happy Reading,

Chiah

PACO

Book 5 in the Night Rebels MC Series

Coming in February, 2018

Paco, the rugged VP of the Night Rebels MC, only stopped for some chow at the diner. He was headed back to Alina. He never intended on staying. But then he saw her sitting alone at the booth next to his. She had on too much makeup and too little clothing for the cold winter night.

Then she looked at him. Her eyes were dark like an endless stretch of midnight sky. In their inky depths, he saw sorrow and pain and threads of fierceness. They drew him in.

He, the man who never looked past one night with a woman, wanted to know about this small woman sitting across from him.

Sensing she was in trouble, he wanted to help her. He knew he should just pay his bill, hop on his Harley, and head home, but he couldn't. She grounded him, and in that one instant, he knew she'd be his. The urge to possess her consumed him.

Misty Sullivan hated the cold nights when she'd have to haul her ass from truck to truck to make enough to satisfy her boyfriend, Bobby. She used to have another name, but that was a long time ago when she was normal and life was good. She tried not to think about it anymore—it just made her life worse.

The stranger who stared at her didn't look like a trucker. He was decked out in leather and denim, and he looked at her like she was a person not a piece of ass. But life experience told her he was probably just as bad as all the other men who came into her world.

Men couldn't be trusted. They acted nice to get a woman where they wanted her, and then they turned mean and ugly.

But the stranger's piercing stare didn't frighten her, and that surprised her. A good-looking, sexy man like him could have any woman he wanted, so why was he wasting his time with her?

Then events throw them together and Misty must decide if she should trust the man who is playing havoc with her heart.

Paco knows that the only way Misty can trust him is to face her past and deal with it. Will she let him help her before her past crashes with her present and destroys her? Can he let her slip away from him?

This is the fifth book in the Night Rebels MC Romance series. This is Paco's story. It is a standalone. This book contains violence, sexual assault (not graphic), strong language, and steamy/graphic sexual scenes. It describes the life and actions of an outlaw motorcycle club. If any of these issues offend you, please do not read the book. HEA. No cliffhangers! The book is intended for readers over the age of 18.

Rough Draft Excerpt for PACO

Please note that this is a very rough draft of part of Chapter One of my upcoming book, PACO: Night Rebels MC. I offer it as a glimpse inside the novel.

CHAPTER ONE

STREAKS OF WHITE hot lightning broke the blackness, ripping the night sky like paper. Seconds later the rumbling thunder came. Another few miles down the highway, the lightning forked close to Paco's Harley. More booms reverberated overhead and then the rain fell. Slow and spattering at first, and then lashing down, torrential, relentless.

Paco slowed down, cursing the semi-trucks as they barreled past him, burying him in a blinding wave of water as their tires hit the puddles. He squeezed the water out of his foam grips and debated about pulling over and taking out his rain gear.

A second series of jagged lightning bolts zig-zagged across the sky. *I gotta get out of this fucking storm.* Riding wet on a bike with lightning too close for comfort was just asking for trouble. The rain came down in sheets, obstructing his vision, pelleting his skin like bullets. The brake lights on several of the large trucks in front of him glowed eerily in the mist, and he decided to follow them, hoping they were headed to the nearest truck stop in the area.

Sure enough, the semis took the next exit and turned right with Paco following behind them. Bright lights filtered through the thin mist and a yellow neon sign read "Eagle Truck Stop" and underneath it, in blue lettering, the word "Diner" flashed. Three of the large trucks turned in and drove to the fuel pumps. After following them in, he veered to the right and parked in front of the eatery. The rain had soaked him, and he opened his saddle bag, took out a plastic bag, and rushed into the diner. Drops of water rolled down his face and neck and his feet squished with every step he took.

"It sure is coming down," a woman behind the lunch counter said as her eyes traveled up and down his muscled body. "You need somewhere to dry off?"

"Yeah. Do you have showers here?" he replied.

She pointed to the right. "You gotta go next door for that. They got showers, a trucker lounge with TV and video games. No laundry, though. The shower will cost you twelve bucks but that includes a towel, washcloth, soap, and a floor mat. Where did you come from?"

The redhead gave him a smile that said she was available. He'd seen that smile more times than he could count. "Thanks for the info." A gust of wind blew past him when he opened the door, and with head bent, he walked next door.

Thirty minutes later Paco was back at the diner in a booth by the window watching the trucks as they moved from the pumps to the parking spaces that lined the large lot. The rain was steady now and he saw several women move between the lanes of parked semis.

"My name's Holly," the redhead said as she handed him a menu. "I see you got yourself all dried off. Nice pair of jeans by the way. When you came back in, I noticed you wear them real good." She licked her pink stained lips.

"Get me a cup of black coffee," he said, looking at the menu.

"You got a name?"

"Yeah. Get me that coffee."

Holly snorted then walked away. Several men came in yelling out greetings to her. Paco watched as she laughed and flirted with them, bending over the counter and playfully smacking a couple of them on their arms when they commented on her tits. Shaking his head, he pulled out his phone and shifted his focus to the parking lot. The door to a truck opened and an arm reached out to help hoist a woman with long dark hair inside.

"Hey, dude," he said to Steel.

"Where the hell are you?" the president answered.

"I got caught in a fucking storm. I pulled into a truck stop. I'm gonna wait it out. If it doesn't get better, I'll have to spend the night drinking coffee in the diner. How's the weather in Alina?"

"Clear. Are you still in Utah?"

"Yeah. I'm close to the Colorado border though."

"How's your sister?"

"Great. She had another boy."

"Here's your coffee," Holly said as she put the cup in front of him.

"I gotta go. I may not be back until tomorrow. Later."

"There's a motel behind the truck stop in case you stay the night. The beds are real comfy too." She undid the top two buttons on her uniform.

"Thanks. I may need a room."

"Holly, bring your sweet ass over here. My buddy Rich wants to ask you a question."

The waitress turned sideways and laughed. "You just hang on. I got a customer here." She looked at Paco and winked. "I'm popular with the men around here."

"I'll have a burger—medium, fries, and a cup of green chili."

Her brows knitted. "You're not very friendly, are you?"

"No. I'm not." He picked up his cup and took a sip. The coffee tasted stale and harsh like it'd been sitting out all day. "Give me a fresh cup of coffee and bring me some cream."

"Don't you ever say 'please' when you want something?"

"No." He scrolled through his texts as she walked away. The majority of his texts were from women he'd hooked up with in the past six months asking when they could get together. Shaking his head, he put his phone down on the table. The truth was he didn't want to see any of them again. He'd had fun for a while, but no one had interested him enough to pursue anything for more than a few weeks. It wasn't that he was against relationships it was just that the one woman who'd captured his heart had also shattered it, and he wasn't looking to have that happen again.

"Here you go," Holly said, placing a steaming cup of coffee in front of him. "And I just opened a new carton of creamer just for you."

"Thanks." He stirred a splash of cream in the coffee. The earthy scent filled his nostrils as he brought the cup to his lips and took a sip. Bitter sweetness snapped at the back of his throat as the hot liquid warmed him.

Glancing outside, he saw three women in short shorts huddled under the eaves of the diner as the rain poured down. A cold rush of wind swirled around him as the front door opened and a woman with too much makeup and too little clothing entered. With bent head, she walked over to the booth next to his and slid. Drops of water trickled down her face and neck, and she grabbed a napkin and wiped them away before running it through her long wet hair.

Then she looked up and locked gazes with him. Her eyes were dark like an endless stretch of midnight sky. A bundle of sorrow, pain, and loneliness swam in their inky depths along with threads of fierceness and pride. They drew him in. Something down deep, very deep, inside him stirred faintly. He sucked in a deep breath. *Damn.*

Upcoming Books
Wheelie's Challenge
Coming Spring/Summer 2018

A member of the Insurgents MC, Wheelie is a chick magnate. Having a ripped body, mesmerizing tats, and a boyish grin, he can have any woman he wants. Except for one: Sofia. Ever since he laid eyes on her, he was taken in by her sparkling eyes, her sweet laugh, and her pretty face.

There's just one very big problem: she belongs to another Insurgent.

He knows that means she's off-limits, but he can't get her out of his mind.

The memory of their kiss consumes him.

He now knows how soft and perfect she is.

Pursuing her will get him kicked out of the brotherhood, and the club is his life. He can't betray another brother even if he's a cruel, cocky jerk. He has to be strong, but the more time he spends with Sofia the more tempting it is to cross the line.

Sofia can't get the handsome biker out of her mind. Married to Tigger, she is unhappy and tired of his cruelty and manipulation. She longs to be in the strong arms of Wheelie, but she knows what the consequences are for him if they give in to their desire.

Tigger made Sofia his old lady years ago and she knows he will never let her go. If she ever leaves him, she has no doubt that he will kill her. He's told her that more times than she can count. Is she willing to risk her life and Wheelie's in order to be happy?

Wheelie's fortitude is waning, and he wants nothing more than to claim

Sofia and make her his even if that means going against another brother. Will he be able to turn his back on the Insurgents MC without any regrets? Is he prepared to love and protect Sofia from the demons of her past and present? Will Tigger make sure Sofia and Wheelie never get their happily ever after?

The Insurgents MC series are standalone romance novels. This is Wheelie's story. This book contains violence, abuse, strong language, and steamy/graphic sexual scenes. It describes the life and actions of an outlaw motorcycle club. If any of these issues offend you, please do not read the book. HEA. No cliffhangers. The book is intended for readers over the age of 18.

Dear Mr. Wolfe

Coming in Early Spring, 2018

For two years I gave my everything to my relationship with Derrick only to have him tell me he isn't feeling it anymore. To add insult to injury, he moves another woman into our place a week after I move out. Yeah… I can really pick them.

I've been dumped, have no apartment, and can barely stand my coworker at my new job. Life is just great. Not.

After feeling sorry for myself to the point where I'm sick of it, I decide to check out an online fantasy site my friend Rochelle tells me about. Well, she actually insists I do it.

No names, no pictures, no phone calls. Just anonymous musings and fantasies between two people. Sounds like the perfect relationship. I have no expectations.

Imagine my surprise when the third guy to contact me sounds intriguing.

His name is Mr. Wolfe. Yeah… I know, real original.

He tells me his desires and I share mine with him. It's liberating to dig deep inside myself and tell a perfect stranger things I'd never even tell my best friend. Very nasty, dirty things.

I look forward to our time together.

We start to exchange photos without showing our faces. Things are heating up my computer screen.

Then he wants to meet me.

And that's when fantasy meets reality.

My sexy pen pal is so not what I expected.

Life just got a whole lot more interesting....

Other Books by Chiah Wilder

Insurgent MC Series:

Hawk's Property

Jax's Dilemma

Chas's Fervor

Axe's Fall

Banger's Ride

Jerry's Passion

Throttle's Seduction

Rock's Redemption

An Insurgent's Wedding

Insurgents MC Romance Series: Insurgents Motorcycle Club Box Set
(Books 1 – 4)

Night Rebels MC Series:

STEEL

MUERTO

DIABLO

GOLDIE

Steamy Contemporary Romance:

My Sexy Boss

Find all my books at: amazon.com/author/chiahwilder

I love hearing from my readers. You can email me at chiahwilder@gmail.com.

Sign up for my newsletter to receive a FREE Novella, updates on new books, special sales, free short stories, and ARC opportunities at http://eepurl.com/bACCL1.

Visit me on facebook at facebook.com/AuthorChiahWilder.

Printed in Great Britain
by Amazon

49441558R00159